THE DREAMER

Highland Heroes
Book Four

by Maeve Greyson

ARE YOU SIGNED UP FOR DRAGONBLADE'S BLOG?

You'll get the latest news and information on exclusive giveaways, exclusive excerpts, coming releases, sales, free books, cover reveals and more.

Check out our complete list of authors, too!

No spam, no junk. That's a promise!

Sign Up Here

www.dragonbladepublishing.com

Dearest Reader;

Thank you for your support of a small press. At Dragonblade Publishing, we strive to bring you the highest quality Historical Romance from the some of the best authors in the business. Without your support, there is no 'us', so we sincerely hope you adore these stories and find some new favorite authors along the way.

Happy Reading!

CEO, Dragonblade Publishing

Additional Dragonblade books by
Author Maeve Greyson

Highland Heroes Series
The Guardian

The Warrior

The Judge

The Dreamer

CHAPTER ONE

Glen Nevis, Scotland
September 1701

"I F YE RIDE any slower, the horses will die of old age before we reach the keep."

Ian Cameron ignored his cousin's jests. In fact, the man could shove them up his arse. After all, Sutherland's views would be a damn sight different if he was the one the MacCoinnich Clan was trying to chain to Gretna Neal.

"They didna say ye had to marry the lass," Magnus de Gray, fellow mercenary and brother by battle, if not by blood, sagely reminded. "They only wish yer help for the poor woman. Those sons of hers need a man's guidance. Yer Christian duty, aye? Helping widows and children."

"Ye truly think me that daft?" Ian cast a dismal glance around as they entered the village at the base of Ben Nevis. The place had become too cluttered, even acquired the stench of a town. It was a great deal busier than its former state of scattered dwellings belonging to a few MacCoinnich crofters. Of course, it had been nigh on three years since he'd been here. He scowled at Sutherland. "Explain to me why Alexander didna choose ye rather than me for this task? Ye darken the halls of *Tor Ruadh* far more often than I, and ye're a MacCoinnich to boot."

Sutherland gave him a sly wink and an even more irritating grin. "Gretna said she wouldna have me nor wished her sons trained up to be womanizers."

"At least it sounds as though the woman still possesses some good sense," Ian grumbled. And it was further proof this had nothing to do with helping three boys become men. This was a blatant marriage trap for certain.

"She's still a beauty, too," Magnus reassured as their mounts wound through a jumble of carts lining both sides of the lane. "Hair shines like polished copper and curves a'plenty. That bonnie lass would keep a man warm through the coldest of winters."

"Then ye marry her," Ian said. "I'll dance at yer wedding, aye?"

Clanging metal and an angry stream of cursing grabbed their attention. A pair of horses, harnessed for pulling a cart, trotted across the intersection in front of them.

"Ye wee bastards! I'll be a'shootin' ye, I will!" A short, disheveled man, hands shaking as he fumbled a rusty pistol free of his belt, jittered back and forth in front of a horseless cart. Pots, pans, and all manner of wares were scattered on the road, while some still swayed from the wagon's racks.

A young lad, accompanied by two smaller scamps, stuck out his tongue, then added a series of rude hand gestures to his taunting dance. "Try an' shoot us! I dare ye, ye scrummy ole baw bag! That pistol of yers is shoddy as the wares ye rob the folk of *Ruadh* with!"

A sense of doom tightened Ian's gut. The trio harassing the traveling peddler looked vaguely familiar. He turned to Magnus and Sutherland. "Gretna's cubs?"

"Aye, cousin," Sutherland confirmed as all three men dismounted. "There be all three of yer charges. Congratulations."

"Congratulations, my arse." He strode between the jeering lads and the cursing man, just as the peddler aimed the weapon that looked too old to fire even if the man managed to pull the trigger. "Hold fast. Ye canna shoot these lads."

"The hell I can't," growled the old coot. He swaggered forward, greatly resembling a disgruntled badger. "Them brats been nothing but trouble to me all summer. Every trip I make through these parts, they pull some such devilry on me. Cause me nothing but grief. Now, they done gone and ran off me team and damaged me goods. Ignored it long as I can stomach."

"Damaged yer goods?" laughed the oldest boy, still spoiling for a fight. "Yer goods already be shite! They barely last 'til yer next trip through, so ye can charge folk double to mend'm."

"Ye see?" The peddler waved the pistol toward the lad. "No respect for their elders. None at all." He thumped his chest, his faded tunic and jacket so grubby that dust puffed out in a small cloud. "And I'm not the only one that'll tell ye them there three need to be horsewhipped and taught what for." He swung the weapon up and down the street. "Ask any a'these here folk. They'll tell ye." He jutted his scruffy chin upward. "And my wares be good as any and cheaper than most. The poor here in *Ruadh* be lost and have to do without if it weren't for old Duff Tamson. Heart a gold, I have. Ask any of'm."

"He's a cheat!" the young ringleader shouted, charging forward.

Ian grabbed hold of the lad's collar and yanked him back. "Enough!" Still holding fast to the boy, he leaned forward and plucked the pistol out of the man's hand. "And that goes for ye as well."

"But…"

"Take it to the meetin' today!" shouted one of the villagers clustered in front of the shops. "Chief'll sort it!" The suggestion brought a rumble of assent through the growing crowd of onlookers.

"A fine idea," Ian said with a backward glance at Sutherland and Magnus. Both men agreed with a single nod. He motioned for the peddler to gather his team. The pair of horses had come to a halt farther up the way. "Fetch your team. To great hall we'll go, and let the MacCoinnich do as he sees fit about this matter."

Tamson darted a shifty-eyed glance in the keep's direction. "Chief MacCoinnich doesna have time for such foolishness as this." He jerked a thumb in the boy's direction. "If'n ye swear ye'll thrash these boys good and proper, I'm a big enough man to accept that as payment for all me damages today." With a labored grunt, he scooped up one of his pots and brushed it off. "Just a bit a dirt it seems. No real harm, after all."

The peddler's sudden change of heart told Ian all he needed to know. Perhaps the lad spoke the truth about the man's business practices. With a firm shake, he stilled the boy's struggling to escape his hold. "Which of Gretna Neal's sons are ye?"

The child glared up at him and stood taller. "I be Evander. The eldest."

"And I be Rory," the next in height said with a cocky toss of his head. "Middle son."

"And yerself?" Ian looked to the smallest of the three red-haired demons.

"I be Finn," the boy said in a quivering voice barely above a whisper. He looked neither as brave nor as pleased to be there as his brothers. He twitched his freckled nose as though it itched. "I be the least of us, but I be nine, sir."

"Well, then." Ian rested his hands on the older brothers' shoulders. "Evander. Rory. Finn. Do the three of ye feel this matter needs airing in the great hall?"

"Aye," Evander belted out. "Let the chieftain rule it."

Tamson snorted out a laugh, then sneered at the boy. "The Mac-Coinnich'll have the three of ye stripped to the waist and whipped in front of all and sundry! Ye want the entire clan seeing ye cry for yer mam?"

"We're not afeared!" Evander touted with a threatening step toward the peddler.

"Aye!" Rory chimed in, while meek Finn shuffled back a step.

"The boys shall ride with me and my kin," Ian said. He took a step toward Tamson. "Gather yer team and meet us at the keep, or I'll send the MacCoinnich guards to fetch ye."

The scowling peddler swallowed hard, then rolled his shoulders. He dared to fist both hands as though readying for a fight. "Who be ye to claim such control of the MacCoinnich guards?"

"I be Ian Cameron, cousin to the MacCoinnich, and a man weary from a long journey and in no mood for liars or cheats, ye ken?"

Tamsin's hands relaxed, and he made a nervous swiping of his palms against his coat. "Aye, then. I see. Reckon I'll get my team now and follow soon as I can." The man took off at a fast gait, arms pumping at his sides.

Ian herded the boys over to the horses, pointing Rory to ride behind Sutherland and Finn to ride with Magnus. "Evander, ride with me. I wish to hear yer side of this day's events." He mounted, then reached down for the lad.

Evander took his hand without hesitation and scrambled up behind him. "That thieving man tricks the poor with smooth words and wares that he's made sure will fall apart by the next time he passes through the glen. Then, when he returns, they have to buy more or pay him to mend them." Evander thumped his small fist atop his knee. "Heard more than one folk say it's so. And Mam Hattie swears to it, even."

"Then why has no one brought it to the chief before now?" Ian halted his mount and checked the lane behind them. Duff Tamson was still in the process of hitching his team to the wagon. The man moved as slow as tree sap in the dead of winter.

"Mam Hattie says it's 'cause the old bastard finds out things about folk and uses it to make them afeared of saying anything. Says he's sly and mean as an egg-sucking stoat. Says she wouldna put any evil past him."

"What things?" Ian found it a little hard to believe the man possessed the ability to blackmail every patron. A belated sense of his mother's long-ago teachings nudged his conscience. "And dinna use the word bastard, ye ken? Especially not around women."

"I dinna ken what things he finds out for certain, but Mam Hattie knows. Ask her. She'll tell ye." Evander fidgeted behind him. "Mam Hattie says those who know better and have enough coin get their goods from Master MacElroy's shop. Those who dinna have the money are left to deal with Tamson and his thievery."

"Ye're telling me that no one, neither the poor he's robbed nor anyone else, thought to bring such a matter to the chieftain?"

"The poor are afeared. Not just 'cause he threatens them, but 'cause without him, they'd have to do without." Evander shifted again, seemingly unable to sit still while they waited for the peddler to join them. "The others dinna care. Mam Hattie says they gots their own fish to fry."

For the life of him, Ian couldn't remember this Mam Hattie, but from the sound of it, the woman was Evander's main source of information. In other words, the village gossip. "Why did ye not tell yer mother? She wouldha told Lady Mercy or brought it to the chief. She has Alexander's ear." He knew Gretna. If folk were being mistreated, she'd never stay quiet or look the other way. She always helped those in need.

"My brothers and me hardly ever see Mama," Evander's bravado weakened considerably, and his voice grew quieter. "If she's no' helping Lady Mercy, she's out with healing or getting bairns into the world." The lad shrugged. "Everybody needs Mama, and they dinna be shy about asking. She says we must nay be selfish 'bout never seeing her 'cause we're old enough to understand that it's her duty to help folk." He sniffed. "So, the boys and me dinna bother her about nothing. We handle what needs taking care of ourselves. But daren't ye say any ill about her. She's the best mam in all the Highlands and loves us fierce. Tells us all the time how she loves us. And she's nay had an easy time of it either, ye ken?" He pointed down the street. "That ole baw bag's finally caught up with us."

Ian urged his horse into motion. He should probably tell the boy not to call an elder an old baw bag but decided to let it pass. At least the boy hadn't said bastard again. It sounded as though Gretna truly did need help with the lads, although Evander spoke with the conviction of a man grown. They definitely needed more guidance than their Mam Hattie. God's beard, what a mess. He felt the MacCo-innich marriage snare cinch a notch tighter.

Shaking away the stifling thought, he focused on the task at hand. His cousin Alexander was a fair and patient chieftain, but patience was easily spent—especially if today's gathering in great hall happened to involve an excess of petty grievances. As they passed beneath the portcullis, he tossed back a bit of advice to Evander, "When ye get in front of the chief, be respectful. Quiet. No outbursts. Answer what ye are asked. Nothing else, aye?" He thought back to the scene in the street. "And dinna be calling Tamson names. Understand? It shows yer arse."

"This isna our first time before the chief," Evander bragged as though such a thing were a badge of honor. "Happens a lot 'cause of our sacred oath."

The boy's words gave Ian pause, while at the same time, triggering a deeper level of uneasiness. Upon reaching the bailey, he helped the lad down but stopped him from proceeding a step farther. "Sacred oath?"

"Ye're no' supposed to tell," Rory warned as he and Finn joined them. "'Tis a secret oath, too, Evander. Ye know that!"

"A secret, sacred oath?" Magnus repeated as he herded the two younger boys to stand beside their brother.

"Swear us in," Sutherland said with a conspiratorial wink. He squatted down in front of Finn. "We three be verra trustworthy." He thumped his chest. "I swear it."

"Dinna mock us," Evander said with the surliness of a snarling dog. He shrugged out from under Ian's grasp and pulled his little brother away from Sutherland. With an angry side-eyed glance at Ian, he made it clear that any modicum of trust between them had just been lost. "Just because we be lads, doesna mean we dinna ken what goes on and what shouldna be ignored."

"Why we'd never mock such brave lads," Sutherland said in the placating tone often used with children.

Magnus groaned and rolled his eyes. "Shut your maw, Sutherland."

Ian stepped between the boys and Sutherland before the man opened his mouth again and worsened the situation. "If I didna believe the three of ye had valid reasons for what ye did, I wouldha left ye back in the street to sort this out yerselves." He held out a hand to Evander as though the boy were a man. "But I can best help if I know *all* the reasons for yer actions, aye? I havena been here for nigh on three years. I've a bit a catching up to do about the goings-on."

All three of them looked like cornered strays ready to fight for their lives.

Hand still extended, Ian widened his stance. "What say ye, Evander? Tell me about this secret oath. I'll do my best to keep it secret unless the chieftain needs to hear of it, aye? I willna lie to ye. If this oath is dangerous, both yer mother and the chief must be told. Ye have my word on it, and the sacred bond of my handshake."

Evander shared a look with his brothers. Rory gave an almost imperceptible nod, and Finn trembled with a shrug. With a step forward, Evander cleared his throat. "We be the guardians of *Ruadh*. We tend to the wrongs that go ignored and help folk who go unheard." He lifted his chin. "We know well enough what it's like when no one listens, and people look through ye as though ye're nay even standing in front of them."

"Evander Shaw Neal!"

"Dinna tell her of the oath, aye? We do it for her sake, too."

Desperation and something akin to a plea for understanding flickered in the boy's eyes. A certainty filled Ian. The certainty that he'd not betray the lads' trust if at all possible. He shot a stern look over at Magnus, then Sutherland. "Not a word—aye?"

Both men gave silent assent, then ducked back a step as Gretna Neal raced down the keep's front steps and flew across the cobblestone courtyard faster than a storm overtaking the land.

"How did she find out so fast?" Ian asked under his breath.

"She always knows," Evander answered with a heavy sigh.

"What in heaven's name have the three of ye done this time?" Gretna came to a halt in front of her eldest son.

Before Evander could begin his defense, Ian stepped next to him and rested a hand on his shoulder. He had to give the boy credit. The child didn't cower nor shake as he stood prepared to endure his mother's wrath.

Ian smiled his most charming smile, made all the easier by the high coloring across Gretna's lovely features. Magnus had spoken true. The lass was still a fiery beauty. Twice widowed, three children, and the passage of time hadn't touched her. If anything, she'd blossomed even more with the full curviness of womanhood and held herself with strength and grace. Damn, she was bonnie. "'Tis good to see ye again, Gretna."

Blue eyes clearer than any Highland sky cut over to him. "'Twould be a fair sight better under different circumstances." Her focus immediately shifted back to her son. "Well?"

"We're in the right this time, Mama," Evander said with the barest lift of his chin. "I swear it."

Her mouth tightened, then she shifted the interrogation to her youngest. "Finn?"

"'Member what we said," Rory whispered entirely too loud.

Snatching hold of Rory's chin, she bent until the tip of her nose nearly touched his. "Dinna threaten yer brother, or I'll take a switch to yer backside, ye ken?"

"Gretna…" Words fled Ian as her angry glare shot back to him. A distant memory of her temper returned with sudden clarity. He cleared his throat. "I dinna ken about the other times the lads have been participants in great hall, but I believe them to be in the right this time. Somewhat," he added as an afterthought. The boys *had* vandalized the man's cart when they should've taken the matter to an adult—if they could've gotten an adult to listen.

"Somewhat?" she repeated as a clanging bell signaled the beginning of the chieftain's hearing of his peoples' grievances.

Never fight a battle ye're no' armed to win. Mercenary wisdom also applied to arguing with women. He'd learned that early on. He motioned to Magnus and Sutherland. "Find the smithy quick as ye can. Have him look over that cart and tell ye what he finds." Movement near the gate behind them caught his eye. "And keep close watch of Duff Tamson, aye?" He pointed to the peddler angling his team back toward the bailey's exit. "The bastard's looking to make a run for it once we all get inside. He has no intention of joining us in the hall if he can keep from it."

"Ye told me I couldna call him a bastard," Evander said.

"Dinna sass yer elders, and dinna ye dare use that word again. Ye know better." Gretna yanked her eldest from Ian's side and gave him a shake. "Now, tell me why Master Cameron is bringing ye to the chieftain. What did ye do? Have ye been nettling the peddler again?"

"I brought him here to keep him from getting shot," Ian interrupted while watching Magnus and Sutherland take their posts on either side of Tamson and escort the man into the keep. As soon as he heard Gretna's gasp, he cringed. Perhaps, he could've worded that better.

"Shot?" She snatched the rest of her brood closer, herding them up the steps while alternately swatting each of their backsides hard enough to make them yelp and step livelier. "The death of me! The lot of ye shall be the death of me. D'ye hear? Are ye set on sending me to an early grave? Are ye?"

Ian's heart went out to the lads, but now was neither the time nor the place to assert his opinion or assistance on the matter. He didn't fear Gretna, but she'd instilled within him a healthy dose of respect long ago. The woman was as fierce as any warrior. He prayed she'd calm enough to reason with once she heard all the details of the day. The boys had meant well. Surely, she'd find comfort and pride in that and grant them a bit of forgiveness.

As soon as they'd pushed their way to the front of those gathered on the fringes of the long meeting hall, he lifted a hand to catch both the chieftain and his wife's attention. Catriona *would* choose this day of all days to join Alexander in the settling of grievances. Their heads turned at the same time, and their gazes settled on him. A chill raced across him as their smiles flashed brighter.

Graham, Alexander's brother, and Clan MacCoinnich's war chief, stood beside the laird's chair, grinning like a fool, too. He winked at Ian. Was everyone privy to this plot to marry him off to Gretna?

"Ah, well. In for a penny, in for a pound," he muttered under his breath as he strode into the area in front of the chieftain and motioned for the boys to join him. Jaw set, Gretna herded her sons forward, then took her place behind them. Evander to the right, Rory to the left, and poor trembling Finn in the middle backed up into the folds of his mother's skirts.

Ian moved to stand beside her, directly behind Evander. Even though he knew nothing about the raising of bairns, he wouldn't let them fight this battle alone. They needed someone other than their mother on their side.

Magnus and Sutherland nudged Duff Tamson into the space, then stepped back and took a stance that left no question they stood guard to ensure no one exited without permission.

Ian resettled his stance and glanced around. The cavernous hall at the heart of the keep was packed. Folk clustered at least three-deep around the sides of the room and in the archways. Some even gathered above in the gallery, leaning over the banister to better view the proceedings.

Alexander lifted a hand, and silence washed across the room. "'Tis good to see ye, cousin. How long has it been since ye graced these halls?"

Not long enough. Ian stifled the selfish thought and forced a polite smile. "Nigh on three years, I think. With Alasdair last time."

With a thoughtful nod, Alexander agreed. "Aye. Three years." His pleasant countenance faded, settling into a dark look, Ian knew all too well from their days of fighting together as mercenaries. Alexander was about to launch a battle plan. He pointed at the boys. "'Tis my understanding ye happened upon an incident ye feel needs my attention."

"Aye." Ian settled a hand on Evander's shoulder and squeezed, hoping both the boy and Gretna would understand what he was about to do. He'd been known to plot a battle plan or two himself. He turned and made a half bow to Duff Tamson. "To take care of any accusations of prejudice due to my ties to yerself, I believe Master Tamson should speak first and present his side of what happened."

Eyes narrowing, the chieftain looked at the peddler. "Master Tamson."

The fidgeting man stole one last hopeful glance toward the exit, then scrubbed his palms on his coat. With a respectful bob of his head, he cleared his throat and shifted back and forth. "Chieftain." He made a sideways jerk of his head toward the boys. "These scamps meddled with me wagon. Made it so my team broke loose, and half me wares ended up in the street."

"Did ye recover yer horses?" Alexander asked.

"Aye, aye." Tamson clasped his hands together. "Only went up the road a short way, they did. Weren't no trouble at all to fetch them."

"Any damages?" Alexander shifted in the ornately carved chieftain's seat, then set his fingers to drumming atop the curved arm of the chair.

Tamson shook his head. "Nay, my chieftain."

Alexander shifted his attention to Ian, seeming not to understand. "No damages and the horses recovered. Why are the lot of ye here? This isna the place to address the pranks of children."

"Aye, that's true," Ian agreed, pleased he'd read Tamson correctly. He'd wagered the man would try to get through this with as little trouble as possible to keep from drawing too much attention to his business. "But shooting the lads seemed a rather severe punishment for their crime. D'ye no' agree?"

"Shooting the lads?" Alexander sat straighter, even leaned forward as though relieved to finally hear something of interest.

Tamson eked out a nervous laugh and gave a sharp shake of his head. "I was nay really going to shoot them, my chieftain. Just wanted to put a little fear into the boys, ye ken?"

"Ye had your pistol aimed right at this boy when I stepped in front of it." Ian made a dramatic sweeping look around the room. His brother Alasdair, Edinburgh's finest solicitor, was not the only member of the family who knew how to play a crowd. A collective gasp from several of the women goaded him on. "Ye didna call them scamps then either. I believe yer exact words were, 'Ye wee bastards. Shoot ye, I will!'"

"I didna mean it," Tamson sputtered, waving both hands as though wishing to wipe away Ian's words. "I was angry. Spoke ill because of me temper. Surely, ye've done that at times? Said things ye didna mean?" He swiped his fingers across his forehead, then pulled a dingy square of linen out of his pocket and mopped his face with it. He shook his head again. "Meant no harm at all. I wouldna have really shot them."

"Ye would, too, ye ole baw bag!" Evander jeered. "Ye tried last month but misfired. Then ye threw it at us. That's why ye've nay got but one pistol left!"

"Evander!" Gretna scolded in a shushing whisper.

"Hush, boy. Let me handle this." Ian squeezed Evander's shoulder again and gave Rory a stern look to keep his wee mouth shut as well. "These boys dinna deny what they did, Alexander. They told me their reasons." He paused for effect. "And after witnessing Master Tamson's behavior, I felt ye should hear their reasons, too."

Alexander nodded. "So be it."

CHAPTER TWO

TEETH CLENCHED SO tight her jaws throbbed, Gretna held her breath as she watched her eldest son. Evander would be the one to speak. Dear, sweet, headstrong Evander always spoke for the three whenever they'd been caught in some mischief. Rory had too much of a temper, and poor, timid Finn sometimes went mute whenever afraid—and the lad was scared of everything.

God bless these three—her heart's reason for beating. But, sweet Jesu, they would have her silver-headed before her time. And they *would* pick today for one of their ill-fated campaigns. She stole a glance at Ian. *Poor man.* Hunted down and brought to heel by Catriona and Mercy's infernal matchmaking. The bait they'd used to draw him in had worked well. Her unsuspecting sons had played right into the matchmakers' hands.

"Evander?" Alexander encouraged. "Ye've always been the one to speak on behalf of yer brothers. Tell me yer reasons, boy."

Evander inched a step forward and threw out his chest. "We did what ole Tamson said we did. Fixed it so his team would run loose and dump his cart." The boy's stern look puckered into an irritated scowl. "Didna work as we planned, though. Not everything fell off like it was supposed to."

A tittering of laughter rippled through the crowd. Inwardly, Gretna groaned. Evander always spoke his mind whether it did him good or not.

Alexander cleared his throat and turned aside for a moment. Fist pressed to his mouth, he appeared to be struggling to breathe. He finally pointed at Ian. "My cousin seems to think I need to hear the reasons for yer plan. The same reasons ye explained to him, aye? *Why* ye did it, boy. Not what ye did."

"The man's a thief," Evander declared. "He cheats the poor. Been up to his evil a long time. Me and my brothers decided to end it by running him out a *Ruadh*."

Gretna understood now. It was the old woman again. Mam Hattie, the elderly spinster who helped with the boys, had to be at the heart of this. She felt sure of it. The gossipmonger had filled the boys' heads with her tales again.

Everyone knew about Duff Tamson. The man didn't do all that much harm. Gretna had even been duped by him. But he served a purpose. When a body didn't have a pair of pence to rub together and couldn't afford MacElroy's goods, they were thankful for what they *could* get from Tamson.

"We mean to keep him out," Evander added. "We're protecting the innocent."

"The boy lies!" Tamson interjected. "I take care of the poor. Price me wares just for them."

"Ye had yer chance," Ian said with a threatening step toward the man. "Shut your maw, and let the lad finish."

Relief and gratitude warmed Gretna. Ian always had been a kind man. Usually, only she defended her boys. While her lads weren't perfect and could nettle a soul to death, their hearts were pure gold, and she wouldn't have them any other way. Not many in Clan MacCoinnich understood that.

"How does he cheat the poor, lad?" Alexander rose and paced slowly back and forth in front of the chief's dais.

"Sells them things made to fall apart. Thin, shabby cast-offs ready for the scrap heap. He knows they'll have to either buy more or pay him to mend them in a few months." Evander shoved a hand into the ratty leather pouch hanging from his belt. He drew out a bent piece of metal and showed it. "See how it bends and snaps?" He folded the piece back and forth a time or two, then snapped it apart with ease.

"That isna mine!" Tamson argued, pointing a shaking finger at the pieces of metal. "Who knows where the boy got that bit a trash?"

Ian strode over to the man and grabbed his arm. "What did I tell ye about staying quiet and letting the lad say his piece?"

Alexander held out his hand. "Hand it here, boy."

Without hesitation, Evander gave it to him.

Alexander studied the pieces of metal, then handed them to Graham before turning back to Evander. "If what ye claim is true, why has no one brought this to my attention before now?"

"He makes folks afeared." Evander pointed at Tamson. "Threatens them, he does."

"I do not! All lies!" Tamson surged a step forward.

Ian yanked him back in place.

Alexander scowled at the peddler long enough to make the silence in the room palpable. He turned back to Evander. "How does he threaten them, lad?" he asked in an encouraging tone.

Evander shrugged. "Finds out stuff they dinna want everyone to know and says he'll tell it." He shot a look of disgust at Tamson. "Makes'm feel all helpless and like they owe him. Tells'm if it weren't for him, they wouldna have a pot to piss in and would have to go begging." He shrugged again. "Mam Hattie knows better than me. Ask her. She'll tell ye all he does."

A unified groan vibrated through the room.

Gretna bowed her head and closed her eyes. Evander had just lost all support and credibility by mentioning Mam Hattie. No one listened to the old gossip. Everyone knew her tales always spun out of control.

Her stories might start with a kernel of truth, but by the time she finished with them, what was real and what was imagined could not be sorted out.

Graham stepped forward and whispered something in Alexander's ear. Alexander gave a slow nod, shielded his response with his hand, then motioned toward the archway to the right of the room. Rather than return to his post beside the chieftain's chair, Graham left the room.

Alexander returned his attention to those gathered in front of him and fixed a dark look on Tamson. "It appears the smithy looked over yer wares, man. Would ye hazard a guess as to what he found?"

Hope rising, Gretna lifted her head and looked over at old Duff Tamson. The suddenly pale man stood with his mouth open.

Ian caught her eye and gave her a reassuring wink.

"Master Tamson," Alexander repeated. "I would appreciate an answer. Now."

Tamson stretched as tall as his squat stature allowed. "Aye. I can tell ye verra well what the man found. But I stand by my goods. 'Tis the only way I can sell'm at a price suited for the folk who canna afford MacElroy's shop."

"Yer goods come from the smithy's scrap heap before he's had a chance to melt them. Castoffs he's paid good money for, I might add. The man recognized several of his pieces that had gone missing." Alexander's face darkened. "It appears ye not only stand accused of cheating yer customers but also of stealing from the smithy."

She squeezed her boys' shoulders. For once, they might escape the great hall as heroes.

"What say ye to these charges?" Alexander asked.

"Nothing," Tamson snapped with a dark look at the boys.

With a motion to the MacCoinnich guards stationed along the wall behind the dais, Alexander nodded. "Verra well. Once the smithy has finished reclaiming what is his, ye shall be escorted from MacCoinnich lands, never to return again lest ye wish to live out yer life chained to the smithy's forge, understand?"

Tamson answered with a downward jerk of his chin.

"I'd be thanking the chief if I were ye," Ian interjected. "He could-ha put ye in stocks or chopped off yer hands for yer thieving."

Tamson's only response was a look filled with hatred as a pair of MacCoinnich guards escorted the sullen man from the room.

Alexander held up a hand to silence the rumbling crowd. "And I shall speak to Hugh MacElroy to see what can be done about making goods affordable to the *entire* community of *Ruadh*, so none shall suffer from want."

A heady mix of relief, pride, and thankfulness bubbled through Gretna as she gathered up her boys in a fierce hug. "I'm so proud of ye," she whispered as she embarrassed them each with a sound kiss on their cheeks. "We'll talk about yer methods later, but for now, just know I'm proud of ye." She turned to usher them out—

"I bid ye wait, Gretna," Alexander said, then snapped his fingers in Ian's direction, where he was attempting to melt into the crowd. "And yerself as well, Ian. Please come stand beside the lady."

Gretna's heart fell, and her happy mood disappeared as quickly as steam rising from a pot. Catriona and Mercy had nearly driven her mad by trying to saddle her with another husband, and poor Ian Cameron was their latest target. Apparently, the two had also involved Alexander in their scheme to see her married to Ian.

The crowd hummed with excitement. She glanced at all the expectant faces. How in heaven's name had everyone found out? Had the wily women enlisted the help of the entire clan?

With an indulgent smile, Alexander stepped back to the dais, took Catriona's hand, and helped her rise from her seat. Heavy with child, Catriona rested a hand atop her swollen middle and beamed at them both.

The need to turn tail and run was strong, but Gretna forced herself to stand firm. *Nay.* She'd not show cowardice in front of her sons. She glared at Catriona, willing the woman to hear her thoughts. How could they do this in front of everyone? A sideways glance at Ian made her feel even worse. *Aye.* She knew that set to a man's jaw. He felt just as cornered as she. Hopefully, he didn't think her a willing party to this mess.

Alexander cast a silencing look around the room, then smiled at each of the boys lined up like peas in a pod in front of Gretna. "How old are each of ye now?"

"Eleven," Evander answered in a leery tone.

"I be ten," Rory said after Evander elbowed him.

"Nine," Finn whispered after both his brothers nudged him.

Alexander's gaze settled on Gretna. "And how long have these poor lads been without a father to look up to and guide them?"

She bit back the sharp retort burning on her tongue. Alexander knew good and well how long it had been since Colin's accident, and that bastard had been a poor excuse for a father. "Six years," she said in the most respectful tone she could manage.

"And I believe this be the fourth time since last summer that these boys have stood before me. Is it not?"

"My boys are not bad—just a wee bit rowdy." She forced a smile. "Just look at today. Whilst I agree they couldha handled it better, they were but trying to help the poor."

Alexander nodded. "And that is why I intend to help both them and yerself."

Ian groaned something under his breath that she couldn't make out, but was certain it wasn't good. Servants, guards, and folk from the village milled around the perimeter of the room, inching ever closer and narrowing the cleared space. She pulled in a deep breath. Merciful heavens, they'd surely smother her if they didn't step back and give her some room.

"And I appreciate the thought. But we are fine, my chieftain."

Gretna made a gracious half-bow and managed another strained smile. Usually, she always called Alexander by name. After all, she was Catriona's closest cousin. She hoped he'd realize the barb intended by her cold use of his title. "Thanks to the Lady Mercy's generosity and my helping Mrs. Bickerstaff with her healing errands, my boys and I have had no trouble at all keeping food on the table and a roof over our heads."

"Nay." Alexander frowned and shook his head. "It is high time these boys were fostered and taught properly. They need a guardian to train them rather than allow them to shoot up wild as weeds. An upstanding man will help them become the best sort of men they can be." His gaze slid to Ian. "And I have just the man. Let it be known from this day forward that Ian Cameron is legal guardian to these three until they reach manhood. Ye will foster them, Ian. Raise them up to be fine young clansmen. Teach them, and…" Alexander paused, and his smile disappeared. "Ye will keep them out of trouble, aye?"

"Far be it from me to refuse my chief and cousin anything, but I must respectfully decline," Ian said. "I have no land. No home. I live my life on my horse's back." He gave a smug nod, then turned to Gretna with a placating smile that struck her ill. "They be fine boys, of that I'm sure, but I'm a mercenary. I canna be foster father to yer lads."

"I didna ask ye to, now did I?" How dare he think her a part of this thinly veiled ploy. "I can take care of my own sons, thank ye verra much." She turned back to Alexander and flipped a hand in Ian's direction. "Ye heard the man. Not only does he not wish to do it, he has no place to keep them. He canna do it."

"Of course he has a place to keep them," Catriona interjected with a sweep of her hand toward a staircase at the back of the room. "He and the boys shall stay in the north wing of the keep. We've already set an entire floor in order for them."

"My lady," Gretna said in a tone she hoped her cousin would heed.

"Has it slipped yer mind that Graham and Lady Mercy reside in the north wing—them and their children?" She'd gone beyond caring that they stood in front of half the clan. This foolishness had to stop.

"They dinna live on the second floor." Folding her hands atop her middle, Catriona gave a self-satisfied nod. "The second floor needed a good cleansing of all the evil once done there. Father William's already blessed it, and it's quite ready to be filled with the laughter of children."

Gretna was taken aback. "So, ye mean to take my boys from me? How can ye do this, Catriona? How can ye do such a thing just to get yer way?" By the saints, she would take her sons and leave *Ruadh* before she'd let them take her babies from her. They'd live in caves if they had to—whatever it took to be together.

Catriona beamed with the smile of a victorious warrior. "We would never attempt to take the lads from ye, dear cousin. They've already lost two fathers. How cruel would it be to separate them from their mother?" Her gaze fell to Finn as the boy shuffled backward even tighter into the protective folds of Gretna's skirts. "Perhaps, ye misunderstand? Father William blessed the entire second floor of the north wing, and the maids have scrubbed *all* the chambers."

"The entirety of the living quarters?" Gretna whispered, the words catching in her throat. Surely, Catriona didn't mean…

"Aye! Ye will live here with the boys, too!" Catriona announced with an excited clap of her hands. Glee rang through her tone like the peeling of a church bell. She cast a stern look around the room and spoke louder. "Ye will share one of the chambers with Mam Hattie, whilst Ian and the boys share the other. Everything will be moral and proper as it should be." Her tone dared anyone to say otherwise.

Ian lifted a hand and shook his head. "Alexander—"

"This is not a request, Ian." Alexander's congenial look hardened into a stern glare. "Yer chieftain bids ye do this, aye?"

"I am sorry," Gretna whispered with the barest turn of her head toward him. "None of this is my doing. I swear it." Could they possibly humiliate her any more? Would they leave her no pride at all?

Ian's strong jaw flexed, and he bowed his head the slightest bit. The man had heard her, but had he accepted her words as truth?

With a shifting of his stance beside her, he swelled with a great intake of breath, then blew it out. "I accept the task then," he said through bared teeth. "But until next summer only. As I said, I earn my way as a mercenary." His scowl was an open dare to Alexander. "Come summer, I will be on my way again. Agreed?"

"For now," Alexander said. The man was not a fool. A sly smile lifted a corner of his mouth. "We shall see how the lads fare by then, aye? I am not an unreasonable man."

Ian shifted in place, obviously struggling to hold his tongue. "Aye," he finally growled.

The crowd hummed all around them, buzzing and stirring like an overfilled hive. Gretna wouldn't be surprised if the meddlesome fools didn't break into cheers at any moment.

"May we go now?" she asked.

"Aye," Catriona answered before Alexander could respond. With a sideways glance at her husband, she touched his hand and smiled. "I shall go now, too, and leave ye to the settling of the people's grievances."

Alexander helped her step down from the dais, then turned back to Ian and Gretna. "'Twill be a fine winter with the keep filled with kith and kin. Aye, cousin?"

"Aye," Ian agreed in a tone that said otherwise. He offered Gretna his arm with a jerk. "Shall we go?"

As far as she was concerned, they couldn't go fast enough. She took his arm and urged the boys onward. "On wi' ye, now."

"We're to live here in the keep? All of us? With him?" Evander asked as they pushed their way through the crowded room.

"Hush now." Gretna herded her brood to walk faster. "We shall talk of it in the courtyard. I've shared more than I ever cared to share with this clan today." Tongues would be wagging all winter long and then some.

She hurried them down the steps and around the back of the keep to the walled-off gardens meant for the chieftain and those closest to him.

"Hold fast, lads." Ian held them back, then sidled his way in front of them and opened the gate. Grim as death, dark brows knotted, his jaw flexed beneath the dusting of his shadowy beard. He gave a polite nod for her to pass through first. "M'lady."

"Mama always opens the gate," Rory argued. His plump, freckled cheeks went red, and defensiveness flashed in his eyes.

"A gentleman always opens the gate for the lady, and she always passes through first." Ian motioned her forward again while still scowling at Rory. "'Tis proper and mannerly, ye ken?"

"They know that," Gretna defended as they entered the private garden. "I've taught my sons their manners." She pointed at a bench tucked between a pair of rowan trees lit with the brilliant red of autumn. "Sit over there. All three of ye now, and be quiet whilst I speak with Master Ian." She pointed a warning finger in their direction as she walked away. "And dinna ye move from that seat, or I'll have yer behinds, ye ken? I'll fetch ye in a bit."

The restless lads lined up on the bench.

Thankfully, Ian followed her without argument. She led him a few steps away, far enough so the boys couldn't overhear. "I had nothing to do with this," she said, wishing to be anywhere but where she stood. Cheeks burning with bruised pride and shame, it took all her strength to take hold of this situation and attempt to manage it. "Ye know me, Ian, or ye should by now. Have I ever acted as though I wished to trap a man and saddle him with my bairns? When Coire died, I found myself forced into a loveless marriage with Colin. It was a grand mistake, but I'd promised—for Coire's peace of mind. Do ye truly think I'd willingly go through such misery again?"

"Nay, lass." He scowled at their surroundings, looking everywhere but at her. "But I dinna see a clear way out of this for either of us just yet." He raked a hand back through his unruly, shoulder-length, dark hair.

The poor man looked travel-worn and weary—as handsome and fine as she remembered but still as though he sorely needed a meal and a bed. His frown settling on the boys, he shook his head. "It's the women. Catriona, Mercy, and I'm sure even Isobel had a hand in this all the way from Edinburgh. Ye know as well as I, they canna help themselves. All three think if ye're not married, ye canna possibly be happy."

"I am blessed with three, fine healthy sons, a roof, and plenty of food in our bellies. How could I not be happy?" She hugged herself, refusing to speak her true feelings. Unfortunately, Catriona and Mercy knew one more thing about her. A weakness that worked to their advantage. They'd weaseled it out of her one afternoon while the three of them snipped herbs for drying. They knew she was lonely. She'd foolishly confessed it. Even told them how she missed the closeness, the precious loving she'd shared with her first husband.

Dearest Coire, God rest his soul. The emptiness he'd left her with when he'd died had only worsened with the forced marriage to his twin brother after the deathbed promise to ease Coire's mind about leaving his bairns behind. Marrying Colin had been a fool's errand. She would not go through another loveless union of duty and convenience. She had her sons. They were all she needed. "I am truly sorry they trapped ye. Especially in such a public way."

"Alexander is sly as a fox and firmly under Catriona's control." Ian gave a weary laugh. "This all happened just as they planned it. I grant ye that."

"Ye know they think we'll eventually marry. Think if they force us together and wear us down, we'll give in and do as they wish." Gretna gathered her knitted shawl closer. A chill had set in. A chill that had nothing to do with the kiss of winter hiding in the autumn breeze. "But at least he didna refuse ye flat out when ye said ye couldna stay until they were grown. He didna say for certain ye couldna leave come next summer. There is that to help ye through the winter." At least Ian seemed to accept none of this was her doing. She wished she could make this better for him.

He gave her a look that clearly conveyed he thought her addled. "Ye know better than that." Thumbs hooked in his belt, he turned and looked at the boys again. "I'm surprised ye've managed to escape a trap such as this for as long as six years. Damn meddlesome clan."

"I believe my working with old Elena to learn her healing helped me avoid the fall of the axe for a while." She joined his study of the boys fidgeting on the bench. Not one of them had the capacity to sit still, but at least all three remained where she had put them. "I'm sorry for ye, Ian." She massaged the side of her throbbing head. A cup of willow bark tea was definitely in her near future. "I truly am sorry. I know ye've much better things to do rather than playing nursemaid to three boys and tolerating me when I've no more desire to be yer wife than I wish to be tossed off a cliff."

"I dinna believe I'm all that terrible a choice, am I?" His disgruntled look swiveled back to her. "Ye make it sound like ye'd rather have the plague than be caught in the same room with me."

"That is not what I meant, and ye know it." Saints alive, she'd forgotten he was the sensitive one. Always had been. She assumed it was because of what she'd heard about how his wife was murdered at Glencoe. The hideous deed was made even worse because she carried their first child. "Ye're a fine man," she hurried to reassure. "But I've been married twice, and dinna wish to lower a third husband into the grave."

"Aye, well..." He cast a glance skyward. "I've buried more than just Janet, and I'm none too keen on burying another either."

"Ye married again?" She hadn't heard that. Of course, it had been over three years since he'd been back to *Tor Ruadh.*

"Not exactly."

Have mercy on her soul. The man looked like one of her lads when they'd done some mischief and were trying to hide it. "What do ye mean *not exactly*?"

"Shall we go to yer croft and pack yer things?" he asked, ignoring the question entirely.

Since the marriage noose hadn't tightened around her neck just yet, she'd leave him his secrets for now.

"Aye." She released the boys from the bench with a wave of her hand. "Home, lads. Time to gather our things. Run and see if Master Simpson will let us borrow his cart, aye? It should do well enough to move what little we have."

She stole a more lingering look at Ian, as the lads charged past them and stormed out of the garden. Had he always been this tall and broad-shouldered? She hadn't remembered him as such. Shooing away the thought as though it was a midge, she concentrated on where they were headed rather than on Ian's good looks. "We've not got much, but we have all we need. It shouldna be too big of a chore to get us moved into the keep." As they passed through the garden gate and crossed the bailey, she caught sight of his horse with several compact bundles lashed behind the saddle. "What about yerself? I assume ye dinna have more than what ye have packed on yer horse?"

For the first time since Alexander had harnessed them with their sentence, Ian gave her a genuine smile. "Aye, 'tis everything I own." His smile widened. "I was right. Ye *are* a canny lass."

"And what is that supposed to mean?" She didn't know whether to be insulted or not.

"Sutherland said ye refused him." He nodded his approval. "I told him that showed ye possessed good sense."

"Sutherland loves women. *All* the women." She squinted to catch sight of the boys, but they'd already sprinted out of view. "I am far too busy to take on the breaking of that randy horse." Someday, Sutherland would meet his match, and she hoped she was around to enjoy that spectacle.

They exited the barbican and maneuvered around a stretch of muddy ruts taking up half the lane. As they topped the first rise, the sight of the boys scampering around Mam Hattie and a cart pulled by a MacCoinnich guard halted her. "What have they done?" She fisted a hand in her shawl. Was nothing private anymore? Had they dared to go through her things without her?

"It looks as though they've already packed yer croft for ye," Ian said as though it was the most natural thing in the world.

"They had no right." She charged forward. They may have meant well, but this was too much. "What have ye done?" she shouted. The realization hit her that for them to have already finished, even though they had little to pack, Alexander must have ordered Graham to send the guard with the cart to her croft while they still stood before him in the great hall. This latest meddling infuriated her. She was not some pawn for the clan's amusement.

Mam Hattie smiled and waved as she toddled along beside the scantily filled cart. Arisaid covering her silver head, a gnarled hand holding it tight beneath her chin, she squinted against the sun peeping through the clouds. "Wait 'til we get closer, lass. I canna hear ye over the racket."

Evander bounced up to her. "All is already packed. Can we be off to play now?"

"Ye may not," she said sharper than she meant. Guilt washed across her. It was not her son's fault their lives had become the MacCoinnich's favorite pastime.

Evander backed up a step and motioned for Finn and Rory to stay back. "Sorry, Mama. What do ye wish us to do?" he asked in a hurt tone that made her feel even worse.

She shook her head and waved him away. "Forgive me, Evander, I'm weary. Of course, the lot of ye may go and play." She snatched hold of his arm before he escaped. "But I beg ye, please stay out of trouble. At least for the rest of the day, aye? Will ye try? Please?"

Evander bobbed his head and smiled. "Aye, Mama. We'll be good. I swear it." He bounded back, gave her a fierce hug, then took off at a dead run, Rory and Finn charging after him.

As Mam Hattie and the cart came up even with them, the old woman pulled a small cloth parcel from a fold in her plaid and held it out. "Almost missed this. Found it tucked away in a back corner of the cupboard. Be it yers?"

Gretna snatched it away and pressed it to her heart. Eyes closed, she shook with a silent sob she couldn't hold at bay.

Damn them. Damn them, every last one.

CHAPTER THREE

IAN HURRIED THE guard with the cart onward, wishing the old woman would go along with him. Gretna had handled the day's events well until the crone had pulled whatever that was out of her plaid. "Who are ye, and who gave ye permission to do this?"

The matron shot him a haughty glare that brought visions of witchery and ill-wishes to mind. "I be Hattie Neal, most call me Mam Hattie. I have been helping Mistress Gretna with her bairns ever since she found herself widowed for the second time." She hitched a step closer, squinting as she looked him over from head to toe. "Ye be Ian Cameron, aye?"

He'd not stand here and yammer niceties with the town gossip while Gretna was more upset than he'd ever seen her. He pointed at the cart, already disappearing into the keep. "Be gone wi' ye, aye? Since ye claim to be her helper, go unpack her things whilst I attempt to undo this damage ye've done."

Her eyes flared wide. "Ye are a rude man, Ian Cameron." She shook a crooked finger in his face. "And ye best learn right now, I dinna take orders from the likes of ye. I'll not be leaving until Mistress Gretna tells me to go, ye ken?" She stomped a foot and sidled closer to Gretna.

"Go on ahead," Gretna said in a hushed voice. She kept her gaze locked on the small, cloth parcel clutched to her chest. "Please, just go and do as he asks, aye?"

The old woman's wrinkled scowl tightened to a darker look as she backed up a step. "If ye're certain?"

"I am certain."

With a disgruntled *hmpf*, the crone gave Ian a growling sneer, then jerked aside and wobbled her way up the lane.

He didn't have a clue why the parcel had Gretna so shaken. He was also at a loss for how to proceed. Nothing was more fearsome than a woman upset about something only known to herself. He shifted his weight from side to side, all the while watching her, hoping she'd recover and return to the earnest, self-assured woman he'd always known. She didn't move. Just stood on the side of the road, staring down at the wee bundle.

"Shall I do away with it for ye?" he finally asked, figuring if he disposed of the thing, it would trouble her no more.

She lifted her head, looking as though she'd just awakened from a dream. "Do away with it?"

"Aye." He nodded toward the package. "Whatever it is, I'll rid ye of it so it canna upset ye anymore."

She gave him a sad smile. "Nay," she whispered. "This is a verra dear thing to me. More than a little precious."

Fingers trembling, she gently pulled free the ties and opened the folds of linen like the petals of a flower. Within the cloth lay a small, dark gemstone, smoky and multi-faceted, surrounded by intricate silver ivy leaves worked into the shape of a petite heart. Gretna's head tilted as she lifted the necklace and held it for Ian to see. "My dearest Coire gave this to me on our wedding day. I never took it off." Her jaw hardened, and her look turned cold. "At least—I never took it off until the day Colin yanked it from around my throat." She lowered the bit of jewelry back into the linen and secured the cloth around it. "With the chain broken, I put it away to keep it safe."

"I am sorry." Useless words, but he had to say something. He knew her pain. Nothing lessened the ache of losing someone you loved. All you could do was learn to carry it through life. He stared off toward the village, struggling for anything to say. A solution better than empty words came to him. "Ye need a chest for it. A wee box." He nodded toward the wadded bundle as she tucked it away in a pocket hidden in the folds of her skirts. "Ye dinna wish it thrown out by mistake for a useless rag."

She patted her pocket and lifted her chin, seeming to shake herself into control. "Maybe someday." She turned back toward the keep with a strained sound meant as a laugh. "I've more important items requiring my precious coins at the moment." With a gentle nod and a wave back at him, she shooed him away. "I best see to getting my things settled. Ye dinna have to help. I suppose ye'll be at the evening meal?"

"Aye."

She gave an exaggerated curtsy. Her usual spirited nature had settled back in place, flashing in her smile. "I shall see ye then, Master Cameron, as I'm sure our matchmakers will expect us to dine at the same table."

"Most certainly." He accepted her curtsy with an equally mocking bow. As he watched her hurry away, he shook his head. What a rare woman. Bullheaded and fierce but so vulnerable when she allowed a scarce peek inside. Maybe she did need a husband to help her. Not him, of course, but a good man. One she could love, and he'd love her back. Aye, that's what she needed. As he strode toward the village, Ian settled it in his mind. Since he was trapped here for the winter, maybe he'd try his hand at matchmaking. After all, he could attack it from the male perspective.

He headed for the street where he'd come across the boys harassing the peddler. Places for trade had lined that street. He couldn't remember what sorts of shops, but there was but one way to find out.

The miller took up the far end of the way nearest the stream running through town. The smallest stone building looked to be an apothecary. A two-story structure connected to the apothecary bore a sign that showed promise: MacElroy's Sundries.

Ian pushed through the door and came to a halt before the bell announcing his arrival stopped jangling. The place was crammed full from floor to ceiling. He'd never seen such clutter. While the building appeared two stories tall from outside, inside, it was but a single floor with high ceilings. A wide gallery above went around the circumference of the room, and that area looked to be packed tighter than a drum, too. Items dangled down from the banisters and even from the rafters. Ribbons, belts, and all sorts of what-nots hung from shelf corners. How the hell did anyone find anything?

"Can I be a helpin' ye, sir?" came a voice from somewhere beyond a daringly stacked mountain of pots, pans, and kettles.

"I need a box," Ian said to whoever might be listening. He turned sideways and slipped by the mound of cookware, and an equally impressive array of crocks balanced atop one another. More obstacles blocked his way. Books, bolts of cloth, bottles, and some items he wouldn't even attempt to identify.

"A box?" the voice repeated. "What sort, sir? I've many boxes here."

Of that, Ian had no doubt. "Where the hell are ye?" He didn't much care for talking to air.

"Behind ye, sir," the quiet voice answered.

He turned to find a man who barely reached the height of his hip. While he was a bit taken aback by the man's diminutive size, he had to admit the gentleman's stealth was impressive. "Ye'd make quite the assassin, sir. Ye're so light of foot, I didna hear ye behind me until ye spoke."

The shopkeeper chuckled as he adjusted his wire-rimmed spectacles higher on his nose. "I have been called many a thing over the years, but I do believe ye're the first to call me an *assassin*." He gave a gracious nod. "I am Hugh MacElroy, proprietor, at yer service, sir." He smoothed his palms down his immaculate waistcoat and smiled. "Now, what sort of box might I help ye find?"

"Ian Cameron, sir." Ian hurried to get the nicety out of the way, then formed a square with his hands and showed the man. "'Tis for a verra special necklace. To protect it. A small trinket box, ye might say."

Hugh tapped his fingers together, eyes narrowing as he turned in a slow circle, then headed down a path winding through his wares. "A small jewelry box. For a lady. Yer wife, perhaps?"

"Aye." Ian shook his head. "I mean, aye, 'tis for a lady—I nay have a wife." He followed the shopkeeper as the man traversed the store with the grace and ease of a stream winding through the woods. "How the hell do ye find anything in this place?"

"While God cursed me in size, he blessed me with the ability to remember everything. Although, in some ways, that be a curse as well." Hugh maneuvered higher on a set of steps Ian hadn't even noticed.

After another adjustment of his spectacles, the shopkeeper pawed through several items jammed on a shelf. "Ah, here it is. The verra one I had in mind." He plucked the item up and descended. With a smile, he proffered a small box. "What do ye think?"

Made from mahogany and hexagonal in shape, its surface was rubbed and polished until the reddish-brown grain shimmered with a rich luster. An intricate carving of knot-work in the shape of a heart covered the lid. Bronze hinges and a latch. Padding of blood-red velvet lined the insides. *Aye*, this would be perfect. Ian nodded. "How much?"

The shrewd proprietor eyed him as though bracing himself for a fight. "A pound. Sterling, not Scot."

Seemed a mite dear, but Ian didn't care. It was for Gretna. He handed over the coin. "Thank ye for yer troubles, sir."

The man smiled and slipped the coin into his pocket. As he disappeared behind stacks of crates filled with books, he called out, "When ye decide to marry her, come back. I've the perfect ring."

Ian left the shop without commenting. If the proprietor saved the ring for that wedding, he'd never sell it. With the box safely tucked in his sporran, he hurried back to the keep. Praise the saints, Alexander's meeting to hear grievances appeared to be over. The main room had emptied of everyone but a few.

Sutherland hailed him from the archway that led to the kitchens. "Alexander sent me to find ye. Thought ye might be plotting yer escape."

"Not yet," Ian said, scrambling to think of a way to lose Sutherland. He headed toward the winding staircase at the back of the hall. "Ye might as well be on yer way. I'm sure there's a lassie somewhere waiting for ye, aye?" He damn sure didn't want his cousin following him. The man gossiped worse than a gaggle of old women. If he got wind of Gretna's gift, the entire clan, clean down to the worms in the gardens, would know about it before nightfall.

"I did spy a new lovely helping with the feast preparations when I walked through the kitchens. Quite fetching, she was. I'll be talking to her later," Sutherland said.

Ian halted at the stairwell and faced the man, unease prickling like needles across his nape. His cousin was a damn sight too happy. Even his grin was more infuriating than usual. "Feast preparations?"

"Aye." Sutherland plucked up an apple from the nearest table and chomped into it.

Ian looked around the hall, noticing the details for the first time. Extra tables and benches had been brought in and arranged in long rows running the length of the massive room. Enough to seat the entire clan and then some.

Sutherland clapped a hand to his shoulder and gave him a playful shake. "The harvest feast. Mabon. Alexander delayed the celebration until we arrived. Tomorrow eve, the festivities begin!"

"Since when does Clan MacCoinnich celebrate a pagan festival?" Ian toyed with the idea of taking Sutherland by the throat and shaking him 'til his teeth rattled. There was more afoot here than the man was saying.

"Since we missed Lammas, Catriona and Alexander felt there was no harm in celebrating Mabon." Sutherland gave him a look that came off as more devilish than pious. "Father William even agreed. The clan has had a good year. A harvest unusually bountiful for the glen. 'Tis only fitting to be thankful." His hand dropped from Ian's shoulder. "Ye should feel honored they wished us to be a part of it." He failed at a devout nod. "I am."

"We just arrived today. How can they have such a celebration ready by tomorrow?" Ian scrubbed a hand down his face, a sudden weariness gnawing at him. He'd always been a patient man, but today had nearly worn it to the very last shred. He would not guarantee courteous handling of this latest game.

"Magnus sent word by Merlin when we left Edinburgh."

Merlin was Magnus's falcon. He and the bird had become inseparable unless Magnus needed a message sent to *Tor Ruadh*. In that case, Merlin happily complied.

Ian tightened his jaw. *Damn them.* He should've noticed the winged hunter hadn't been with them during their journey from Edinburgh to Ben Nevis. The small but effective bird rode on Magnus's shoulder when he wasn't in the air. "So, the feast is tomorrow?"

"Aye." Sutherland motioned toward the stairs. "And I had them put yer things up there." He grinned. "In the quarters ye'll share with the boys." He leaned closer and lowered his teasing tone. "And maybe sometime soon…with the lovely Gretna."

He'd had enough. Ian slammed both hands on Sutherland's chest and shoved him back against the wall with enough force to send the man's half-eaten apple flying. His cousin was nearly his equal in brawn and height, but Sutherland was no match when Ian's temper fueled his strength. "I have had my fill of ye," Ian warned through clenched teeth. "I understand ye find my situation amusing as hell, but I'll not spend the winter with yer jabbin' at me, ye ken?" He bounced Sutherland against the wall a second time. "Yer time will come, ye irritatin' bastard. Mark my words. Yer time will come when the MacCoinnichs tire of toying with me and shift their sights to ye."

Sutherland gave him a genuinely apologetic look. "Forgive me, cousin." He leaned back against the wall and didn't struggle to escape Ian's hold. In a quiet voice filled with no guile, he continued, "I meant no harm. Truly. It appears once again, I've carried my mocking too far." He dipped his head in a contrite nod. "'Tis one of my many failings, but I assure ye, I'll nettle ye no more about Gretna and her sons."

Ian shoved him aside and stepped away. "See that ye don't." He pulled in a deep breath and blew it out. "Now, if ye dinna mind, I'll be heading upstairs to see how they've padded this cage they intend to keep me in." Before Sutherland could speak, Ian thumped him on the chest. "And ye're not welcome to accompany me, ye ken?"

His cousin retrieved his apple from the floor, wiped it on his jacket, then saluted with it as he turned and headed back toward the kitchens. "I understand completely." He paused and tossed back a wink. "Besides, I believe it's time for a visit with that new wee lovely whilst she chops carrots."

Without responding, Ian headed up the stairs. He rolled his shoulders, noticing he didn't feel quite as tense as before. Maybe he should've shut Sutherland's maw a long time ago. His stomping lightened to a regular step.

As he entered the second floor, an acrid stench caught in his throat and set him to coughing. Catriona had said the maids had given the wing a good scrubbing, and she hadn't exaggerated. The odor of lye water almost singed away his nose hairs. He left the door to the stairwell open, praying extra air might help dilute the potent smell of cleanliness.

He eased into the area, confused as he looked around. The second floor of the north wing wasn't like the others. It didn't have a hall and a series of doors. Instead, it consisted of an overlarge sitting area fitted out as comfortably as a chief's solar. Ian supposed that made sense. After all, this wing had once belonged to Catriona's father, Chieftain Neal. A series of tapestries depicting hunting scenes decorated the walls. A woven rug, opulent with a rich red and gold pattern, covered most of the floor. Couches, benches, and chairs overflowing with pillows sat around the space. Shelves of books. A desk, and praise God, what looked to be a long buffet with an ample supply of full decanters. A cheery fire burned in the hearth between a pair of open doors. From what Ian could see, each of those led to the private bedchambers of the living quarters.

Voices came from the room on the left. Ian stepped closer and listened. It never hurt to be prepared.

"Once ye're good and settled, we'll see to making them more," Catriona said, "My seamstress will help. And ye know Mercy will, too. They're growing boys. We canna have them running around bare-arsed in the dead of winter."

"Quick as I get new trews stitched for them, they've already out-grown them," Gretna complained. "Faster than weeds, they're shooting up, and rough as can be. I canna keep the rips and tears mended. They look like poor orphans half the time. Makes me ashamed."

"What are ye standing there spying on them for?" Mam Hattie emerged from the room on the right. "I said it before, and I'll say it again, ye're a rude man, Ian Cameron."

Damned if he didn't feel like a bairn caught stealing bannocks. "I just got here," he lied.

"Ye did not," the old woman argued. "I been standing here a

watching ye."

"Then ye're just as rude as I am, aye?" Ian strode over to the line of decanters and poured himself a whisky. A large one. Lord knew he'd earned it. "Dinna be calling me a spy when ye did the verra same."

"What is going on out here?" Catriona hurried into the sitting area, Gretna following close behind.

Hattie pointed at Ian. "He has been standing there listening to every word ye said without ye knowing it." She shook her head with a haughty snort. "Sneaky as an egg-sucking stoat, he is."

"I just got here," Ian repeated, downed his drink, and poured himself another. "I was merely waiting a wee spell before I entered the room." He returned the crone's damning glare. "'Tis rude to interrupt."

Catriona waved the matron forward. "Now, Hattie. Come to the laundry with me, aye? Ye can help me set the maids aright about the extra linens needed for the rooms." She looked back and gave them both an unsettling smile. "Gretna can show Master Cameron the layout of the chambers to see if they meet with his approval."

Meet with his approval. Ian swallowed a bitter laugh. As if his approval meant a damn thing in this entire farce.

Hattie responded with another huffing snort, then flounced out the door on Catriona's heels.

"Ye've made a braw enemy there, ye ken?" Gretna took hold of the linen bunched across her arm, shook it out, then folded it.

"Aye, well...I've had worse." He nodded toward the decanters. "Shall I pour ye something? Yer day has been just as trying as mine."

Gretna smiled. "Aye, that would be nice."

Something occurred to him as he poured her a glass of port. "I thought ye tended Lady Mercy? Stayed at her side most of the time? I've nay caught sight of her since I arrived."

With an almost embarrassed look, Gretna shook her head. "Lady Mercy doesna really need me. At least, not nearly as much as she did when she first lost her sight." She draped the folded linen across the top of a chair. "King William sent her another lady's maid almost a year ago. A fine girl named Fenna. That sweet lass takes care of Lady Mercy's every need and even helps with her bairns." She stared down at her hands folded atop the linen. "I am little more than a charity since I've no husband to provide for my sons, and my work with old Elena pays verra little." Her irritated gaze lifted. "They think me blind to their ways. Pretending Mercy still needs me is their poor attempt to spare my pride so they can give me coin." She smoothed her hands across the cloth again. "Their pity chokes me most days."

He could kick himself for mentioning it. What a damned fool he was. He gave her the port, then lifted his glass for a toast. "Ye are not a charity, and I'm sure they dinna think that." He raised his glass higher. "A toast to ye, Gretna Neal, strong woman that ye are. Dinna ever change nor think yerself a burden to others, aye? *Slàinte mhath!*"

"*Slàinte mhath!*" She took the tiniest sip of the port, then wrinkled her nose. "Dinna tell Catriona, but I've never cared for port. Too sweet."

"Then, I shall remedy that." Ian took the port from her, cast a glance toward the stairwell, then poured it back in the decanter. He winked. "No one will ever know." He pointed at the other choices lined up on the cabinet. "What shall it be, m'lady?"

Gretna gave a soft laugh and looked more relaxed. "Whisky, kind sir."

"Whisky, it is." Ian filled a glass and brought it to her. "*Slàinte mhath*—for true, this time."

"Aye." She tapped it to his and took a much healthier sip than she had before. "*Slàinte mhath*—for true."

Remembering his mission, Ian set his whisky aside. He couldn't wait to see how pleased she'd be with what he'd found. "Now, set yer dram on the table, and close yer eyes."

Gretna frowned, looking at him as though he'd gone daft. "What?"

"Ye heard me," he said. "I've a surprise. Close yer eyes and hold out both yer hands."

A doubting look still firmly in place, she grudgingly complied. With her drink on the table and her eyes closed, she stood with her hands locked at her sides. "I am none too keen on surprises. Nor any other kind of foolery, ye ken? Never have been. Give me a hint before I trust my hands to ye."

He stepped closer, easing the trinket box out of his sporran as he moved. "This is a good surprise. Ye can trust me. I swear it."

"Verra well then." She took a deep breath, blew it out, then held her hands, palms up, in front of her. She resettled her stance and lifted her chin. "I am ready."

Proud and anxious to share his find and witness her happiness, he placed it in her hands. "Open yer eyes."

Curiosity knotting her brow, Gretna hurried to open her eyes. Gaze locked on the box, her lips parted, and her brow smoothed. She cocked her head to one side as she flipped the latch with her thumb and eased open the lid.

"It's for yer wee necklace!" He couldn't stand it any longer. Surely, she had to prize it. It was perfect for keeping her dear memento safe.

Gretna caught her lip between her teeth and closed the lid. Fingers trembling, she cradled the box between her hands, then slowly hugged it to her chest. "Ye bought this for me? For the necklace Coire gave me?"

"Aye." Ian swallowed hard and gave her his best smile. Something had gone wrong. He felt it in his bones and even heavier in his gut.

A sheen of tears brightened her eyes, and her voice broke with emotions. "For the necklace?" she repeated with a tremulous smile. "To keep it safe?"

Lord Almighty. He'd most assuredly erred. "Do ye not like it?"

"Not like it?" The dreaded tears escaped and raced down her cheeks. She turned away and bowed her head. "How could I not like it?" she said so softly he barely heard her. "'Tis the most thoughtful thing anyone has done for me since…" Her voice trailed off, and her shoulders shook with silent weeping.

Shite. He hadn't meant to make her cry. "I'm sorry, Gretna. I didna mean to upset ye." The wee gift had made things worse for her rather than better. *Dammit.* "I just thought—"

She whirled and wrapped her arms around him, squeezing him in a fierce hug. Face tucked into the crook of his neck, she whispered, "'Tis perfect. Finer than fine." She squeezed him even harder until he became increasingly aware of just how soft and enjoyable her curves against him felt. When she released him and stepped away, he immediately missed her warmth, almost painfully so.

"This means more than I can say," she said as she gave the box a series of gentle pats. "So verra much more." With a hard swallow and another sniff, she set the box on the corner of the buffet and opened the lid. She pulled the cloth parcel from her pocket, unwrapped the necklace, and placed it in the box. A peaceful look settled across her as she closed the lid. "'Tis perfect, for true. Coire would be pleased ye treated his gift with so much kindness and respect." She glanced up at him. "Many say I should put all my memories of him away and only worry with making new ones. I dinna feel it's wrong to remember those we love. Do ye?"

"Nay." Ian took hold of both her hands. "Nay, lass. I agree whole-heartedly. Remembering those we loved honors them and keeps them with us 'til we see them again."

"Ye're a good man, Ian." She smiled. "I shall do my best to make yer stay this winter as tolerable as possible. I promise." She kissed his cheek, then patted his hands, and hurried to gather up the linen she'd left on the chair. "Best put this away," she said as she hurried into the room on the right, the room he assumed she'd share with that irritating crone.

Ian watched her until she disappeared. He pulled in a deep breath and held it, doing his best to sort through all he felt. Her touch. Her softness pressed against him. Her scent and warmth. All these things had burned themselves across his senses in a way he'd not expected. *Tolerable*, she had said. This stay at *Tor Ruadh* had already become more *tolerable* than he'd ever dreamed—and it scared the living hell out of him.

CHAPTER FOUR

"WE EACH OF us get our own?" Evander gave her a dubious look, then turned back to stare at the three cots lined up on either side of the hearth. "No more a Rory's kicking or Finn's pissing the bed?"

"Yer verra own bed," Gretna reassured. Poor lads. They'd always slept three to the pallet, but at least they'd kept each other warm on cold nights. "And since ye're eldest, ye get to choose first."

Without hesitating, he pointed at the bed in the farthest corner. "That one. Rory'll want to be by the hearth, and Finn'll need to be closest to the door, so's ye can get to him when he has his bad dreams." Without another word, he climbed into the bed and pulled the covers up to his chin.

"What if I dinna want to be by the hearth?" Rory argued. "I can pick my own bed, thank ye verra much."

"Stop spoiling for a fight. It's late, and we're all of us weary." Gretna gave a light swat to the lad's rump. If the wee imp wasn't sparring with someone, he wasn't happy. "Ye know as well as I that ye're always cold." She pointed to the cot closest to the hearth. "Get ye to bed."

Not fazed by the scolding, Rory grinned as he plopped down on the cot, bounced up and down for a moment, then slid under the blankets.

"Finlay Drake?" She only used his full Christian name when she was determined to share some of her own strength with the timid mite. Poor wee Finn didn't handle change well. To be honest, he handled few things well. This youngest child of hers struggled with life itself. Small for his age, he looked like any normal child, but she knew in her heart, he was not quite as he should be. God bless him. She didn't care what was wrong with him. He was her dear, sweet bairn, and she loved him fiercely.

"Get ye to bed, son. I'll be just outside the door in the sitting room with my mending for a while. Then Mam Hattie and I will be right in the next room should ye need us."

"Will ye be able to hear me if'n I call out?" Finn asked, rocking back and forth from one foot to the other.

Lord help her troubled child. Whenever Finn took to his rocking, he was more than a little anxious. He'd done it even as a wee babe. "I'll leave the doors ajar just to make sure, aye?" She gave him a quick hug and kissed his cheek. "To bed with ye now, so's I can tuck ye in."

Steps dragging, he made his way to the bed, then froze in place, his unblinking stare locked on the pillow.

"Get in bed, Finn," Evander ordered from the corner. "There's naught to fear here in the keep, and if anything does try to bother ye, me and Rory'll whip its arse for it."

"Aye, Finn," Rory chimed in. "And we'll hold it down and make it smell the cracks of our arses when we break wind!"

That brought a smile and a giggle from the lad.

Praise be. "In the bed, Finn," she urged before the brotherly spell wore off.

The child slid under the blankets, curled into a ball, then continued his rocking from side to side.

At least he was in bed. Once he grew accustomed to the new arrangement, he'd settle down enough to sleep. Gretna tucked each child in snug and kissed their brows. "Ye're my world, lads. I love ye forever and a day. Never forget." She spoke this same blessing over them each and every night, praying they'd always remember just how much she loved them.

She eased out of the room, leaving the door ajar just as she'd promised. Movement beside the far window caught her eye. Ian. Drink in hand. Staring up at the stars. God help that poor man.

Mercy and Catriona had attempted to snare first Duncan, then Sutherland for her. She had flat out refused both and prayed that would be the end of it. Apparently, those two failures had served only to hone the matchmakers' determination. And now this kind soul was trapped—at least for a little while. Without a word, she fetched her mending basket and settled in a chair closest to the boys' room. She couldn't lay down her own head until she knew her bairns slept.

Ian turned from the window. "The old woman said to tell ye she'll help with the mending tomorrow. Said she was too weary to make a straight stitch and has gone to bed." He took a sip of whisky, then added, "thank God."

She pulled the candelabra on the table closer, angling the dark trews in the flickering light to better show the rip. "So, the two of ye are still fighting, I take it?"

"We dinna fight." He moved to the buffet and refilled his glass. "We just dinna like each other." He nodded toward the line of decanters and pitchers. "Care for a drink?"

"A bit of ale would be nice." She pulled the line of stitching tight, knotted the thread, and cut it close with her teeth. "Anything stronger, and I'll not get the proper mending done." She set aside the completed garment and pulled another from her basket. As she adjusted her thread, she nodded down at the seemingly endless pile. "If ye've anything in need of mending, pop it in the basket. I dinna mind."

He set her drink on the table beside her. "Thank ye, but I usually tend to my own mending." He gave a twitching shrug. "There's not always someone available to handle it for me." He meandered around the room, sipping at his whisky as he walked.

On his third pass in front of her, Gretna pointed to the chair on the other side of the table. "Either sit and entertain me with tales of yer adventures or get ye to bed. Yer pacing rattles my nerves."

"After today, I'm surprised ye've got any nerves left." He shot her a pouting scowl but lowered himself into the chair.

"And dinna perch on the edge and sit there bouncing yer knees either. Ye fidget worse than Finn." She'd forgotten that not only was Ian the most pensive of the seven who had shown up at the keep on that long-ago winter's day, he'd also been the most restless.

"Might I remind ye I am not one of yer sons? I dinna require constant scolding, ye ken?"

He was right. The realization triggered a flash of remorse. "Aye, that's more than true. Forgive me." She pulled the stitch tight and stabbed the needle into the cloth. "I would blame it on the day, but that still doesn't make it acceptable." A heavy sigh escaped her as she sank deeper in the chair and allowed the mending to rest in her lap. "I'm sure the winter would be easier for both of us to bear without my nagging."

Ian scooted back in the chair and stilled his jittering. "I should not have spoken so sharply. Forgive me, too, aye?"

She lifted her glass and gave him a smile. "To forgiveness all around."

Matching her smile, he leaned over and clicked his glass to hers. "Aye. To forgiveness."

They both drank, then set their glasses on the table. The silence between them grew, becoming an uncomfortable beast that filled the room. She had to think of something to say to vanquish it. *The boys.* She should tell him about the boys. Especially Finn. She shifted in the chair, turning to face him. "I dinna ken if ye've noticed, but Finlay— my wee Finn, is...special. He's not like most boys his age."

Ian stared at her, eyes narrowing. "I had noticed," he finally said. He frowned, still studying her. "Has he always been so…odd?"

"Dinna call him that!" She hated that word. *Odd. Touched. Addled.* She'd have none of those names attached to her sweet bairn. "He struggles more than most, but he's quick-witted. He'll learn whatever task ye charge him with and keep at it until he has it perfect. Just be patient and give him a chance. Never mock him, or ye'll have me to deal with, understand?"

"I would never mock him, lass," Ian said quietly. "Not ever." He nodded toward the bedchamber door. "I'll have all three of them made into fine warriors before I leave. Ye have my word on that."

A terrible memory surfaced. "Dinna take him hunting." She shoved the unfinished mending back into the basket and scooted to the edge of the chair. "Promise ye willna take him hunting nor kill any animals in front of him, aye?"

"Why? What happened to the lad?" Only concern and kindness shone in Ian's eyes, urging her to relax. "Tell me so I can help him."

"The day before Colin's accident, the fool decided he'd had enough of his son's meekness. He killed the rabbit Evander had caught for Finn to keep as a pet. Finn had loved that rabbit dear. Even named it and held it all the time." Her throat ached with a knot of emotions. "Colin gutted it in front of him." She swallowed hard, determined not to weep. "Finn screamed for hours, and didna speak for nearly two years after that." Lingering rage and unresolved vengeance shook through her. "If Colin *had* returned from his trip, I planned to slit his throat and gut him the same way."

"Heartless bastard deserved to die."

Ian's quiet outrage warmed her heart. He looked the avenging mercenary she'd heard him to be. Teeth bared. Strong jaw flexing. Hands clenched and ready to unsheathe his sword. Her heart beat faster. What a fine man to find herself tethered to for the winter. A man not only of strength but of kindness.

"Every day, I thank God Almighty for taking care of the matter for me." She rose and moved to the bedroom door. "I best check on them one last time before I seek my own bed."

No sound came from the room, dimly lit by a single candle on the mantel and the fire in the hearth. She eased inside, listening as she waited for her eyes to adjust to the darkness. Finn had stopped his troubled rocking. The only sound in the room was the slow, steady breathing of her boys deep in their dreams. She turned down the covers of the large bed beside the window, then returned to the sitting room.

"All are asleep if ye wish to get in yer bed now. I turned down the covers for ye since I'm now off to seek my own."

Ian stared at her with a strange expression.

"Is something wrong?" She hoped she hadn't insulted him by preparing his bed. 'Twas true they'd been unwillingly saddled with each other, but there was no need to make the worst of it. "Did ye not wish me to fix yer bed for ye?"

He blinked as though waking from a dream. "Nay, lass. 'Tis fine. Thank ye. I'll retire in a bit." He held up his half-full glass. "I never waste a dram. Rest ye well and dream of only good things."

"Aye...and ye do the same." An eeriness rippled across her, like the touch of a restless ghost. It wasn't unpleasant. More like a vague memory, a good memory, struggling to be recalled and enjoyed. She shivered away the strange feeling. Such silliness. Her weariness played tiresome tricks on her sometimes. "Good evening to ye," she said as slipped into her bedchamber.

"Aye, lass. Rest ye well," he repeated.

A DELICATE HUMMING pulled him to full wakefulness. He never slept deeply. Hadn't since Glencoe. He blinked, clearing his vision. The room had gone dark. The night candle must've spent itself or blown out from the partially opened window. The fire in the hearth had reduced to glowing coals. He sat up in bed, listening, pinpointing the sound. *The sitting room. Maybe.* With stealth born from years of fighting, he moved to the door and opened it wider. Flickering firelight from the sitting room hearth danced into the bedchamber and fell across young Finn's bed. It was empty. Concern tingled through the hairs at the back of his neck. *Nay. The lad's fine.* Surely, he'd just gone to his mother. Hadn't he?

Ian stared at the small pair of boots beside the bed. Finn was troubled. Troubled but bright. Ian had noticed that even before Gretna had mentioned the young lad was quick-witted—just a mite different. Well...she'd not said *different* and had made it clear she found the word *odd* offensive. So be it. He'd do what he could to help the boy. God help him. He'd best locate the bairn just to be sure all was well. It surprised him the child had moved with such silence.

The sitting room was empty, but the soft lilting hum that had awakened him continued. He followed the sound to Gretna and Miss Hattie's room, hestitating at the door. It stood wide enough for him to squeeze through without opening it further. But, perhaps he shouldn't. The sweet tune faded in and out, then splintered off into silence. Naught sounded amiss, but what of wee Finn? What if he wasn't in the room with his mother? Gretna could've been humming to soothe herself after the day they'd all had. He slipped inside.

A whistling snore came from the bed closest to the door. The generous mound rising, then falling in tandem with the snoring assured him his enemy, the crone, rested well. He squinted, surveying the large room lit only by the fire in the hearth. The bed beside the window was empty. Covers thrown back, pillows askew. He eased past the foot of Mam Hattie's bed, freezing in place as she breathed out a long, mumbling groan, then farted. Praise God, she didn't wake.

Once past the old woman's bed, he circled around the chairs in front of the fire. He came to a halt. There she was. Cross-legged on the floor. Arms locked around Finn, who was curled in her lap. Poor Gretna was sound asleep while propped against the chair behind her.

God bless her. Mouth ajar, hair tumbling down around her shoulders, Ian couldn't remember the last time he'd seen such a precious sight as this. The firelight's glow danced across her fair skin and enlivened the coppery fire in her hair. He swallowed hard, noticing for the first time just how much her thin chemise revealed. *Christ Almighty.* He should go.

As he stood there, her arms gradually relaxed. Her laced fingers eased apart, and her hands came to rest on the floor beside her legs. Finn shifted, snuggling down more comfortably in the nest of her lap. How on earth could she sleep so soundly in such a position? He couldn't leave her like this. She wouldn't be able to move come morning. Ian made up his mind. *Aye.* He knew exactly what to do. Duty and honor demanded it. He'd put them both in the bed.

Silent as a shadow, he slid his hands under Finn, all the while watching for Gretna to waken and ready to calm her as soon as she did. She remained motionless. *Poor lass. Exhausted.*

The backs of his hands brushed her thighs as he bettered his hold of the lad. *Lord have mercy.* Warm, sweet-smelling, and soft as silk. Ian held his breath, struggling to keep his thoughts on the task at hand. He lifted the boy and settled him against his chest. Gretna still didn't rustle, and the sight revealed by moving the boy made him swallow hard to keep from groaning. Chemise bunched up around her thighs, from the knees down, her shapely legs were exposed.

Ian quick-stepped to the bed and settled the child among the pillows. He looked back at the area in front of the hearth. He should wake her so she could join Finn in the bed. *Aye.* That's what he'd do. He slipped back to the chairs and squatted down beside her, adjusting his entirely too interested cock that was tangled in the folds of his léine. "Lass," he whispered and gave her arm a gentle shake.

Her only response was a deeper breath and tucking her head more comfortably against the chair.

There was no helping it. He couldn't leave her on the cold floor. It would be rudeness itself. He slipped his arms around her and stood, cradling her against him. She exhaled an alluring, purring sound and snuggled closer, nudging her cheek into the dip of his shoulder. He had to get her to the bed before his raging cock crippled him completely.

As soon as he placed her among the pillows, she rolled to her side, tucked an arm around Finn, and melted into the covers. He stared down at her and the boy. Relaxed. Peaceful. A rush of bitterness almost choked him. Fate had denied him such as this. Robbed him of Janet. Snatched away his child. How different would life have been if he'd only had the chance to look upon his own loved ones sleeping like this?

He shoved away the unfairness of it all and pulled the blankets up over them, gently tucking it around their shoulders. Damned, if he wasn't tempted to crawl in beside her. Just to hold her. Just to keep the aching loneliness at bay for one night. He scrubbed a hand down his face and shook himself. What a damned foolish thing that would be. Without a sound, he slipped from the room, clicking the door shut behind him. He leaned back against the wall and blew out a heavy sigh. "God give me the strength to survive this winter without losing my mind," he prayed. "Or my heart," he added with a groan.

He pushed away from the wall and shook himself again. He would get through this, then leave come summer as he'd planned. But by damned if he wouldn't be at risk every minute of it and have to be on his guard. Gretna might not realize it, but the rumors about her were true. She was a witch. Powerfully so. The pull of her magic dared him to do his best to win her and claim her family for his own. He shook his head against the dangerous urge. *Nay.* As cursed as he was, 'twould be folly for certain. And neither his heart nor his soul could survive another loss.

CHAPTER FIVE

GRETNA HURRIED UP to the next floor. She had to admit, tending Mercy would be a great deal easier with them both living just a floor apart in the north wing. A wailing three-year-old met her at the door. Little Effie. Graham and Mercy's youngest child.

"What's wrong, lassie?" Gretna scooped up the little girl and hugged her.

"Maxel broke dolly again!" Effie shouted between squalls, not a tear in her eyes. Wee Effie wasn't heartbroken. She was enraged. Maxwell MacCoinnich was the eldest of Catriona and Alexander's youngest set of twins, and apparently, Effie's arch-enemy at the moment.

Even though sightless, her mother crossed the room with ease. Calmness itself, Mercy held out her arms for her daughter. "Effie, come to Mama."

The little girl dove into her mother's embrace, and Gretna smiled. The two made a heartwarming picture. Dark hair, amber eyes, Effie Marsalla was the spitting image of her lovely mother, and no one could reason with her as well as Mercy.

"Forgive us," Mercy said to Gretna with a smile as she swayed and bounced with the child. "We refuse to nap, torment the other children while they try to sleep, and have poor Nanny at her wit's end."

"Poor Nanny indeed," Gretna said. The dear old woman had her hands full with the twins and Effie. Luckily, Alexander and Catriona's older twins and Graham and Mercy's seven-year-old son had outgrown the nursery and earned the run of the keep.

A sturdy young girl with light brown hair clipped short appeared in the doorway to the adjoining room. Gretna admired Fenna's bravery for cropping her hair. It suited the girl's temperament perfectly.

"Well, ye are here," the maid said. "I didna think ye'd come today what with yer family just moved into the keep. Thought ye'd need more time for settling." She strode across the room and held out her hands to Effie. "Come to Fenna, aye? We'll go downstairs and find some bonnie treats for ye."

The doll forgotten, Effie jumped into Fenna's arms. The maid shifted the toddler to her hip, then sidled closer to Mercy. With a sympathetic nod in Gretna's direction, she advised her mistress, "Dinna forget to tell her what I heard. I'll do what I can to help, aye?"

"I shall address it," Mercy said, her usual serenity replaced with a worrisome hardness around her mouth.

"Off to find treats," Fenna announced as she bounced out the door and closed it behind her.

"Address what?" Gretna repeated. She'd had her fill with matters needing to be addressed and didn't possess the patience or willingness to face anymore.

"We should sit. This could take a while."

That comment made her feel even worse. She followed Mercy to a pair of cushioned chairs flanking a small table in front of the window. Bright sunlight helped Mercy make out shapes and colors in her world of shadows.

"Is this going to call for something stronger than ale?" Gretna detoured over to a long, narrow table against the wall. Pitchers and bottles, as well as tankards and glasses, were neatly arranged and waiting.

"Probably. I'll have a bit of port, if you don't mind pouring?" Mercy seated herself and folded her hands atop the table.

"Verra well." Gretna filled a short glass with whisky and a goblet with port. She placed their drinks on the table, then settled in the chair opposite Mercy. "Now tell me what Fenna was talking about." Gretna considered the lady's maid a trusted friend. Whatever the lass's dire reminder had concerned couldn't be good.

Mercy sipped her wine then frowned. "It appears the rumors have already started."

"Rumors?" Gretna risked a sip of her whisky, then blew out a short, bitter laugh. "Can ye narrow it down a bit, m'lady? Ye know as well as I that *Tor Ruadh* is always astir with rumors." She cupped her glass between her hands. "If ye're speaking about the one where everyone thinks I'm a witch because my herbs and healing are so much better than old Elena's, that story's been around a while. In fact, I'd lay odds Elena Bickerstaff started that rumor herself." She paused for another sip and waved Mercy's worries aside. "Dinna fash yerself. Alexander keeps that mess at bay as best he can. Ye know how some folk can be."

As long as those closest to her didn't believe the foolish tales, that's all that mattered to Gretna. Well...that, and the fact that the rumors were never allowed to grow strong enough to have her lashed to a stake and burned.

Mercy shook her head. "No. Not the accusations of witchery." Her face was filled with sympathy and concern. "The talk of your morals in choosing to share quarters with Ian without the benefit of marriage."

"I didna choose it!" Gretna thumped her glass on the table. "Alexander ordered it so. Ask Catriona." She banged the glass against the table again. "Mam Hattie and I share one of the bedchambers whilst Ian and the boys share the other. The entire clan knows this. Catriona announced it at the meeting in great hall and made it plain as day, so there'd be no unseemly talk."

Mercy held up a hand. "I know. Graham told me everything that happened." She started to say something else but stopped herself.

"What?" Gretna toyed with the idea of refilling her glass, then thought better of it. *Nay.* She needed to keep her wits about her. More was astir here than the lady was telling. "I would hear it all, Mercy. Tell me now. This ruinous game canna get much worse."

"Fenna told me of the rumors, and Graham confirmed them after he and Alexander discovered the boys fighting in the stable."

"Fighting already?" Gretna sagged back in her chair. "Which ones?" It was a pointless question. She knew it had to be Rory and Evander. Rory had a temper as fiery as hers, and Evander never allowed his brother to fight alone.

Head bowed, Mercy's mouth tightened with displeasure at the topic. "All of them, actually. It appears some of the children had been taunting poor Finn with rude names about you. They cornered him, roughed him up a bit, and had him screaming. I'm sure you can figure out the rest." With a shake of her head, her frown deepened. "Graham said if Evander and Rory had not shown up, the poor child would've taken quite the beating. The smithy's sons are heartless ruffians." Mercy lifted her head. "Rest assured, I've charged Graham with seeing that their father takes them in hand immediately."

"When did this happen?" Gretna could care less about the name-calling; she was worried about her child. "Did Evander and Rory thrash those ill-mannered beasts?"

"Earlier today." Mercy brightened. "According to Graham, they did quite well even though the smithy's boys are twice their size. I believe Evander walked away unscathed, and Rory ended up with a bloodied nose, but considered it a badge of honor." She took another sip, set her glass back to the table, then fixed Gretna with a stern look. "But you know as well as I this isn't the end of it. You just moved into the keep, and the boys already have to defend your honor—and each other."

"I shall speak to them about the fighting." She had the sudden feeling Mercy was scolding her and about to pronounce her punishment. "I'll tell them to ignore the other boys, but I canna say I'm not proud of them for standing together and taking care of their brother."

Mercy reached across the table, found her hand, and clasped it tight. "They shouldn't have to live like that. You know they already have so much trouble getting along with the other children. Especially little Finn. I'm not saying it's their fault, I'm just saying they've had so many scuffles that now they always hang back. Keep to themselves. You've said so yourself and told me you worry about it as well. Have they ever spoken of any friends?" She squeezed Gretna's hand again. "It's as though they're outcasts. Graham and I worry about them. Worry about you."

"Then tell Alexander and Catriona to reverse this ridiculous sham and allow me and my boys to move back to our croft." She pulled free of Mercy's grasp and rose from the chair. "The lot of ye have gone too far this time. Have ye no other way to amuse yerselves?" How dare they accuse her of being a poor mother. She loved her lads. Loved them more than life itself. "I can take of my boys without any help from anyone, thank ye verra much."

"It is not amusement to attempt to help those we love. It is our wish for a dear friend's happiness." Mercy rose, holding out both hands. "Please don't be cross. You are the sister I never had, and I pray you understand that everything I say to you, I say with love." She took a step toward Gretna, hands still extended, waiting for Gretna to take them. "The boys had trouble before you moved into the keep. I don't think moving back into your croft will help. Be honest, Gretna. You know it's true."

"Then what do you suggest?" Gretna ignored Mercy's outstretched hands, her heart aching. "I am damned if I do and damned if I do not. Tell me, foster sister of mine, what is best for my boys?" She hated the way she sounded. Bitter. Lonely. Ungrateful. But she couldn't help it.

This situation had pushed her beyond all she could bear.

With a heavy sigh, Mercy drew back her hands and clasped them to her middle. "It is my belief that at the feast tonight, you and Ian should be handfasted in front of the clan. Graham suggested it. I spoke to Catriona, and she agrees. It's the only way other than saying vows in front of Father William to extinguish at least some of the rumors." She shrugged and shook her head. "I've yet to come up with a way to squelch the lingering rumblings of witchery unless you're willing to have Father William sprinkle holy water on you during the next clan gathering."

"Handfasted." Gretna ignored the holy water remark as she massaged her temples. Her head pounded, and it had nothing to do with the whisky. She glared at Mercy, willing her to understand. "I opened my heart to ye. Told ye the tales of my cold, loveless marriage to Colin. Ye say ye care for me? Love me like a sister? I doubt the truth of those sentiments if ye're so cruel as to suggest I go through the pain of such an existence again."

"It would be different with Ian." Mercy sounded like a mother attempting to soothe a fretting bairn. "He is a good, kind man. You already like each other. Didn't you tell me you barely knew Colin when you wed because he was always off seeking some sort of trouble to get into? Find himself an easy fortune?" She eased a step closer. "And no one knew of his cruelty because you hid it so well." Mercy lifted her clasped hands as though about to pray. "Think how much such a commitment with Ian could help your boys."

"I canna believe ye'd suggest such a thing." If not for the fact that she loved Mercy, she would've already stormed out of the room to never return. But she couldn't do that. Mercy had been her dearest friend for years and never treated her ill. At least, not until now. Gretna lowered herself to a nearby couch and sagged into the cushions. "I canna do what ye ask of me, Mercy. I can not."

Mercy joined her. "It's handfasting. Little more than a betrothal, really. Alexander would remind everyone it would only last for a year and day." She paused, a daring smile creeping across her lips. "Unless, of course, you and Ian decide to make it permanent, and then I'm sure we'd have a fine wedding with Father William to seal the union properly."

A peck on the door interrupted them. It cracked open enough to allow Catriona to peep inside. "Has she agreed?"

"Nay, she has not agreed!" Gretna jumped up. "I will ask ye the same thing I asked Mercy. Do ye not have anything better to amuse yerselves with other than my life? I've about had my fill with the lot of ye!"

They had her so nettled, she didn't know what to do. Should she stay in the keep? Would her refusal of the handfasting make it worse for the boys? If she moved back to the croft, would they suffer shame there, too? Should they leave Glen Nevis completely? If she did, how on earth could she provide for her wee lads? How would she feed them? Clothe them? Keep a roof over the heads?

She dropped back to the couch and cradled her head in her hands. "Ye've addled me so, I canna think straight."

Mercy scooted closer and wrapped an arm about her shoulders. Catriona scurried across the room, seated herself on the other side, and hugged her as well.

"We just want to help," Catriona said, catching hold of one her hands and squeezing it. "We mean no harm, lass. We love ye. Please believe us."

Gretna couldn't bear the both of them beating her brow. She pushed them away. "This is madness. Ye understand that, aye?"

"It's nay madness," Catriona argued. She shifted her focus to Mercy. "Did ye tell her of the year and the day?"

"I did," Mercy defended. "I explained it all."

"Dinna talk as though I'm not sitting right here betwixt ye!"

Catriona gave her a hard look. "Did ye stop and think that if ye handfasted with Ian, a MacCoinnich cousin, 'twould make yer ties to the chieftain even stronger? Ye're already my cousin. This would make ye doubly tied to the head of the clan and, hopefully, grant the boys some better treatment from all they meet."

"Knowing this clan, they'll probably be treated worse!" Gretna rose and moved away from their smothering circle. "Why are the lot of ye so damned and determined to join me with Ian Cameron?"

"Because the two of ye would be good for each other!" Mercy retorted. She fidgeted on the couch, clutching her hands in her lap.

Catriona supported the statement with a jerking dip of her chin. "Aye. The both of ye need each other whether ye know it yet or not."

Gretna forced herself to rein in her emotions. Arguing with these two was futile. But she knew something they didn't. She knew Ian would never agree because he felt the same as she did. More so, in fact. He was determined to resume his mercenary life of travel and warring for coin come summer. She folded her arms across her middle. "I will agree on one condition."

"Which is?" Catriona asked, leeriness in her tone.

"No promises or threats to make Ian agree. If he agrees of his own free will, I will do so as well. I willna have a man forced to join with me. Never again. Leave me a bit of pride, aye?"

"Agreed," both women said as one.

"Gretna agreed."

"Ye lie." Ian emptied his tankard, then leaned sideways to peer around Graham and Magnus. Gretna's cubs were still in place. They sat pouting beside the hearth. Ian had ordered the wee imps to sit where he could see them, since every time they disappeared, they got into trouble. They'd already been caught fighting in the stables with the smithy's sons. Shameful—sort of.

He had to admit the boys had done themselves proud. And when he'd heard the reason for the fight, he didn't blame them a damn bit. They were good lads. Had it been him, he would've pummeled the smithy's wee bastards, too. He thumped his tankard on the table. "There is no way Gretna agreed to it. She doesna want such a tie any more than I do."

"Maybe so," Graham argued. "But that was before she discovered what a new mess of troubles this current situation has caused the lads." He tossed a glance back at the boys. "Poor bairns. Their lives have never been easy." He tapped the table, then pointed at Ian. "Ye could make their lives better, ye ken?"

"It's just a simple handfasting," Magnus chimed in, his oddly whitish-blonde hair reflecting the candles and lanterns already lit for the feast. "Just a year and a day commitment so everyone, adults and bairns alike, move on to spreading rumors about someone else. It would give the lads a welcomed break. Help them feel more settled. Accepted."

"And if ye do it tonight in front of all those gathered for the feast, 'twould squelch the rumors good and proper," Graham added.

"I dinna consider sleeping in a room with three boys and an old woman as living in sin with a brazen woman." Ian waved his tankard for a refill. The smiling girl emptied her pitcher by filling all three of their mugs.

"Where there's a will, there's a way," Magnus observed, watching the girl's swaying curves as she walked away. "And everyone knows that, aye?"

Merlin gave a sharp chirp of agreement.

Ian glared at the small but regal falcon perched on Magnus's shoulder. "Must ye bring that bird everywhere?"

"Agree to the handfasting, and I'll put him to bed early in my room." Magnus grinned as he took another healthy swig. He plunked the tankard back on the table. "Alexander has already said he'll play it off as if it were planned this way all along. That way, all the rumor-mongers will look the fool."

"And how will he explain what Catriona said during great hall about Mam Hattie? About how the woman would stay with us in our quarters to show all was proper?" He was not a dullard. Magnus and Graham were making this up as they went along.

Magnus gave a noncommittal shrug. "He'll just say Catriona misspoke." He leaned forward, stole a look around, then lowered his voice. "After all, she's already huge, and this bairn's not due 'til the dead of winter. He'll play it off to her pregnancy. Everyone knows a woman goes a little daft what with all their troubles during that time."

Ian laughed. "Ye better pray she never hears ye say that."

Movement beside the hearth caught his eye. Finn had disappeared, Rory was about to slip away, and Evander looked ready to bolt. Ian rose from the table and strode over to them. He pointed at their stools beside the fire. "Sit."

Both lads complied without argument.

"Where is yer brother?" he asked after a glance around the hall failed to provide him any clue as to Finn's whereabouts.

"Went to take a piss," Rory said in a sullen tone. "I need to go, too."

"Me, too," Evander said. "I'll go with him, and we'll gather up Finn and return quick as we're done, aye?"

Ian glared at the lads. They *had* been in the hall for quite a while. He could use a step outside himself. He motioned for them to follow. "Come. We'll fetch Finn together."

"Ye dinna trust us?" Rory sniped.

"Nay." Ian led the way. "I need a piss, too."

They headed down the corridor to a side door that opened out to the bailey between the dovecote and the outside kitchen. Ian cast a side-eyed glance at the boys. "Yer fight today. I heard it was because those boys called yer mother an unsavory name and were picking on yer brother. Is that true?"

"Aye," Evander said in a tone that sounded as if he felt it pointless to defend himself to Ian.

"It's good ye stand up for yer mother and brother." Ian pushed the door open, and they all stepped outside. Finn was nowhere to be seen in the area considered acceptable to use as an outdoor garderobe. He gave them both a warning look. "If ye lied to me, I'll thrash ye. I canna abide with liars. Where is he?"

"We didna lie," Evander defended with a scowl. "He's probably hiding because he heard the door slam and got scared."

"Finn!" Rory bellowed with his hands cupped around his mouth. "Come out, ye wee bugger!"

"Dinna call yer brother a bugger," Ian ordered, his patience running thin. Damnation, how many other swear words did they know? A faint scuffling in the shadows beside the dovecote caught his attention. "Finn?"

"Aye," came a hesitant whisper. The young lad stepped into the torchlight. "I'm sorry I left the hearth, Master Ian. I know I wasna 'posed ta, but I had ta go."

"Ye shouldha asked me. I wouldha said yes and not thought ye were trying to disobey me." Ian stared at the lot of them lined up next to the wall like a trio of prisoners. "Ye'll find I am not an unreasonable man. Ye can ask anything ye like, and I'll help ye if I'm able."

The boys shifted in place, giving each other pointed looks in their silent communication.

"While I piss, all of ye decide who has the courage to say what's on yer minds, ye ken?" Ian gave them his back and relieved himself of all the ale he'd drunk. When he turned back around, Evander stepped forward. He'd figured Evander would be the one. He'd learned the boy was the representative for the trio. "Evander?"

"Some say ye might be handfasting with Mama tonight at the feast." He flexed his hands and resettled his feet. "Others say ye would never promise yerself to Mama 'cause ye know her to be a witch and a whore, and ye swore ye never wanted nothin' to do with bairns or marriage ever again." He jerked his chin in Ian's direction. "What say ye?"

Ian sucked in a deep breath, folded his arms across his chest, and broadened his stance. Valid questions that demanded the truth as best as he could give it to them. "I have known yer mother for almost ten years now." He nodded toward Rory and Finn. "About as long as the two of ye have walked this earth." He took a step closer to the boys. "She's not a witch nor a whore, and I'd never think such vile things about her. I know her to be a canny, fearless lass who I'm proud to call friend."

"Then what about never marrying again? And about never wanting any bairns around ye?" Rory taunted.

"I was married once," Ian said quietly. "For a little while." He shifted in place, determined to make them understand. "Barely a day after my sweet Janet told me she carried our first bairn, a heartless bastard slit her throat at Glencoe. I held her in my arms and watched the spark of her life drain away." He swallowed hard. "I would give anything to see my Janet again. Meet our child. I loved them both fierce." He looked at each of the boys and gave them a sad smile. "It's not that I didna want any bairns nor wish them around. It's that my verra own bairn was taken from me."

The boys shuffled in place, looking first at each other, then down at their feet.

"We're sorry, Master Ian," Finn whispered, swaying back and forth.

"Aye," Rory agreed, voice hitching. He coughed, then cleared his throat. "Sorry for certain."

"And the handfasting?" Evander asked. "What of that rumor?"

A thought occurred to Ian. These poor lads had always been the victims of circumstances. Considering all they'd endured, the trio probably resented never having a choice. It could be part of the reason why they were always into mischief. At least mischief was something they could control. "What do ye think I should I do, Evander?"

"Eh?" The boy stared at him.

"Should I go through with a handfasting to yer mother? Would the three of ye support such a thing or make life a living hell for all of us?" Ian felt it a valid question. "It would only be for a year and a day, mind ye," he hurried to add. No sense making the boys think this would in any way be permanent. "I am a mercenary. I've battles to profit from once my time here is over. What say ye?"

"Ye're asking us?" Rory said, eying Ian as though he thought the man a confirmed liar.

"Why are ye asking us?" Finn chimed in. It was the first time Ian had heard the boy speak loud enough to be heard clearly.

"Ye're her sons. 'Tis yer right to agree or refuse." And he truly believed that. Gretna was all they had, and they were all she loved and needed. The choice belonged to the boys. Ian started with the youngest. "Yay or nay, Finn?"

"Yay," Finn said without hesitation. The lad even managed a shy smile while he chewed on the corner of his thumb.

"Rory?" Ian asked. "Yay or nay?"

"Yay," Rory said after scowling at Ian for a long moment.

He turned to Evander. "If ye're not all of one mind, it willna happen. What say ye, Evander? Are ye willing to make it unanimous?"

Still looking bewildered, Evander gave a weak shrug. "Aye. I reckon I'm for it."

Ian herded the boys toward the door. The realization of what he'd just done hit him in the gut like a punch. *Damnation. What the hell was I thinking?* He hurried them. "Come along, lads. I need to speak with Graham and Magnus before the festivities begin."

"Can we go to the kitchens? Sometimes Cook saves us scraps for our traps," Rory said.

Not entirely sure he wanted to know, Ian halted them in the corridor between the kitchens and the hall. "What exactly do ye trap?"

"Rats!" the boy exclaimed proudly. "We keep'm as pets and race them like horses. Folk even bet on which of'm will win." He gave a sad shake of his head. "The last lot got away. Chewed a hole in their basket and ran clean off."

"There's nay time for that tonight," Evander admonished. "We best go wash our hands and faces before Mama and Master Ian plight their troth."

God have mercy on my soul. Ian swallowed hard against the panic rising in the back of his throat. "Aye. A fine idea. Follow yer brother, and do as he bids."

He waved them away as they entered the hall. He needed more ale. Lots of ale, and definitely some whisky. He returned to his seat across from Graham, Magnus, and that damn bird. "I canna believe what I just did."

Both men sat taller and watched the boys until the trio disappeared into the stairwell.

"What?" Magnus asked. "They dinna look as though they just got a thrashing."

Ian propped his head in his hands. "I didna thrash them. I agreed to handfast with their mother."

Graham reached across the table and smacked Ian's shoulder so hard, he nearly knocked him from the bench. "Well done, man. I'm proud of ye."

"And I, too," Magnus said, pounding a fist against the table. "Whisky, lass! Bring us whisky."

"Aye," Ian agreed. "I need whisky. Badly." He still didn't know quite how it had happened. The words had just spilled from his mouth. How could he have agreed to such? He lifted his head. "They do know it's naught for but a year and a day. They know I'm leaving after that," he defended his actions more for his own benefit than theirs.

Both men nodded.

"It's good to be honest with the lads," Magnus agreed as the girl brought them three glasses and an unopened bottle.

"Ye looked as though ye needed a fresh bottle," she teased with a glance in Ian's direction before sauntering away.

Graham filled the glasses, then lifted his into the air. "To Ian. *Slàinte mhath!*"

"*Slàinte mhath!*" Magnus echoed.

Ian gave a half-hearted wave of his glass, then downed its contents, and poured another. It would take more than good health to get him through this.

Graham thunked his empty glass on the table, then rose from the bench. "I'm off to tell Alexander." His smile faded as he gave Ian an up and down look. "Ye might think about gettin' yerself cleaned up, aye?" His smile returned. "After all, it's not every day a man gets handfasted."

"Thank God for that," Ian mumbled under his breath. He glanced down at his clothes. The man was right. He pushed himself up from the bench and snatched up the bottle.

"Ye're taking the whisky?" Magnus complained.

"Aye." Ian topped off Magnus's glass, then tucked the bottle in the crook of his arm. "I'm thinking, I need it a damned sight more than ye do."

Saluting with his glass, Magnus nodded. "God be with ye, man. God be with ye."

CHAPTER SIX

"**Y**E TRULY AGREED to this of yer own free will?" Gretna found that hard to believe. She knew Ian. He'd been widowed longer than she and had also sworn he had no interest in ever marrying again. "Truly?" she stressed as quietly as she could, considering she felt like roaring at the situation. He had been her only out. If he had refused, she could've used that against Mercy and Catriona.

"Aye," he said, his unblinking stare locked on Alexander winding a strip of the MacCoinnich colors around their clasped hands.

"Ye both need to hush and get on with it," Alexander warned under his breath as he finished securing the cloth. With his hand resting atop theirs, he raised his voice so all gathered might hear. "In front of these witnesses, these two are bound one to the other."

"For a year and day," Gretna reminded in an urgent whisper. He'd forgotten to say for a year and a day so everyone would know the terms without question.

Alexander smiled, stepped back, and lifted both hands to quieten the packed room. "And now we would hear their vows."

Hear their vows? She caught her bottom lip between her teeth, as she faced Ian and clasped his other hand atop their tied ones. If she said half of what she felt right now toward this entire gaggle of meddlers in her life, they'd probably oust her from the clan. She swallowed hard and stared at Ian. Thank the Lord, the man usually went first. *Poor Ian.* Looked like a trapped animal ready to gnaw off his limb to escape.

"I..." He paused, smacked his lips, then ran the tip of his tongue across them as though attempting to find enough spit to speak. He swelled with a deep intake of breath, then blew it out. "I, Ian Frances William, take thee Gretna..." He stopped again, then leaned forward and whispered, "I dinna ken yer full Christian name."

"Evaline Merideth."

"Ah." With a nervous smile, he dipped his chin and squeezed her hand. "Best start again, I reckon." He cleared his throat and resettled his stance. "I, Ian Frances William, take ye, Gretna Evaline Merideth, to be my lawful helpmate and partner."

Gretna smiled her encouragement and relaxed a notch. Praise the saints, the man hadn't used the word *wife*.

Returning her smile, he continued, "I share with ye all my worldly possessions and swear to protect ye. I shall remain faithful and true through sickness and health, good times and bad, and fight at yer side during any battle this life may bring."

Her heart hitched hard enough to shake her. The look in Ian's soft gray eyes had changed. His tone had taken on a meaningful depth. The firm, reassuring squeeze of his hand sent an unspoken message. Ian meant every word he said.

He lifted her hand and brushed the gentlest of kisses to it. "I plight thee my troth," he finished quietly, then nodded for her to speak her words.

"Aye." The word came from her unbidden. Her turn. All in the hall remained silent, their expectant stares piercing through her. She settled herself with a deep breath, then let it ease out. Ian had remained brave. She could do this, too. "I, Gretna Evaline Merideth, do take thee, Ian Frances William, to be my lawful helpmate and partner."

He squeezed her hand.

Aye. She could and would do this, but her words needed to be a mite different from his. "I share with ye all the joys and sorrows of helping me raise my sons, along with what little I possess in this world." A myriad of past choices, both good and bad, stormed through her mind as she continued, "I swear to protect ye and remain faithful and true through sickness and health, good times and ill, and fight at yer side during any battle we meet." She bowed her head, closed her eyes, and sent up a silent prayer for strength. This was all beginning to feel too real. It was just for a year and a day. Done to silence the harpies and their rumormongering. To help and protect the boys. She had to keep that in mind. Opening her eyes, she straightened her shoulders and lifted her head.

"I do plight thee my troth," she said, sinking into the safety of his gaze and pushing all else from her mind.

He leaned toward her, pausing the span of a heartbeat right before brushing his lips across hers. His mouth still within a hair's breadth, he paused again as though warring with indecision. The chaste kiss had held unimaginable power, making it difficult to reason. She had felt it, too. With a hushed groan, he claimed her with a proper kiss, a fiery seal fueled with the loneliness and need they shared.

The crowded hall echoed with cheers. Those sitting at the tables against the walls banged their tankards and stomped their feet. The place shook with their thundering.

Still recovering from the kiss, Gretna heard nothing. All she knew was the man's touch. The heat of him so close. His taste. May God have mercy on her soul. What had just happened?

"Music!" Alexander shouted, clapping his hands overhead. Chanters, bagpipes, bodhráns, and fiddles came to life.

With a gentle tug, Ian led Gretna back to their table placed adjacent to the chieftain's in their honor. Evander, Rory, and Finn sat grinning as though they'd just received extra treats for Yule.

Before they took their places, Sutherland met them with a silver, two-handled cup held high so all could see. At his nod, the musicians halted their song.

"A drink to bless this union! A drink from the *quaich* for protection." He lowered his voice so only they could hear. "And an oath from me to support ye in any way I can instead of nettlin' ye with my poorly chosen jests. My apologies again, cousin. I want all to be right between us, aye? A blessing to ye both." He took a quick sip from the vessel and held it out.

Confused, Gretna looked to Ian. "What does he mean?" Sutherland had always been an annoying tease and the first to make a jest. Everyone knew that and ignored him.

"I'll explain later," Ian said as he took the *quaich* and offered it first to her. He gave her a reassuring smile. "To our adventure, aye?"

"Aye." If he were determined to make the best of it, then so could she. She took a sip of the fine MacCoinnich whisky, smooth but fiery. "To conquering beasties," she added with a side-eyed glance over at her sons. She offered the vessel back to Ian.

"Aye," Ian agreed with a wink. "To conquering *all* the beasties." He drained the *quaich*, then gave it back to Sutherland.

Cheers shook the rafters again, and a lively reel filled the air.

"Shall I remove the bindings of yer vows so ye might dance?" Magnus asked from behind them, shouting to be heard.

Ian gave her a worried look and leaned in close, sending a shiver down her spine as his warm breath tickled her ear. "I dinna do that well when it comes to the dancing. If ye value yer feet, I dinna recommend it."

She guided their bound hands closer to Magnus and gave him a nod to free them. Watching as he unwound the sash, she smiled. "I'd like to sit with the boys for a bit first. We'll attempt a dance later." They had to dance. It would be expected. The perfect plan came to mind. "We can dance as a newly formed family. With the boys, ye ken?" She watched to see if Ian would realize that the sight of her three boys hopping along with them would draw the attention away from any missteps or stumbles he might make.

He brightened and gave a quick nod. "Aye. That'll do nicely."

Magnus pulled away the last of the sash, then escorted them to their seats.

Ian nudged Magnus aside and held the chair for Gretna. "My dear one."

My dear one. The sentiment stirred long ago memories of Coire and the closeness they'd shared. She shook free of the foolish spell. Ian was acting for the crowd's sake, and so should she. She gave him a regal nod as she seated herself and scooted closer to the table. "Thank ye, kind sir."

Servants hurried to refill their glasses and replace the remnants of the dinner feast they had already enjoyed with fresh bread, cheeses, and fruit.

She glanced down the table at the boys. All three sat with their cheeks stuffed full as they reached for more. "Dinna make yerselves sick," she admonished. "And mind yer manners, aye? Ye act like ye've been starved for a month of Sundays." She sidled a look at Ian deep in conversation with Magnus and Sutherland, then turned back to the lads. Thank goodness for her three sons.

With them in their quarters, there'd be no privacy that might make Ian feel as though their oath should be consummated. She looked at him again and swallowed hard. Surely, he'd not feel such. A mixture of disappointment and lost wishes fluttered across her. What in heaven's name was wrong with her? If she wished this handfasting to be just for show, then she shouldn't hope for Ian in her bed.

"Mama." Evander tapped her elbow.

She leaned closer to hear him over the din. "Aye, my lad?"

"Lady Catriona and Lady Mercy said they made us our verra own barracks in the guard tower for tonight. William and Ramsay, too. Willa might even be there, 'cause she swears she's better than her

brother with a sword and the bow. I dinna ken. I dinna know them
that well. Master Graham said the lot of us would be the keep's special
guard for the feast tonight. He's clan war chief. He'd be there for a
while, too." He stared at her in earnest. "Can we do it? They seem like
they want to be our friends."

Gretna bit back the coarse words she'd forbidden her sons to use.
Catriona and Mercy were more meddling than any pair of sisters she
never wanted to have. The marrow of their thinly laid plan knotted in
the pit of her stomach. She emptied her glass, glaring at the women
over its rim. The conniving wenches would stop at nothing.

"Can we, Mama?" Evander repeated.

"Can we?" Rory chimed in as the current song finished and made
talking a bit easier. "We've never done nothin' like that before. And in
the guard tower itself. They dinna allow just anybody in the guard
tower."

She leaned to see Finn. "Well, Finn? Do ye wish to go, too?" She
wouldn't force her meek lamb to do it if he didn't wish. He was also
her last hope for a shield against her own scandalous stirrings.

Wide-eyed and resembling a frightened hare, Finn gave a quick
nod. "Aye, Mama. I dinna want them thinkin' I'm a wee bairn too
scairt to leave ye for a night. I can do it if'n ye'll let me try."

Aye, well, he might be brave this time, but she wasn't. The boys
were her skirting wall in case Ian decided to storm her keep, and she
weakened enough to lower her drawbridge. At least there would still
be Mam Hattie. The old woman had already moved her things into
the north wing. Surely, Hattie hadn't had time to move back to the
home they'd shared since Colin drowned. She looked closer at her
three wee beasties. She loved them so, and they dearly needed
acceptance and friends. "Ye may go. As long as ye swear to take care of
each other and mind yer manners. Ye must heed what Master Graham
and the guards say—like good MacCoinnich warriors, aye?"

The three lit up with wide smiles, bouncing on the bench to be off and join the other children.

"Master Graham said we could go any time now. The guards are a waiting for us," Evander said as he swung a leg over the bench. "Can we go now?" Rory and Finn followed suit.

She couldn't bear to tell them no, even though she'd promised Ian their diversion during a dance. He'd just have to be brave and get through it as best he could. After all, that's what both of them were doing. She nodded. "Ye may go now on one condition."

All three flinched in unison, waiting for her to name it.

She held out her arms. "Yer cost is a hug for yer mother."

Evander jumped into her embrace and squeezed her hard. "Thank ye, Mama. Thank ye ever so much."

Patting his back, she hugged him harder. "I love ye, Evander, and I want ye happy. I know it doesna seem that way at times, but I do."

He pecked a quick kiss to her cheek. "I'll even give ye extra payment. A kiss!"

Not to be outdone, Rory and Finn did the same.

"And where are my wee dance partners going?" Ian asked as the boys bounded away.

"It appears our matchmakers have outdone themselves." She waved her empty glass at a passing maid.

"Let me fetch the wine pitcher, miss," the girl said with a polite bob.

"Whisky, if ye please, Anne," Gretna corrected.

Anne grinned. "Lady Catriona said to bring ye the bottle when ye asked. I willna be but a moment."

"Whisky?" Ian arched a brow. "It must be serious. What else have they plotted? We're handfasted, as they wished."

"They've tempted the boys away for the night. Playing MacCo-innich warriors with their verra own barracks in the guard tower."

Both of Ian's dark brows rose. "I see," he said. He reached for the bottle as the maid sat it on the table along with two glasses. "Definitely a call for whisky."

At least he felt the same. "Dinna worry. Yer favorite person in the keep should still be there as moral guardian," she promised as she accepted the glass he'd filled.

He gave her a strange look. "'Tis my understanding that Mam Hattie has already been moved back to the village. Said they didna wish yer place left empty."

She nearly choked on the sip she'd just taken. With a hard swallow, she patted her chest. "Surely, ye jest? They havena had time. They just fetched the rest of her bundles up here yesterday."

"And they carted them right back. Graham told me earlier." Ian downed his glass, refilled it, then waved the bottle toward hers. "Top ye off, aye?"

Without a word, she plopped her glass on the table and slid it toward him. "Aye." There was not enough whisky in the keep tonight.

The music grew louder, increasing to a thunderous roar with everyone's clapping and stomping. All eyes were on them. Apparently, the crowd had waited as long as they would for the newly united couple to dance.

Ian rose and held out his hand. He had the expression of a man headed to the gallows. "Hopefully, they're too drunk to notice how I step. Mind yer toes, aye?" he shouted.

She forced a smile. The simple reel was the least of her worries right now. She took his hand and allowed him to lead her into the first set. They stepped and spun, then stepped and spun some more. As they linked arms and whirled around in a circle, she became more aware of just what a handsome man Ian Cameron was.

It wasn't just his braw, muscular stature that caught her attention most. Nor the way his waistcoat and kilt outlined his trim waist and powerful legs. It was his kindness, the understanding in his eyes, and a lingering sadness shadowing his smile. This fine Highland warrior tied to her for a year and day always looked as though he'd grudgingly resigned himself to his fate. She knew that feeling well. It came upon you when life stole away your dreams and turned them into nightmares. She felt a kinship with Ian. They had both lost so much.

Arms crossed at the wrists, they linked hands and spun around some more. Thank the Lord she'd not had enough time yet to drink all the whisky she intended to consume before they retired to their quarters. But the longer they spun, the more she realized that Ian seemed to be enjoying himself. She loved his deep laugh as the tempo increased, and they whirled faster. The longer they danced, the more she found herself laughing along with him. This was not so bad at all. It had been a long time since she'd let go and felt this lighthearted.

Much to every dancing couple's relief, the reel finally ended and allowed them the chance to catch their breath.

Gretna gasped for air, "Mercy sakes! I'm winded."

"I, too," Ian laughed as he led her back to their table. "I dinna remember it being so hard to last the length of the song before. I must be getting old."

They drank a while, then danced some more, unable to carry on even half a conversation due to the boisterous festivities. Even though pleasingly light-headed with drink, Gretna kept an eye on the trio of feast candles burning on the chief's table. Alexander had established a practice long ago when he'd first become chieftain. When the row of tapers at the head table burned out, the revelry ended. At that time, the hall would be cleared, and all merrymakers were sent to their beds. She'd always felt it a good practice—until now. Now the flames ate up the wax entirely too fast.

As they finished another dance, Ian tugged her to the side of the room, behind the privacy of one of the thick stone pillars. With a covert glance around, he took both her hands in his. "We should go upstairs now whilst everyone is busy with their own merriment." He looked around again. "If we wait until the end, they'll all be deep in their cups, and several of them will more than likely be a damn sight cruder and more worrisome to us."

The thought made her heart pound, but he was right. They need-ed to go now. She pulled away, wove through the revelers, and snatched up a fresh bottle of whisky and wine from the cabinet behind the chief's table. She'd not retire to their rooms without extra fortification for their decanters.

Ian waited beside the stair, standing watch as though they were thieves. Thieves, indeed. More like horses attempting to escape their master's stable. She prayed that after today, their matchmakers would find another way of amusing themselves.

He nodded his approval as she swept past him and hurried up the stairs. The closer they drew to the second floor, the more her steps slowed. She pushed on, attempting not to dwell on it. As they entered their quarters, the first thing she noticed was the silence. Compared to the uproar they'd just left, the place was quiet as a tomb.

"My goodness." She eased deeper into the room. Even her foot-steps seemed muffled as her shoes sank into the rug. "After the noisiness of the hall, I feel as if I've been struck deaf."

Ian went to the wide wall of windows and pushed one of them open, lifting his face to the fresh air like a hound seeking a scent. Without looking away from the night sky, he shook his head. "Aye. The quiet here is better." A weary chuckle escaped him as he turned and gave her a lazy smile. "Reckon our keepers are happy now?"

"Who knows?" She poured them some whisky, moved to the pair of plush chairs angled in front of the hearth, and held up his glass. These seats would be less suggestive than the couches. "Ye do want this, aye?" She set it on the small table between them and made herself comfortable.

"Most definitely." He sauntered over, scooped up the glass, and held it high. "To my lovely partner and helpmate."

She looked at him sharply. Had he said that as a resentful jest? She lifted her glass. "And to the braw, handsome man saddled with my family and me for a year and a day of his life that he'll never get back."

"I'm not bitter, lass," he said quietly, then put his glass on the table as he took a seat. Brow furrowed, he studied her until she felt the need to fidget.

"I must look a fright after whirling about like a leaf caught in the wind." She patted her hair and yanked at her bodice. How long had it been since a man's perusal had made her feel so unsettled?

"I never appreciated just how lovely ye were until this day." He tore his gaze away and stared at the flames dancing in the hearth. Eyes narrowing, he kept his focus on the fire as he lifted his glass for another drink. He turned and faced her. "Ye've always been here, Gretna, and yet today is like the first time I've ever truly seen ye." He shook his head, speaking barely above a whisper that tickled across her like a caress. "Damnedest thing I've ever felt. I've known ye so long, and yet I dinna know ye at all." His smile seemed thoughtful. Almost shy. "Ye were married to Colin when first we met. After Glencoe." A scowl swept his contented look aside. "Then ye became his widow in the summer after Graham and Mercy's son came." He emptied his glass and took hers, then crossed the room and refilled them. "Ye mentioned earlier that ye didna wish another loveless marriage. Said ye were tricked into marrying Colin. How so?" He held out her freshened drink. "If ye dinna mind speaking of it."

"I dinna mind." She accepted the whisky, but put it on the table for later.

The memories seemed like so long ago. Another lifetime, really. She never spoke about it, but Ian deserved to know the story from her lips. "Coire, my first husband, my true love, his dying was not easy nor quick." She paused and steadied herself. The dark memories of her dear one's suffering still pained her even after all these years. "He wasted away for weeks before passing." She clasped her hands in her lap and watched the fire. The flames helped her handle the troubling memories. "I was huge with Rory, and Evander was but a wee bairn.

Just a little over a year old. Coire knew he was going to die, but he didna fear it nor ever complain of his pain. The only thing that worried him senseless was leaving us behind. Me. His bairns. Leaving us with no means to get by."

"Sounds like he was a good man." Ian placed his glass on the table beside hers and leaned forward with his hands clasped, watching her, waiting.

"He was a good man," she said softly. The senseless grudge she bore gave her strength to continue as the darker memories surfaced. "Coire was a much better man than his shiftless twin brother." She'd burn in hell for the malice she still held for Colin and all the troubles he'd caused her. "Coire promised to give Colin all we had if he'd marry me and provide for our children." She met Ian's gaze, not flinching against the hatred she heard in her own voice. "He agreed, and the priest heard our vows in front of Coire right when he died to send him on his way in peace." Her hands tightened into fists. "Thank God I was only married to Colin a scant three years before the bastard did me the courtesy of dying, too."

"And how did he die?"

She almost laughed. Ian sounded as though he feared she had killed Colin. She'd already told him she had planned to do it. Bitterness filled her. Calmed by the candlelight's reflection in her swirling whisky, she forced a civilized tone. "Drowned." She paused for a sip of her drink, wickedly tempted to toast the statement. "He and a few others had been charged with taking several MacCoinnich horses to their new owner in Glasgow. They stopped in Finnich Glen to water the stock, but rains had flooded the gorge and made it too dangerous. At the Devil's Pulpit, the fool stepped too close, and the ground gave way. The waters took him. They never found his body."

"I'm sorry."

"Dinna be sorry." She sat taller and looked Ian in the eyes. "I'm not." He might think her heartless, but at least he'd know the truth. It was time to change the focus to him. "Will ye tell me of yer wife?"

Drink cupped between his hands, he rolled it back and forth, his gaze locked on the swirling liquid. "Janet and I had not been wed long, but we'd known each other since we were bairns." He paused, his eyes tightening, almost as though he flinched against the memories. "The night before Glencoe, she shared that she carried our first child. The next day, during that bloody massacre, a bastard slit her throat."

The suffering and loss in his voice tore through her. The rumors had not done justice to his pain. She went to him, perched on the arm of the chair, and hugged an arm around his shoulders. "God bless ye and ease ye, ye dear, sweet man. I am so verra sorry." She tucked her head against his and held him, hurting for him.

Without a word, he slid his glass to the table, then scooped her into his lap and settled them both deeper into the cushions. With an arm around her, while his other hand held the bend of her knees, he shifted with a heavy sigh. "Ye're a fine woman, Gretna," he said softly. "I promise to do right by ye."

"I know ye will." She brushed a light kiss to his temple, then rested her head against his again. This felt so right. So safe. She breathed in the warm, tempting scent of him and smiled. *Whisky. Loneliness. Need.* She wondered if she smelled the same. Undeniable proof of Ian's yearning hardened enough to make itself known through the layers of her skirts. Brazen or not, she made up her mind. "Will ye share my bed tonight?"

"I'm nay so sure that would be a good idea, lass." His deep voice was low and mesmerizing as though casting a spell. His arm tightened around her. "I dinna wish to dishonor ye. Nor lead ye astray. Ye know I still mean to leave next summer, aye?"

"Aye. I do." His refusal stung no matter the reason, and she'd not belittle herself by trying to change his mind. 'Twas a matter of pride. What a fool she'd been to ask. She pushed to rise from his lap, but his arm hugged her back and held her in place. She shifted to look at him.

"Do ye not think it best I return to my own chair then?"

He gave a half-hearted shrug. "Nay. Not just yet. Do ye mind?"

"Do I mind?" she repeated. "Ye refuse my offer to share my bed, but ye'll grant me the honor of sitting in yer lap with yer stiff willy poking me in the thigh? Why would I mind?" Perhaps, that was a mite sharp, but the man had hurt her feelings. She glared at him. At least he had the decency to turn a bit red.

"I nay refused because I dinna want ye." With a defensive tilt to his chin, he shot back her glare. "Ye can tell that well enough by what's poking ye." His smug look made her itch to smack him. "What if I get ye with child? The last thing ye need is a fourth bairn to see after once I'm gone."

A fair point indeed. A possibility that both the whisky and her loneliness had chosen to forget. *Damn him.* It was her turn to dismiss his words with a shrug. She relented and settled back against his chest. "Aye, well, there is that."

Her gaze traveled to the open door of her bedchamber. Such a large bed in there. A cold, large bed. Common sense pushed its way through her pouting. A lusty tingle of anticipation set her mind to plotting. She had herbs. If the possibility of a child was all that was keeping him from her bed…

CHAPTER SEVEN

IAN DIDN'T WISH to lose her soft, tempting weight in his lap, but he recognized it for the dangerous thing it was. He should release her, allow her to move back to her chair. Even so, his arm tightened around her, and his man parts throbbed harder, demanding relief. He hadn't been with a woman since Lettie, his precious harlot in Edinburgh, had died. After she passed away, he'd sworn off the fairer sex for a while. First Janet. Then Lettie. Best to leave women alone rather than risk that sort of pain again.

A glance at the table showed his drink within reach, but he feared if he downed it, Gretna might offer to fetch him another. Then what would he say to keep her close? She shifted, rubbing against his poor aching cock. He had to risk a drink. Lord, he needed it. Badly. With one smooth motion, he scooped up his glass and emptied it.

Just as he feared, she sat up, wiggling her fine round arse against the length of his suffering member. She turned and set her feet to the floor, then squirmed her delectable bum against him again before standing. Damnation, was the woman trying to kill him?

"I'll fetch us both another, aye?" she offered with the hint of a devilish smile.

"Aye," he forced out. He cleared his throat and adjusted his position, spreading his knees farther apart to provide his man parts with some much-needed air. Why the hell had he pulled her into his lap? And even more importantly, why the hell had he refused her when she'd offered her bed? He scrubbed a hand down his face. *Because I am a damned fool on both counts, that's why.* Unable to control himself, his gaze returned to her as she fetched their drinks. Damned if the mouthwatering line of her full breasts didn't stretch her bodice in the most tempting way.

Pounding on the stairwell door caused them both to jump. "Ian! Come to the door, man! Now!"

"That's Sutherland." Gretna rushed across the room, beating Ian to the entrance. As she reached for the latch, the door rattled again with another hard hammering.

"Ian! 'Tis urgent and not a jest. Come to the door at once!"

Ian pulled her back behind him. As she opened her mouth to argue, he held up a hand. "I dinna give a damn what he says, I smell a trap. Ye know as well as I the tricks they do to newly joined couples. I'm in no mood for such nonsense, and I dinna think ye are either."

Much to his relief, she didn't argue, just nodded and retreated a step.

He braced himself and eased the door open a crack. "If this be a jest, I'll wring yer damn neck for ye. Understand?"

Sutherland looked a great deal more sober than he should considering the hour and level of festivities still going on. "I wish it were a jest." His bared teeth made the slow shake of his head even more ominous. "Alexander sent me to fetch the both of ye and take ye to the private library. At once."

The man seemed serious, but Ian still didn't trust him. "We'll not be going anywhere until ye tell us why."

With a nudge to the door, his cousin fixed him with a grim look. "Then let me in. Gretna needs to hear this, too."

Satisfied that Sutherland was serious, Ian stepped back and allowed the door to swing open wide. Whatever had happened, it must be urgent. Sutherland rarely looked so dour.

As he stepped inside, Sutherland gave Gretna a polite dip of his chin, then settled his tight-jawed scowl on Ian. "Alexander bids ye both come to his library because ye've an unexpected guest." With a flinch that made him look as though he were in pain, he forced his gaze back to Gretna. "Well…he's actually here to see ye."

"He?" Gretna repeated, her color rising and temper flashing in her eyes.

"Colin," Sutherland spit out the word as though clearing it from his throat.

Gretna's high-spirited coloring left as quickly as it came, and she stumbled back. Ian caught her before she sagged to the floor. He glared at Sutherland. "What the hell are ye playin' at, man?"

"Colin is dead," Gretna gasped, one hand fisted in Ian's shirt as she leaned against him.

"I laid eyes on him myself." Sutherland swiped his hand across his mouth as though trying not to retch. "Several folks in the hall did. Sobered up the lot of us and set the keep to buzzing."

"The boys. Finn." Gretna pushed away, her hands fisted. "Do the boys know?"

Sutherland's look told them both what they feared before he spoke. "Aye. They were in the guard tower when the men stopped him to find out who he was."

"I must go to them," she said in a panicked whisper.

Ian grabbed hold of her and pulled her close. "We need to talk to the man first." Without releasing her, he looked to Sutherland. "Fetch the lads and bring them here while we go to Alexander. Stay with them, aye? Find out what ye can from them since they were the first to greet Colin."

"I'll see to it." Part way out the door, Sutherland stopped and looked back. "We took him into the library as quick as we could, but many still saw him."

Ian tucked Gretna into the curve of his arm and held her. The woman looked ready to faint. "We'll be there shortly. See to the boys now."

With a nod, Sutherland left.

"I canna believe that devil rose from hell to torment me again," she whispered. She lifted her gaze to his, her panic reaching out to him. "And my poor boys, Finn especially. They were so happy earlier."

"And they will be again," Ian reassured. A protective rage rose within him. He'd fought the thought of wintering here, fought the notion of fostering those three young imps, and considered the handfasting nothing more than a ruse. But by damned, now that he'd accepted and committed to it all, he'd sure as hell not allow some conniving son of a bitch hurt those he'd promised to protect. "Come. Let's get to the bottom of this."

Gretna gave a weak nod.

They hurried to the inner staircase to avoid the main hall. Ian had no doubt the news had already spread through the entire clan. There were probably already bets being placed on what would happen.

"How could he be... They swore he drowned," Gretna said. "They told me no man could have survived those waters that day." She grabbed hold of Ian just as they reached the closed door of the chieftain's private library, located behind the main hall. She shook him, fear in her eyes. "And where has he been for the past six years? Why now? Why did he come back now?"

Ian's heart hurt for the lass. He wished her fears were a tangible thing he could slash away with his sword. "I dinna have those answers, but I mean to find out. I promise ye." Hand on the latch, he looked to her. "Ready?"

Her bottom lip caught between her teeth as she gave a quick nod.

"I'll be right beside ye. No matter what," he promised as he pushed through the door.

"Wife!" The man in question stood beside the hearth across the room. As thick and short as Ian remembered, Colin's broad smile rounded his freckled face even more as he charged toward Gretna.

Ian stepped between them and shielded her. "Give the woman a chance to breathe, aye?" He pointed at the hearth. "Back there with ye. Now."

Resentment and ire flashed across Colin's features, flaring his face red. His tight-lipped smile made a poor attempt at masking his anger as he bobbed his head. "Aye. Forgive me. I'm sure the sight of me does come as quite the shock." He shoved a hand through his faded hair that had once been a rusty red. Most Neals and MacNeilages bore a reddish mane. 'Twas their bloodline's stamp. He held out a hand in greeting. "Ian, is it? Ye remember me? Colin Neal."

"Aye." Ian folded his arms across his chest. He wasn't about to shake the man's hand. Especially not after all Gretna had told him about the bastard. "I remember ye." He nodded toward the other side of the room again. "Back to the hearth with ye now, aye?"

As Colin retreated, Gretna eased up beside Ian. She took hold of his arm and leaned into him. It warmed his heart the way she trusted him, and he wouldn't let her down.

Alexander sat at his desk, leafing through a loose stack of papers that looked as though they'd just been unfolded. "He arrived this past hour, bearing these papers from a physician, a solicitor, and a minister. All from Inverness."

"Where have ye been?" Gretna asked, her voice quivering. "Six years ago, they claimed ye dead. Said the waters of the Devil's Pulpit had claimed yer body and refused to spit it out. Now ye show up here. Back on my doorstep. Expecting to be greeted with open arms as if ye just returned from a stroll through the Highlands." She lifted her chin and squared her shoulders as she released Ian and took a step forward. "Ye shouldha stayed in Inverness."

Colin's eyes narrowed, and his mouth tightened.

Ian could tell the man was straining to hold his temper. He resettled his stance. *Lose yer temper with her, ye bastard. I dare ye.*

Taking a step toward her, Colin twisted his worn tam between his hands. "I thought I was dead," he said with a pat to the back of his head. "When the water took me, I couldna breathe, nor regain any footing. The rocks bashed me about 'til everything went black." With a failed attempt at looking pitiful, he tucked his hat into his belt and stood as contrite as a criminal at the gallows. "When I came to, lying there where the water tossed me out, I couldna remember a thing. Not my name. My clan. What day it was. Nothing."

"And now all of a sudden, ye know who ye are?" Gretna didn't attempt to hide her contempt.

He shifted in place, staring down at the floor. "I didna know who I was 'til a week ago this past Sunday."

"A week ago this past Sunday?" she repeated. "What happened a week ago this past Sunday? Did ye receive a sudden epiphany from Almighty God whilst in church? Did angels speak to ye?"

Ian couldn't resist smiling. What a fine, braw woman. How had he not appreciated her before now?

With an irritated look, Colin patted the back of his head again. "While steadying the minister as we walked from the rectory to the church, I was the one who slipped on the wet pavers. My feet flew clean out from under me. And when I went down, I hit my skull on the retaining wall beside the path. Everything went dark again, just like in the water six years ago. When I came to, all my memories had come back to me." A forced smile accompanied his shrug as he eased a step toward Gretna. "That's when I knew I had to come back to ye. I couldna wait to reunite with the dear family I'd lost. I missed ye, Gretna."

"Missed me," she repeated in a dangerous tone. "*Missed* me?" Her fists trembled at her sides. "Have ye forgotten the many times ye told me ye considered me punishment for yer sins? Or how ye wouldha rather been castrated with a rusty knife rather than married to me?

How many times did ye wish the boys dead so ye could have some peace and quiet? Did those memories fail to return to ye when God knocked ye in the head?"

Colin hung his head. "I was a fool," he said quietly. He cast a quick, embarrassed glance over at Alexander, then at Ian. "I am a changed man, wife. Six years of helping serve the poor taught me how blessed I am to have ye and the boys." His face brightened. "How are the boys? Finlay? How is my son? I didna get to speak to them before the guards hurried them away from the gate."

Before she could answer, Ian interrupted. "Alexander, what say the papers?" Not that it mattered. Affidavits could be easily falsified.

"They support his story." Alexander fixed Ian with a pointed look and added, "Of course."

Good. Alexander didn't believe Colin Neal either.

"I am a changed man. A better man. I swear it." Colin sidled back and forth in front of the hearth like a trapped animal. "All I ask for is a second chance to prove I can be a good husband and father. A provider. The kind of husband my dear brother wouldha wished me to be—God rest his soul." A simpering smile twitched his mouth as he held out both hands. "Please, wife. Give me another chance."

"She is my wife now." Ian edged up beside Gretna, meaning every word more than he'd ever meant anything before.

"The way I see it," Colin stood taller, his humble facade disappearing. "Yer union is forfeit. She canna have two husbands at the same time."

"I will never return to the life I endured with ye," Gretna said, disgust dripping from her tone. "And I willna put my sons through such misery either."

"Finn is my son."

"If ye go near my precious Finn, I'll kill ye." Teeth bared and eyes flashing, Gretna shook her fist. "Stay away from all my sons."

Alexander rose from his chair.

Ian stayed him with a shake of his head. He rested a hand on Gretna's stiffened back, praying the support of his touch would lend her a bit of his strength. "The way I see it," he said in a mocking tone, using Colin's own words against him, "ye deserted yer family for over six years. That dissolves any and all claims ye may have. But if the court's view differs, I feel sure a divorce on the grounds of abandonment can rectify the matter." He gave Alexander a respectful nod. "I'm sure in the eyes of Clan MacCoinnich, they will side with Gretna and her wishes."

"Unlike the two of ye, the *Neals*, the true ones of this keep and clan, are my *blood*. When I married her," Colin jabbed a finger at Gretna. "*All* my brother's possessions, his trade transporting the *Neal* horses, and her and them two boys became my property. My brother signed a paper saying as such. The old priest filed it in the chapel records." He stuck out his swelled chest. "And I sired Finn— although..." he snorted out a mean-spirited chortle. "If he didna outgrow his strange spells, ye can have that little dullard and keep him with my best wishes."

Ian charged forward, wrapped his fingers around Colin's throat, and slammed him back against the stones of the hearth. "Mind yer tongue, fool, or I'll be knocking yer memories back out yer head for ye." He tightened his hold, squeezing while the man fought and clawed at his hand. He shoved his face closer. "Ye will stay away from my wife and my sons. All three boys, ye ken?" He clamped more pressure. "We'll get the legalities cleared away soon enough, but from this day forward, ye have no claim on Gretna, Evander, Rory, or on Finlay. All are mine and under my protection. Do ye understand me?"

Colin sputtered, beating at Ian's arm. His face changed from a bright red to purple.

"Dinna kill him, Ian," Alexander advised quietly. "He's nay worth the effort to rid ourselves of the body."

Ian lessened his hold the barest bit but bounced Colin back against the hearth one last time for good measure. "Have I made myself clear to ye?"

Both hands still latched tight to Ian's wrist, Colin managed a lowering of his chin and expelled a wheezing, "Aye."

Ian released him and stepped back to Gretna's side as the fool dropped to his knees.

"I wish ye wouldha killed him," she whispered as she hugged herself to his side and pressed her cheek to his chest. He held her close, the urge to finish the man off barely containable.

"What about my business? My croft?" Colin rasped and coughed, still crouched on the floor, one hand to his throat. "Chief Neal signed an agreement with my brother stating him and his would always have the job of taking the horses to their buyers. That paper be filed in the chapel records as well. It is my right!"

"Clan *MacCoinnich* has no further need of yer services, Master Neal." Alexander returned to his seat behind the desk. "And yer croft became ours when we absorbed Clan Neal. The agreement betwixt yer brother and Chief Neal was also nullified due to yer six-year absence. Everything became the lady's property once ye were assumed dead." He scooped up the handful of papers and held them out. "Ye may take yer papers and go. Our business here is finished."

Pushing himself up from the floor, Colin snatched the papers out of Alexander's hand and shoved them inside his jacket. He glared first at Ian, then Gretna. "Ye've nay seen the last of me. None of ye. The MacCoinnichs have enemies, ye ken? And ye sorely erred by adding me to their ranks. I'll have my day. Ye'll see." He jerked his chin in Gretna's direction and shifted his snarling focus to Ian. "Keep the nagging bitch. It willna take long 'til ye'll wish ye gave her and those three little bastards back to me."

Without a second thought, Ian punched Colin in the jaw so hard, he knocked him back to the floor. The man stirred for a moment, then crumpled into a heap and went still.

"It appears I've made a mess in yer solar, cousin." With the toe of his boot, he flipped Colin to his back. "Looks to be out for a while. Shall I drag him away, or do ye wish to have the honor?"

Alexander stood and peered over his desk. "I'll have one of the lads dispose of him." He relaxed back into his chair and settled a concerned look on Gretna. "A confusing man, this Colin Neal. Claimed all he wanted was to be reunited with ye and yet, when ye refused, seemed more concerned about any holdings he might still be owed rather than the loss of his family. What do ye make of it?"

Gretna edged her way closer to the hearth, rubbing her arms as though chilled. "He's always been a greedy man. Greedy but fearsome lazy." She frowned down at the fool, her eyes narrowing as she studied his still form. "Quickest and easiest way to get coin. That was the reason for everything he did. His travels. His *adventures*, as he used to call them. Coire always said Colin would fall in with the wrong sort someday and end up with his throat cut. There's no telling what plot he had in mind by coming here." She shifted her pained scrutiny to Ian, and her look softened. "Thank ye for all ye've done. Please hear me when I say, I'm so verra sorry. This is such a mess. Ye are a good man, Ian, and I am grateful. Truly."

"I'm not sorry for any of it." He went to her and gently pulled her into his arms. "I meant every word I said, Gretna. Every. Word. I consider ye my wife and the boys my sons."

"But..."

He cut her off with a long, urgent kiss that he hoped would convey what he couldn't put into words. He'd never been so sure of something in all his life, but he'd also never been so afraid. If his curse kicked in and he lost her or any of the boys—he kissed her harder, concentrating on the sweet taste of her to silence his own demons.

Alexander cleared his throat. "I shall send a letter straight away to Alasdair, aye? He can see to the preparation of the divorce papers."

"Nay," Ian said as he reluctantly broke the kiss, but kept Gretna close as he turned and faced Alexander. "We've still time with the mild weather for a trip to Edinburgh. We can have a good visit with the family, whilst Alasdair files the papers to ensure the divorce is proper and my guardianship of the lads is recorded and provable should aught happen."

"Catriona will be delighted to have a wedding to plan even though the two of ye are already as good as married." Alexander shook his head. "She never sleeps what with the bairn's kicking and all. Swears this one'll be dancing a jig soon as it's born." He rose and stepped around the desk. "Let me be the first to congratulate ye both." He gave Gretna's hand a polite kiss, then took hold of Ian's forearm and pulled him into a manly hug. "I'm glad for ye, cousin. Truly."

"I need to see the boys now," Gretna said softly, edging toward the door. She frowned back at Colin's unconscious form. "Do ye think he'll just go and leave us alone? He was always a spiteful man bent on revenge against any who crossed him."

"He'll leave if he wishes to live." The sentiment might be harsh, but Ian didn't care. He opened the door and ushered her out into the hall. "I'll send up a pair of lads to clean up the mess," he said as Alexander joined them at the door.

As they walked away, Alexander called after them. "Ye willna leave for Edinburgh 'til after the feasting, aye?" He gave them a grave look. "Catriona will have my arse if ye miss the full seven days of all she has planned."

"Seven days?" Ian repeated.

"Aye." Alexander pushed away from the doorframe. "I told ye she never sleeps. Constantly plotting something."

"We'll stay the full sennight," Gretna promised, pulling on Ian's arm to quicken his step. "Now, I must see to the boys. I fear what Colin may have said to them no matter what he said about seeing them at the gate."

"I'll tend to having Colin hauled away," Alexander said. "Go now and see to the lads."

Ian lengthened his stride to keep up with his newly acquired wife, amazed at the speed with which she moved. Conversation was impossible, but maybe that was for the best. They could talk later. When it was just the two of them. Anticipation heightened every sense. *Aye.* They would talk.

Avoiding the main hall at all cost, they managed to reach their quarters without encountering anyone. It was a miracle since revelry still vibrated through the keep.

Gretna was first through the door. As soon as she entered, she dropped into a crouch and squeaked out a high-pitched cry.

A separate piercing sound filled the room. Ian recognized the shrill, chattering call. It was Magnus's damn bird.

"Merlin willna hurt ye, Mama," Finn reassured as he approached her with the falcon perched on his outstretched arm.

Magnus's long, heavy glove swallowed the lad, reaching clear to his armpit. Face aglow with pride, the child gently brushed the back of a crooked finger against the bird's creamy breast streaked with darker feathers.

"He likes me. Master Magnus says I can help him take care of this fine new friend of mine." His voice softened as he gently swayed from side to side. "Master Magnus says Merlin can be fierce whenever he needs. He can protect me. He's braw and brave and can even fight with his talons."

The look on the boy's face paired with the teary-eyed storm of emotions in Gretna's eyes softened Ian's regard for Merlin considerably. Maybe the bird was not so bad after all.

"He is a fine bird," Gretna agreed while still keeping her distance. "I was but startled when he flew overhead. I'm proud ye've befriended him. My goodness, ye're such a brave lad." She edged deeper into the room, her attention still locked on the feathered wonder perched on her son's arm. "Evander, Rory, be ye as well as yer brother and his new acquaintance?"

Ian's concern for them returned in full force when neither unsmiling boy answered. Both Magnus and Sutherland gave a warning shake of their heads. Perhaps the sharing of what had happened in Alexander's solar was in order to allay the lads' fears. Or at least *some* of what happened. He moved to Gretna's side and settled an arm around her waist. "I believe our announcement will help settle any misgivings yer earlier encounter with Colin Neal caused ye."

"Did ye kill him?" Rory asked, sounding hopeful.

"Nay, lad." Ian waved them closer. "Come over here. The lot of ye, aye?"

Magnus and Sutherland nudged the boys forward. Finn joined Evander and Rory in line.

"Go to Master Magnus," he whispered to the bird. Merlin complied, returning to his usual spot on Magnus's shoulder. Finn slipped off the oversized glove but hugged it to his chest, looking lost and forlorn as his side to side rocking increased.

Ian's heart went out to the lad, to all of them. "Have ye ever been to Edinburgh?"

Gretna latched hold of the hand Ian had rested at her waist. She squeezed his fingers.

The boys looked at him as though they thought him either addled or drunk.

"I'll take that as a nay." Time to seal his commitment further. "After the festival, we'll all be going to Edinburgh to visit my brother Alasdair. He is a solicitor there. The finest in all of Scotland."

Magnus and Sutherland gave each other a side-eyed look that held the hint of victory.

The young trio remained silent, still looking bewildered.

"Yer mother's divorce from Colin Neal must be properly filed before Father William can hear our vows in the chapel, and so must the papers regarding my claiming the three of ye as my sons."

Evander was the first to fully understand. His eyes widened.

Ian gave them all an encouraging smile, hoping if they couldn't come to accept him as their father, they would at least accept him as their friend. "The legal papers will make it official, ye understand, so I can protect ye."

Rory cocked his head. "What about Da?"

"I'm not sure where Master Neal will go." He pulled Gretna closer. "And I really dinna give a damn." He pressed a quick kiss to her temple. "My attentions are better spent tending to my new wife and three sons."

Finn's rocking stopped, and he stepped forward. "So, ye will be our da? Instead of that mean one?"

"Aye." Ian waited, allowing the news to fully sink in. He didn't expect to win their trust or wipe away their fears immediately, but hopefully, this was a start. He nodded at their surroundings. "I'm sure the chieftain will let us live here in the keep until we figure everything out."

That triggered a few daunting worries of his own, but he'd fight those battles when he came to them. For now, easing all of them into this new way of life was more important. Almost as an afterthought, he looked to Gretna. He'd have to work on the habit of including her opinion in his decisions now. After all, it wasn't just him anymore. "That would be all right, aye?"

She sniffed, patting at the corners of her eyes as she blinked faster. "Aye. I've no problem with living here at the keep." She glanced up at him with a worried smile. "The keep will be safer for the boys and makes my tending the Lady Mercy easier."

"I will do my damnedest to protect all of ye." Ian gave them all a sweeping look. "I swear it."

"And we'll be yer kin, too," Sutherland said as he made a playful tap atop each of their heads. "Ye'll have our protection as well."

"Aye," Magnus said, and Merlin joined in with a stirring chirrup.

"So…" Evander stood taller, looking as though he was spoiling for a fight. "Ye going to make us call ye *Da* or *Master Ian* or *Master Cameron*…or what?"

Ahh…the first test. Ian shrugged. "I willna *make* ye call me anything. But what I will require is that ye're always respectful, ye ken?"

"I'll call ye *Da*," Finn announced, his twitchy back and forth swaying growing less pronounced.

"Thank ye. I'm honored, Finn." And he meant that. He gave the boy a nod.

"Rory? Evander?" Gretna's tone held a gentle warning. "Ye will be respectful to Master Ian. He's a good man, and we're thankful to have his protection."

Both lads nodded but remained silent.

"The hour is later than late," Magnus announced as he headed toward the door and motioned for Sutherland to follow. "Merlin and I must seek our rest."

Sutherland paused and turned back to the boys. "Do ye wish to return to the guard tower with the other children?"

All three looked to Ian.

"Do whatever ye wish. It's yer decision." He had mixed feelings about it himself. He feared Gretna would be uneasy about their safety and would not be able to relax enough to…well, whatever she felt inclined to do. But if the boys stayed here… He shook away the thought. They'd figure something out. He chided himself. *That* should be the least of his worries right now.

"We can stay here if we want? In our own beds? Where we're safe?" Finn whispered.

"If that's what ye wish, then absolutely," Ian said in a tone he hoped the boy would take as genuine reassurance. "All of ye may stay or just yerself, Finn. It is entirely up to each of ye."

"I wish to stay," he whispered and took hold of his mother's hand.

"Me, too," Rory announced, sounding subdued for the first time.

"Evander?" Sutherland asked.

Evander shifted in place and squared his shoulders. "I'll stay, too, and make sure these two dinna cause any trouble since it's yer first night handfasted and all."

Magnus smiled and ushered Sutherland out the door with a wave of his hand. "Then we shall leave ye to yer new family. All of ye, rest ye well, and may God bless yer new life together."

Ian nodded. Blessings were all well and good, but he'd rather God gave him wisdom. After all that he'd just agreed to do, he was damn sure going to need it.

CHAPTER EIGHT

Gretna's heart pounded. It was a wonder its fierce beating didn't quake her out of her shoes. She pressed her hand to the cool glass of the window and hung her gaze on the silhouette of the jagged mountain against the star-spattered sky. "There's naught but a few hours of night left," she said more to herself than to Ian. She stole a glance back at him. He'd waited in her bedchamber while she'd settled the boys in their beds. Now, here they were. Door closed. Room softly lit by the hearth and a pair of candles on the mantel.

He sat by the fire, whisky in hand, staring at the flames. "Aye."

A seed of nervous worry took root and sprouted. She moved across the room to the chair beside him but didn't sit. "Are ye wishing ye'd nay said the words? Regret the burden ye've accepted?" What would she and the boys do if he did? What if he changed his mind and decided to leave next summer as he'd already planned?

Without answering, he rose from the chair and set his drink on the mantel. After a brief moment of staring down into the fire, he turned and held out his hand. "I am not sorry for my oath, lass. Please...come to me."

Whether it was the gentle caress of his deep voice or the loneliness in his eyes that pulled her, she didn't know. Nor did it matter. At that moment, she realized they were kindred spirits. Their souls had been tempered by the same pain. She slipped her hand into his and stepped closer.

"Ye offered yer bed to me earlier," he whispered as he brushed his fingers along her temple, then trailed them deeper into her hair. "I was a fool and refused. Does yer offer still stand?"

She slid a hand into the open throat of his shirt, savoring the warmth of his flesh and the braw hardness of his muscles. "Aye," she breathed out as she pushed aside the cloth and dared to skim a trail of kisses to his chest.

He scooped her up into his arms and walked to the bed. Holding her above it, he smiled down at her. "I carried ye like this last night. I ached to lay with ye then."

"I thought it was a dream," she said as he lowered her into the pillows. She held fast to his powerful shoulders, pulling him to join her.

"Nay—not yet." He eased away, stripping his tunic off and letting it fall. Belt and kilt fell away, too. Boots were already gone. The candlelight shimmered across the taut ridges of his muscles—the part of him she could see anyway. With the light at his back, all else teased her from the shadows.

She sat up to rid herself of her shoes, then scooted to the edge of the bed and stood. "Perhaps, I should tend to my clothes, too." It had been so long since she'd had a man. She felt awkward, as uncertain as a virgin.

As Ian turned toward the light, the golden glow of the candles revealed him in all his glory. *Merciful heavens.* A heat she'd not felt in a long time flashed through her. She hurried to let her skirts drop to the floor but paused when nothing remained but her chemise. Would he find her lacking? She was not some fair, untouched lass who had never born a child. Her body reflected her life. Even though she wore the marks of motherhood proudly, she feared he might not feel the same.

As if hearing her thoughts, Ian picked her up again and lay her back in the bed. "Ye're a fiery beauty, *m' eudail*. Never doubt that." He lowered himself down beside her, propping on his side as he allowed his gaze to rake across her. "I can scarce believe ye're mine." Caressing her cheek, he smiled down at her. "And I'm thankful it's so."

She reached up and pulled him closer. "I'll always do my best to make ye happy," she whispered before sealing the promise with the kiss she'd craved since he'd claimed her earlier. The warm maleness of his scent. His hardness. His strength. The velvet of his flesh teasing against hers. All made her feel alive. She ran her hands across him, reveling in the reawakening, the searing promise of what was to come.

He released her mouth and resumed the searing kiss down her throat and across her breasts, treating each of them with breath-stealing reverence and tingling nibbles. Shifting, he gathered her chemise and slipped it over her head. "Such beauty." His rumbling tone made her squirm. He licked his way down her body, moving to kneel between her legs, and pushed them open wider. He smiled, then bent to the task, kneading her buttocks and thighs as he teased with light flicks of his tongue, then dove in with delicious fury.

She bit her lip to keep from crying out, clutching the bedclothes in both hands. Merciful heavens, such bliss would surely kill her. She bucked and shuddered. Her body no longer under her control but Ian's. Ecstasy consumed her, spinning her into a glorious abandon.

Just when she thought she could bear no more, he kissed and licked his way up her body.

She wrapped her legs around him and squeezed, stretching upward to stroke him again and again.

"I must have ye, *mo ghràdh*."

"Then take me." She dug her nails into his buttocks and arched to greet him.

When he plunged inside, she lost the ability to do anything but feel. All thoughts and reasoning disappeared, and only mindless delight remained. She met him thrust for thrust, building speed. Ecstasy crested, then exploded with wave after crashing wave. She cried out her joy. She couldn't help it.

He hammered harder, then roared. Arms locked around her, he shuddered. After what seemed like an eternity of pounding heartbeats, he sagged to the side and rolled to his back, pulling her along and draping her atop him. Breath coming in ragged gasps, he hugged her tighter. *"Mo chridhe."*

"Mo leannan." My lover. My sweetheart. Contentment hummed through her. She pecked a kiss to his throat, smiling at the salty, sweet taste. *Aye*, this is what she'd missed for so very long—a precious connection with another.

He slipped the covers up over them, keeping tight hold of her in the process. "Ye asked me if I regretted my words."

Pleasant drowsiness, a floaty weariness threatened to overtake her. She struggled to pay attention. "Aye."

"I told ye I did not." His fingers tickled up and down her back, hypnotizing her deeper into a sweet lull. "What about yerself? Do ye regret finding yerself caught in such a marriage?"

"I am more than contented." She nestled her cheek more comfortably into the dip of his shoulder and hugged a leg around him as she settled in beside him. "And thankful to be so blessed." A yawn escaped her. "Forgive me." A vague worry of seeming callous stirred through her dreamy fog. "Ye've made me feel so safe and warm, sleep is about to overpower me." If he only knew how contented he'd made her feel. Not just with the loving. But with all he'd done for her and the boys.

"Sleep, lass," he whispered, kissing her forehead and hugging her close. "Now, we have a lifetime together."

As soon as she allowed her eyes to close, it was as though her inner demons considered it a call to action. The peaceful drowsiness disappeared, and her mind whirled, tumbling across the less enjoyable moments of the past few hours. She ached to rise and pace out her thoughts. What was the real reason for Colin's reappearance? What did the devil really want from her?

The slow, rhythmic shifting of Ian's chest beneath her cheek assured her he slept. She eased away, untangling herself as gently as possible. There was no way she could remain in the bed with so much on her mind.

"What troubles ye, lass?"

She toyed with the idea of lying about needing a visit to the chamber pot but decided against it. Ian deserved the truth. Always. "Forgive me. I didna mean to wake ye."

"Dinna fash yerself. I havena slept well since Glencoe and do fine on verra little rest. Now tell me what troubles ye?" He pushed upward, elbowing the pillows behind him as he sat up and leaned back against the headboard.

"I dinna trust Colin." She retrieved her shift and slipped it on, then fetched her knitted shawl to pull around her shoulders. The air held a sudden chill. "He came back here for a reason, and that reason had nothing to do with missing the family he always despised." She glanced back at Ian and immediately felt the fool.

Here she was with a braw, handsome man, her husband by oath, and once the paperwork was sorted out—they'd stand before God and Father William to make it official for the church. Yet, all she could think about was the heartless arse who'd caused her nothing but pain. She couldn't help it. More was at stake here than just herself. Her precious lads had already endured so much. "Forgive me," she repeated.

"For what?" Even in the shadows, she could tell he looked confused. He climbed out of bed, padded over to the fire, and stirred the coals to coax a higher flame. After adding wood, he straightened, brushing his hands together. Fine and tempting in his nakedness, he held out a hand. "Come closer to the fire and tell me yer worries." He gave her a lopsided grin. "And stop apologizing. I told ye—I need verra little sleep."

"It's not for yer loss of sleep that I beg forgiveness. I'm sorry I've tainted our first night together with my fretting." She took his hand and clutched it to her chest, then ran her fingers across the scratchy stubble of his day-old beard.

She'd shave him when morning came—if he'd allow it. She looked forward to a lifetime of tending to her husband in the little ways only a wife knew. It was the least she could do after all he'd done for her. "Ye deserve better than an anxious wife."

He seated himself and pulled her into his lap. Arms wrapped around her, he settled them both more comfortably into the cushions. "I dinna know that I *deserve* anything, but I do know I promised to protect ye and the lads. We've plenty of time to chase away the uneasiness of the past." He touched his head to hers. "And my mam always told me to never put too much weight on any one unpleasant-ness, aye? It takes a fair amount of highs and lows to create a lifetime of rich memories." He hugged her closer. "With any luck, ye and I will have more highs than lows. I'd say we're due, ye ken?"

The fresh wood popped and shifted deeper into the fire, sizzling as its sap heated and bubbled through its splits. He scooped up her hand and tapped a kiss to each of her knuckles. "Tell me, if ye can, any other reasons ye know of that might tempt Colin to return? How might *Tor Ruadh* benefit him?"

"For the life of me, I dinna ken." She considered fetching them both a drink but didn't wish to rise from Ian's lap. The way he was idly tracing circles against her hip was quite pleasing. "I've no money. No land other than a small plot big enough for a few sheep and some hens. And as Alexander said, the land and the croft truly belong to Clan MacCoinnich now—not me." She shook her head, scowling at the fire. "There is nothing here for him to claim or barter away."

"He seemed intent on reclaiming his duties for seeing after the horses that were sold, assuring they were properly transported." With the lightest touch, he slid aside her shawl and shift, baring her shoulder to his kisses.

"But that was barely a living because he made so few trips. Rarely did he travel with the stock himself. Usually, he was one of the herders moving them about the glens." She would've shrugged, but Ian's attention to her shoulder and neck was too pleasurable to interrupt. Instead, she pulled her shawl away and dropped it to the floor. "He was a lazy man. Always found others to go in his place."

"Dinna fear, lass, nor waste any more time worrying after the fool. He'll be watched, I assure ye." He slipped a hand inside her chemise and cupped a breast.

She leaned back, closing her eyes as she wiggled her bottom back against the promising hardness in his lap. Perhaps Ian was right. She shouldn't waste her time worrying when there were much more pleasant distractions at hand.

One hand to her breast, the other between her thighs, he nibbled and kissed her bared shoulder as he stroked and dipped his fingers inside her. *Sweet Jesu*, his fingers were as talented as his mouth. Grip locked on the arms of the chair, she squirmed, bucking upward into his hand as she lay back across his chest. "I need ye," she gasped.

He lifted her up, faced her away from him, then sat her back down, thrusting deep inside her as he kept a hand between her legs, still stroking, teasing.

Rocking back and forth as he worked his fingers faster, her senses reeled. She'd never known of doing such. Where had he learned this rapture? As she whirled into the sweet abyss, he bucked higher, lifting her. She gave herself to wave after wave of bliss, then fell back against him gasping.

Without a word, he wrapped an arm around her waist and stood. He walked them over to the bed, gently draped her belly down across it, then pounded away, rumbling with a groaning growl until he shuddered and emptied inside her. He fell across her, brushing her hair aside to nuzzle a kiss to her ear. "Into the bed now, aye? Ye've made me weak in the knees."

"I *am* in the bed," she teased, twisting to treat herself to a long, slow kiss.

"Vixen." He flipped her over, tossed her deeper into the pillows, then climbed in beside her.

She threw a leg over him and curled into the curve of his arm. A sigh escaped her as he pulled the covers back over them.

Ian hugged her tighter and pressed a kiss to her forehead. "Dinna worry," he admonished. "I swear all will be well."

Stretching to kiss his cheek, she smiled. "'Twas a sigh of contentment. I promise."

He shifted against her with a deep sigh of his own. "Good."

She settled back down, her gaze on the flames flickering in the hearth. *Aye. This is good.* As her eyelids grew heavy, then finally shut, a blood-curdling scream split the night.

⟫⟫⟩⟨⟪⟪

IAN ROLLED OUT of Gretna's embrace, cursing as he stumbled across his boots while searching through his discarded clothes for his dagger. Why in hell's name hadn't he set some of his weapons on the table by the bed? What a damned fool. He'd sworn to protect them, and instead, he'd allowed his cock to override his common sense.

The chilling scream rang out again.

"Ian, stop!" Gretna had already yanked on her shift and was partway to the door. "It's Finn and one of his dreams."

The terrified wail sounded like the child was being skinned alive. Ian held tight to his *sgian dhu.* "Stay behind me just in case, aye?" Unabashedly naked, he vaulted around her, cracked open the door, and scanned the sitting room for intruders. All was quiet until Finn squalled out another high-pitched keening.

"He does this when he's had more than he can handle during the day," Gretna explained in a hushed tone. She stormed forward and entered the boys' room ahead of him.

God's beard. How could such a sound come from such a meek lad? Ian followed her.

Evander and Rory crouched on either side of their brother, attempting to block him safely in the center of the narrow bed while he thrashed and fought as though being attacked.

"I'm here now," Gretna said in a calm, soothing voice. She took Rory's place at Finn's side, hugging him out of the way. "Well done, son. Well done, indeed. Get ye back to yer bed."

Rory yawned, spared Ian a sleepy glance, then climbed back under his covers as though his brother's actions were as normal as drawing breath.

Feeling utterly helpless and hating every moment of it, Ian moved to the foot of Finn's bed. "What can I do?"

"Fetch him a fresh léine, if ye would. Poor lamb. Looks as though he's wet through this one." Gretna leaned over her son, crooning softly as she gently patted his shoulders and touched his head. The child's wild fighting weakened. "It's all right, lad. We're all here. Come back to us. Come back to where it's safe."

"And dinna ye dare make fun of him," Evander warned as he glared back at Ian, then returned his attention to his brother. "He canna help it." He pulled extra linen from the side table and held it ready to slide under Finn.

While Ian understood and admired Evander's love and loyalty to his brother, the boy's warning still stung. "I would never do such a cruel thing," he said as he hurried across the room and fetched Finn's dry clothing. The damned feeling of being more hindrance than help increased as he laid the fresh shirt on the end of the bed and stood there.

"Go to bed, Ian. There's nothing ye can do here," Gretna whispered as though sensing his discomfort.

Nay. Ian took that as a challenge. He'd promised to help and protect, and that's what he'd do. As Gretna eased the boy free of his terrors and cleaned him up, Ian returned to their bedchamber. He placed the dagger on the table beside the bed and donned his own tunic, frantically trying to come up with a way to help. He returned to the lads' room and found Evander already back asleep. Finn sat on the edge of his bed, calmly leaning against his mother.

"I'm sorry, Master Ian," Finn said in a weary whisper.

The boy's words cut his heart. Ian sat on the edge of the bed beside the lad. "I thought ye were going to call me, *Da?*"

Finn shrugged. "I didna think ye'd still want me to after what I just did." He kept his voice so low, Ian had to lean closer to hear him. "I'm sorry," he whispered again.

Pain for her child's suffering creasing her brow, Gretna remained silent. She hugged him closer and pressed her cheek to the top of his head.

"Ye've nothing to be sorry for. Ye battled a demon and won," Ian said. "Every warrior screams a war cry to send fear coursing through his foe."

Still tight in his mother's arms, Finn watched Ian as though deciding whether to trust him. "What's yer battle cry?" he finally asked.

"The MacCoinnich cry," Ian said without hesitation. *"Je ressuscite!"* he shouted.

"What does it mean?" Finn asked, sounding a little stronger.

"It means *I rise.*" Ian stood. "A MacCoinnich never allows anything to suppress them or hold them down in any situation." He held out his hand. "Would ye like to sleep in our chamber tonight? There's nay much night left, but ye can either sleep alone, or myself and yer mother will snug ye in between us."

Finn straightened out of his mother's arms and looked at her. "Can I, Mama?"

Gretna nodded, then gave Ian a grateful smile. "Yer da said ye could."

With Finn between them, they returned to their chamber. Once inside, Finn looked up at Ian with a leery look as if expecting a cruel prank. "Ye said I can sleep with Mama if I want, aye?"

"Aye, lad." Ian squatted down and looked Finn in the eyes. "I shall never lie to ye, boy. Ye have my word, ye ken?"

Finn's eyes rounded even more, then he lunged forward and wrapped his arms around Ian's neck. "Thank ye, Da," he whispered, the tremor in his voice taking full ownership of Ian's soul.

Ian picked the lad up, placed him in the center of Mam Hattie's bed, then climbed in beside him. Gretna settled in on the other side and pulled the covers up over them all.

Finn smiled and snuggled down between them. Within minutes, he was fast asleep.

Closing his eyes, Ian concentrated on the peaceful sound of Finn's faint breathing. Just as it had mesmerized him into a peaceful state of relaxation, he felt the softest touch to his cheek.

"Ian? Are ye still awake?"

He smiled. Gretna's soft whispers in the darkness were sweet as any song. Without opening his eyes, he answered, "Aye, love. What's wrong?"

"Absolutely nothing," she said. After a long pause, she added, "Again, I'm sorry we're such a burden, but I thank ye from the bottom of my heart. I dinna ken what we would do without ye."

He pulled in a deep breath and blew it out. "Do something for me, love."

"Anything."

"Stop thanking me and no more apologizing for being a burden, aye?" He turned his head on the pillow and found the sparkle of her eyes in the shadows. "I dinna wish to listen to such for the rest of my life, ye ken? Neither yerself nor the boys are a burden."

She stroked his face again, then shifted close enough to lay her hand on his shoulder. "I shall do that, my love, but I fear those words must be replaced by some I willna stop saying no matter how often ye ask."

He covered her hand with his, unable to fathom the answer to her riddle. "What words?"

"I love ye, Ian," she whispered. "And I know in my heart, I shall love ye for all time."

Her quiet declaration both surprised and thrilled him. His response came unbidden. "I fear I love ye, too, lass." He'd not said those words to anyone in a very long time, almost ten years, in fact. He'd not felt the need until now. "God Almighty, what the hell do we do now?"

In the darkness of the room, he sensed her smile more than he saw it. She squeezed his shoulder. "We sleep. Such a quandary is better saved for when we're rested."

Wise advice. "Aye." Ian awkwardly patted her hand and closed his eyes, fatigue winning out over panic. "Sleep well, love."

"Sleep well, dear one," Gretna whispered, then rolled to her side. "Sleep well."

CHAPTER NINE

W ITH A YAWN so wide his jaw popped, Ian faced the crisp wind combing across the mountain. He'd not struggled this much from lack of sleep in a while. Of course, a lot had happened in the past few days. Rubbing the corners of his eyes, he blinked against the weariness, then snorted out a laugh. While it was true he was tired, oddly enough, he felt more settled and at peace then he had in years.

"I'll damn sure not tell anyone but Gretna," he swore to the breeze whipping at his kilt. Nothing was more irritating than hearing some wise arse saying, *I told ye so.*

He strolled along the walkway atop the skirting wall, viewing the busyness below. Alexander had spoken the truth. Catriona had outdone herself by pulling together so many activities in so little time. He shook his head, remembering his brother Alasdair's sage advice: never underestimate the furious capabilities of a woman with child.

Cheers rang out from the south yard. Archery contests. Stone put. Caber toss. All manner of games meant to entertain every age from wee bairns to the aged had been set up and were in full force. Food and drink were everywhere. It would be a wonder if enough stores were left to survive through the winter.

He scanned the people milling about, both within the protective walls of the fortress and across the outer grounds. The nearest allied clans had been invited as well, and all had come. One last great celebration before winter set in. This many folks gathered in one place set him ill at ease. Especially with Colin Neal's reappearance and the man's true intentions yet unknown. Old instincts tensed Ian, readying him for battle. The sound of footsteps made him turn around. His tension tightened when he saw the look on Sutherland's face. "Did ye find him?"

"Aye." His cousin gave a curt nod. "At the pub. Slurring Gretna's good name to any and all who'll listen."

"Bastard." Attention shifting to the town farther down in the glen, Ian walked the wall to the point where it joined the barbican. His gut told him to march down there and silence the man with a good beating, but common sense forbade it. At least for now.

Legally, Neal was still Gretna's husband. Even though he'd disappeared for nearly six years, Ian felt sure many in the village would say Neal still had a claim on her. The hypocritical arse worms would also think if Gretna was a good Christian woman, she'd welcome back the worthless cur with open arms. After all, death hadn't parted them, and neither had divorce—yet. He glanced at Sutherland. "What are the rumors so far? I'm sure the gossips have outdone themselves."

"Mixed lot." Sutherland propped against the parapet, squinting at the crowd below. "Few tolerate or look kindly on Master Neal. They know him for the lying cheat he is. He owes several people money. But he's a wily one, I'll give him that. The conniving bastard has already convinced many Gretna shouldha paid off his debts when she thought him dead. He's called her a lying, adulterous Jezebel." He shot a concerned scowl at Ian. "But I dinna think that's the worst of the rumors he's stirred."

"Divorce papers and a wedding in the keep's chapel will steal the thunder from those rumblings, and I can cover the bastard's debts, if that's what it takes to be rid of him." Ian fixed his glare on the town, wishing he could clear the place of any who dared treat Gretna so disrespectfully. "Ye said that's not the worst of it? Out with it, man. I would hear all of it."

"He's feeding the witch accusations. Swears he belongs to a group from Inverness. Some kind of witch hunters. Even brought some of them with him. Spied them myself—dressed all in black with crimson cloaks. Neal is fueling those rumors fierce." Sutherland fisted his hands atop the crenel. "I even overheard one old cow say that Neal swore he'd been dead all this time, and Gretna raised him from the grave." Sutherland barked out a humorless laugh. "He even went so far as to describe his time in heaven." Sutherland shook his head. "As if that son of a bitch would ever make it past St. Peter."

"Perhaps I should send him back. Then there would nay be a need to go to Edinburgh."

"Just dinna leave any witnesses. Ye canna swing a cat in that village without hittin' one of his kin. They may not like him, but blood is blood. There are also some who still consider the MacCoinnichs as conquerors of the Neal clan rather than saviors. The man's found every dissenter and united them, but I'm damned if I can tell ye his next move." A dissatisfied silence simmered between them. His cousin finally jerked a thumb westward. "If ye're nay too weary from last night's celebrations, Alexander asked that we check on the lads tending one of the smaller herds close to the loch. They shouldha brought them back to the glen for wintering by now." Sutherland looked in that direction. "There's been no word from the runner sent to tell them of Catriona's gathering either."

"When was the messenger sent?" Ian asked. The weather had been mild. The man shouldn't have experienced any trouble.

"Several days before we arrived. Long enough for him and the other three herders to get a dozen or so of our best breeding stock home in time to raise a glass at last night's feast. They're not that far from here." Sutherland shook his head as he scratched the beginnings of a beard. "I've never understood their taking the broodmares out like sheep or cattle to forage through different glens, but old man Aber-feldy swears that makes the bloodline stronger."

Aberfeldy was brother to the late Murtagh Aberfeldy, the original stable master integral in developing the highly sought-after breed. MacCoinnich warhorses had become known as the best in all of Scotland and made the clan one of the wealthiest and most powerful in the Highlands.

Ian spotted Gretna as she emerged from the side garden with an overflowing basket of herbs hanging from her arm. His spirits immediately lifted. His precious Gretna. As soon as she left his embrace, he needed her back in his arms. And she loved him. He smiled. Damned, if he didn't love her, too, and wasn't quite sure how or when that had happened.

An anxiousness followed the realization, a worrisome urgency. The rumors of witchery Sutherland reported could be dangerous, especially if Colin Neal kept stoking them. Gretna needed to stay within the walls of the keep until all this was settled. Ian made up his mind then and there. He'd not allow fate to rob him a third time. With a wave, he caught her eye and motioned for her to join them.

Gretna's smile both eased, then tightened the knot in his chest. The day was brighter with her in it, but that alone reminded him how dark it would be if anything happened to her. Damned, if he'd not felt such a mess of feelings since Janet. How the hell had Gretna and her sons managed to pry their way into his soul?

"Have ye ever seen so many?" she asked as she tiptoed to look over the outside of the wall, then turned and looked back down at the inner bailey. "We've never had such a turnout before." She shook her head. "Poor souls in the kitchen. Cook's beside herself and shouting orders like a warrior in the heat of battle."

"Aye," Sutherland agreed. "She threw a pot at me yesterday just for speaking to one of her scullery maids." He pushed away from the wall, took hold of Ian's shoulder, and gave him a friendly shake. "I'll meet ye in front of the stable. Within the hour, aye?"

"Aye." A heaviness blanketed Ian. He dreaded sharing Sutherland's news with Gretna. "I'll be there in a bit."

Sutherland nodded his farewell to Gretna. "M'lady."

"Sutherland," she dismissed with a leery tone, then shifted the short handle of her basket from the crook of one elbow to the other. "Ye're off to somewhere today?" she asked as Sutherland strode away.

"Alexander asked Sutherland and me to check on one of the smaller herds that has yet to return to the glen for the winter." He offered his arm. "Walk with me, aye?"

Her smile disappeared as she took his arm. "No word from any of the men? Several always guard the stock whilst moving them."

"Not a word from them nor the messenger sent to tell them of the celebration and fetch them back sooner." He pulled in a deep breath and hissed it out, delaying the news he really needed to share. "Graham must stay here to oversee this crowd. A gathering this size always brings problems of its own." He shook his head and patted her hand. "Sutherland and I can handle the task. Probably just a matter of a few horses separated from the herd and needing to be found before they pen them up close to the mountain. If it turns out evil's afoot…reivers or such, we'll return to fetch enough guards to quash it."

"If ye feel it a simple task, then why are ye so ill at ease?" She cocked her head and gave him a look that called him a liar. "A wife has the right to know what's troubling her husband." She waited for his answer. "Ye listened to my woes last night." A rosy blush accentuated the fire in her eyes. "And chased them away quite nicely, as I recall."

His man parts roared to attention, ready to take over the conversation. "Shame on ye, wife. Ye do me a great disservice." He hugged her closer, purposely brushing his fingertips against the side of her breast in the process. "Teasing me with such suggestions when I canna properly respond."

She stopped walking and backed up against one of the parapet's tall merlons, pulling him with her. "Shall I grant ye a kiss as a promise for more later? Will that do for my penance?"

"Aye, that'll do...for now." He leaned into her, pressing against her softness as he poured all his own heat and wanting into the kiss. He didn't give a damn who saw them. Let them watch and hate him for what he'd claimed as his own.

When he drew back, the sight of her plump, kiss-reddened lips made him need her even more.

"Now, tell me yer troubles," she whispered, one hand cradling the side of his face. "*All* of them."

He stepped back, wishing he didn't have to sully the moment. "Sutherland reports Neal has taken up a post in the pub to besmirch yer name to all who'll listen."

She looked away, eyes narrowing, and mouth tightening into a hard line. "I am not surprised." Her gaze falling to the basket, she pinched off the tip of a leafy sprout, rubbed it between her fingers, and brought it to her nose. The refreshing, minty scent reached him as well. She turned aside, resting her basket in a crenel, and picking through its contents. "Several in the village dinna like me. I'm sure he'll find them and unite them to his cause—whatever that cause may be." She continued idly crushing leaves, staining her fingers green, as she stared out over the parapet in the town's direction. "My former husband was always a vengeful man. I'm sure he feels he owes me a great deal of misery."

"He's feeding the accusations of witchery. Giving them strength." Of all the rumors, those worried him most. Many an innocent soul had been brutalized and killed because of such. "Sutherland has discovered a group of witch hunters have accompanied him from Inverness. They're feeding the crowd with tales of the horrors they've committed in the name of God and country."

She blew out a bitter huff. "I dinna understand what I ever did to deserve such treatment from this ungrateful lot. I help them. Heal them. Bring their bairns into the world and ease the pain of their dying while they're headed to the grave. Old Elena said I was the best she'd ever trained." With a sad shake of her head, she tossed the bruised, tattered herbs to the wind. "And for all that, they call me *witch* and threaten me."

"Dinna go to the village anymore, aye?" He leaned around in front of her and forced her to look him in the eyes. "I dinna care who's birthing, dying, or ailing. I dinna wish ye to leave the safety of these walls until I get this matter settled. The boys stay here, too. There's not a need for them to go down there either."

"They willna hurt me. Alexander silenced their hateful mutterings before. I'm certain he'll do so again." Her chin lifted to its familiar stubborn tilt as she turned aside. "I willna give them the satisfaction of making me cower. I willna bow to them. Not ever."

He took hold of her arm and pulled her back. He had to make her understand. "Magnus's mother felt the same. She was a renowned healer. A white lady. She refused to heed the danger of such rumors and ended up slowly crushed to death beneath a plank laden with stones. They piled them on her. One by one. Until they squeezed out the last of her air and silenced her screams forever."

Unshed tears made Gretna's eyes a more vibrant shade of blue. She looked away, but he forced her to look back at him. "I willna allow that to happen to ye. Stay inside the walls, Gretna. For yer sake. For the boys' sake. But most of all, for mine."

All defiance left her. Her lips parted as she searched his face with tenderness in her eyes. "For yer sake?"

"Aye." He eased out a breath. "For mine. I told ye last night I loved ye. It scares me something fierce—the thought of losing ye. I love ye, lass, and I dinna say that lightly."

"Neither do I, my love," she whispered. "Ye've captured my heart, too."

"So, ye'll stay inside the walls, aye?"

She squeezed his forearms and failed at a brave smile. "Ye know as well as I that Alexander and Catriona would never allow any harm to come to me."

"And yet I hear a quiver of doubt in yer voice. I hear yer worry." He leveled his gaze with hers. "Promise me ye will stay within these walls until I settle the matter of Neal and this talk of witchery. Swear it, wife, for my precious wife ye are, and I refuse to bury another." He swallowed hard, forcing the words past the fearsome knot in his throat. "As I said before, I canna bear another such loss. I beg ye, *mo ghràdh*, swear it for me and the life we might share if given half the chance."

Tears breaking free, she framed his face between her hands. "I swear it, *husband*. The boys and I shall stay within these walls until ye tell us 'tis safe to leave them."

He covered her hands with his, then pressed a kiss into each of her palms. "All is good then." He took her hands and clutched them to his chest. With a relieved smile, he forced a laugh. "I go now to seek strayed horses." Reluctantly, he released her and eased away. "If aught goes awry, seek Graham or Magnus's help until I return, aye?"

"Aye." She rushed and pulled him into a kiss that made him groan. As she eased a step back, she brushed the tears from her cheeks and locked a fierce glare upon him. "Back by morning. No later, ye ken? Dinna make me have Graham and Magnus fetch ye."

"Aye, m'lady." After a formal bow, he strode away, wishing he didn't have to leave her. She still amazed him. He'd known her for almost ten years, but in the past few days, she'd taken hold of him with a ferocity he'd never expected.

He found Sutherland waiting with the horses in front of the stable. As he launched himself up into the saddle, he scanned the top of the wall, needing one last sight of her before he left. There she stood. Right where he'd left her. One hand lifted in farewell, the other holding tight to the shawl around her shoulders. He gave her a slow nod, then forced himself to look away. "I've orders to return by morning," he said before thinking.

Sutherland just laughed and shook his head as they rode out of the keep.

Ian smiled. His cousin was a man of his word. He'd promised no more teasing, and to his credit, he had kept his vow.

They headed for the western pass leading toward Loch Linnhe. A tolerably cool day and the wind at their backs, Ian watched the sky as they traveled. This time of year, a storm could blow in at any time. A wise man always kept an eye out for any possible shelter were it to be needed.

Late in the day, as they worked their way down an incline leading into a shallow valley, movement farther down the way caught Ian's attention. Four horses. Two with riders and two with some sort of bundles tied across their backs. He recognized the shape of those bundles. They were bodies wrapped in MacCoinnich plaids. One of the riders hunched forward as though injured. The other man, the one in the lead, sat tall in the saddle, the butt of his musket propped atop his thigh, ready to take aim and fire.

"Two dead, one wounded," Sutherland observed as the men approached.

"And not a MacCoinnich horse to be seen other than those they're riding." Ian looked around, scanning their surroundings. "Reivers, I'm sure. Thievin' bastards."

"He canna ride much farther," the man with the musket said as soon as they reached them. He shoved his weapon in its holster and slumped forward. "He's lost too much blood. I dinna ken if he'll last 'til morning."

Ian feared the same. Blood dripped from the wounded man's boot, and his entire left side was soaked dark red. As soon as his horse halted, he slipped out of the saddle and hit the ground. Ian could tell without checking the man was dead.

The lone rider remaining shook his head. "Leaves behind a wife and five weans. God rest his soul."

Sutherland glanced to the west, then pointed toward a rocky rise. "Dark soon and cloudin' up. A bit a'shelter over yon. Might as well make camp for tonight."

Ian dismounted. "Help me wrap him and get him back over his horse. We'll return the three of them to their families tomorrow."

The remaining herder clambered out of the saddle and lent a hand with the somber task. Once they had their clansman secured across his horse, they walked the animals to the spot Sutherland had chosen. It didn't take long to make camp.

"What happened?" Ian asked as they sat around the fire, sharing a much-needed dram.

Rannoch MacNeilage took a deep draw from the bottle and shook his head as he stared into the fire. "Never seen nothing like it. They came from every direction and blocked all the passes. 'Twas as though they knew the land. Rose up out of the verra earth itself. They attacked smoother than any damned army, Highland or otherwise. Had all the horses herded up and away right before our very eyes."

"How many?" Sutherland asked.

Rannoch twitched a shoulder. "Eight. Maybe more." He shrugged and heaved out a weary breath. "Couldha been a dozen, and the more we shot, the harder they came." He shook his head again. "I've never failed my chieftain before. Never in all the years I've been watching over the horses. Reivers dinna usually trouble us this time of year."

Ian held out the bottle, the man needed another drink badly.

He waved it away and leaned against the wall of boulders at their backs. "Nay. I've failed my chief. I dinna deserve as much as I've already drunk."

"Ye did all ye could, man," Ian reassured, looking at Sutherland to confirm the belief as well.

"Aye," Sutherland hurried to agree, holding out an oatcake to go along with the drink. "Four against a dozen or more is poor odds indeed. I'm surprised they allowed ye to live."

The man touched the side of his head. Blood encrusted his hair. It had dried in a trail down his forehead and cheek, attesting to the blow he'd taken. "I dinna ken why I'm alive either. They probably thought me dead after one of their horses kicked me down, then stomped me for good measure when I ran out of lead." He held his ribs as he scooted to a more comfortable position against the rock. "We managed to send at least three of the thieving bastards to their Maker."

"Did they wear any colors?" Ian realized it was a weak hope to identify the clan responsible for the reiving. But any clue could help them recover the stock.

"Nay." Rannoch winced as he bit into the oatcake. Spitting out the bite, he reached into his mouth and yanked a broken tooth the rest of the way out. "Damnation. Bastards cost me another tooth." He spit again, then closed his eyes, and leaned his head back. "Dressed all in black. Coats. Trews. Boots. Not a one wore plaid."

Ian feared as much. "Sleep, man. We'll rise in a few hours and head back. At least we've got ye to return to yer family."

"Wake me when it's my watch," the weary man muttered, his words fading as sleep overtook him.

Ian rose to his feet. "I'll take first watch." He scanned the area. Visibility grew worse as nightfall strengthened. Gathering clouds blotted out any light from the rising moon.

"I'll join ye. I'm not sleepy." Sutherland pushed himself up from the ground, glancing back at the sleeping herder. "Should we try to find the reivers he said they downed?"

"No need. If they took enough care to wear black, I doubt their carcasses would tell us much." Ian moved to higher ground, taking his post on the rise behind their camp. He doubted aught would trouble them. The reivers had gotten what they wanted.

Sutherland settled on the boulder beside him, leaning forward with his elbows propped on his knees. "I smell snow."

"It's too early." But Ian had caught the crisp, biting scent to the air, too. An early snow would make taking Gretna and the boys to Edinburgh ill-advised. A messenger would have to carry the papers to Alasdair instead.

"Mother Nature doesna always heed the calendar," Sutherland retorted. He scrubbed his hands together and lifted his nose. "Definitely snow. Soon. I'm never wrong when it comes to that."

And he wasn't. Ever since they'd been wounded, starved, and stranded in the snow after the massacre at Glencoe, Sutherland could predict snow as if he called up the storms himself.

"I'd hoped to get Gretna and the lads away from *Ruadh* and the Neal mess for a while before the weather hit. Maybe even winter in Edinburgh if she'd been willing. Isobel's babe is due in January. She could help her." Ian heaved out a disgusted sigh. "I suppose it's best to face the fools head-on though. Deal with them now rather than later."

Sutherland shook his head. "Ye've more than simple fools to deal with. Neal is a dangerous man. He knows how to stir people and sway them with lies. He's after something here. Either gold, revenge, or both." Head tilting as though pondering a puzzle, he resettled his arse on the boulder. "And I counted a half dozen of those crimson cloaked bastards from Inverness before we left. I'd not seen that many with him in the pub, but ye canna miss that bloody garb when they're moving about the village."

"Half dozen," Ian repeated. He wished the feasting had already ended, and everything returned to normal. Less people to watch. Less opportunity for danger to hide. "Whatever Neal planned to do as far as Gretna and his family are concerned, he planned long before he returned here to lay claim to her and anything she might own." He scrubbed his hands together. "How else could so many from Inverness suddenly appear?" He itched to ride back to the keep this very minute and pull Gretna into his arms to know she was safe. "I pray the divorce, then the wedding will settle this mess. Maybe then folk'll go on about their business and forget the other. Leave us all in peace."

"For Gretna's sake, I hope so, cousin."

"For my sake, as well," Ian amended, praying this time fate would treat him kindlier.

CHAPTER TEN

"NEARLY A FORTNIGHT, but the last of the visiting clans finally left today. Poor Catriona. Funerals for the three herders cut short all she planned for the gathering." Gretna idly smoothed a fingertip back and forth across Ian's collarbone. "My days should grow quieter now. Less folk in the keep to mend, and no more foolish games that tempt the older men to forget their age." She lifted her head to make sure she wasn't musing aloud to a man who already slept.

"And the guard we sent out recovered all the broodmares. Some of the reivers escaped, but most fell." Ian pecked a kiss to her brow. "See? I am awake and listening to every word that falls from those precious lips."

Gretna couldn't help but giggle as she snuggled back down, safe and warm despite the sleet and rain pelting against the window. "The storm strengthens." She splayed her fingers across his chest, stroking his hard landscape of muscle. A sheen of sweat from their recent loving reflected the light from the hearth, lending a polished glow to his skin.

"Ye warmed stones for the lads' beds, aye? In case their hearth loses its coals before morning?"

She responded with another mirthful snicker.

"Heated stones for the bairns' feet are amusing?" He hugged her closer with a stern shake.

"My sons and I have survived many a bitter winter, dear man. I promise I take good care of them." She'd not taken offense, merely found it endearing that Ian had taken to fretting after the boys like a mother hen.

"I'm glad we were able to convince that bastard Colin to go ahead and sign the papers. Thankfully, we got them sent to Edinburgh before the storm hit."

Gretna smiled. Ian always changed the subject when he knew he'd lost at making his point.

"Ye know as well as I yer gold is all that convinced him to sign so quickly and leave without a fuss." Colin's extortion still infuriated her. They had paid the fool entirely too much. "Ye filled his pockets. Paid off his debts. Even gave the man one of the finest MacCoinnich geldings. 'Tis more than a little shameful to have to do such when right is on our side. I dare say that's probably why he returned after all this time." The storm rattled the windowpanes as though agreeing with her. "At least he's finally gone. Hopefully, forever this time," she added. Moving on to a more pleasant subject, she relaxed back in place. "Do ye feel all will be official so we might marry by Hogmanay?"

"I pray so."

The leeriness in his tone unsettled her. "What is it?" She raised up and looked him in the eyes. "Do ye fear the storms will keep us from getting word from Edinburgh?"

"Nay." Ian smoothed his hand down her back. "My fear is Colin didna truly leave and may yet attempt some mischief. Neither he nor his witch hunters were actually seen leaving *Ruadh*. Their departure was reported by the alewife's son and no one else. Ye can bet, the lad was given coin to make certain we believe they're gone."

She pondered this possibility, watching the firelight dance across

Ian's body. "I suppose ye'll still wish me to stay close to the keep for a while longer then. Until we're certain he's not here?" It wasn't that she minded overly much. She understood his concern and considered it a treasured gift. But with winter all but upon them, she'd hoped for at least another trip or two down into the village before the worst of the weather hit and confined them inside for everything except the most necessary tasks.

"Aye." He squeezed her bum. "The boys, too. I'd not put it past the bastard to seek revenge by using them to cause us pain."

That terrified her more than worrying about her own safety. She pushed up to a sitting position, unable to lie down any longer. A need to see her sons safe filled her. "I'm going to check on the boys, aye?"

Wrapping a throw around her, she padded across the room. The creaking bed and sound of footsteps close behind made her smile. "Stay abed where it's warm. I willna be long." She glanced back and caught her breath. *Naked. Bold. Fierce.* Ian moved with a predatory grace that made her ache to lie beneath him or straddle him and ride. She didn't care as long as he took her again as soon as she returned to their room.

"All the fires need wood."

She allowed him the lie. He'd tended the fires in both the sitting room and the boys' room right before he'd tended hers. A delicious shiver hurried her steps. She'd check on the boys, and then perhaps they'd return to the rug in front of the hearth in their room. It had served them quite nicely earlier.

The sight of the tightly closed bedroom door warmed her. Finn hadn't felt the need to rock nor had any of his screaming dreams since the one from several days ago. Even the keep's constant buzzing about Colin's presence hadn't triggered any of his spells. Just one of the many reasons that told her the joining with Ian had been the right thing to do. Aye, one of many reasons. Each day, her tenderness for him deepened. It thrilled as well as frightened her. He was a mercenary, a warrior at heart. If anything happened to him, she couldn't bear it.

She pushed away the thought and clutched her wrap tighter. Easing open the door, she moved as silent as a shadow. Her heart swelled as it always did at the sight of her angels. She smiled. Aye, the three were angels when they slept. More like wee demons when awake, but that didn't matter. They were hers, and she loved them.

All she could see of any of them was the tops of their heads. They'd each burrowed deep into their layers of blankets. She peeped under Finn's covers. He lay curled in a tight ball, his feet against the stone she'd used to warm his bed. He hugged his long leather glove to his chest. The glove Magnus had fashioned just for Finn to use when he helped with the falcon.

She hurried to brush a kiss to each of their heads, turning as the door creaked open wider.

Ian eased inside. "Are they well? Warm enough?" he whispered.

She nodded, shooing him back out the door as she hurried to follow. After clicking it shut behind her, she smiled up at him. "Ye fret about them as though they're yer own."

"As far as I'm concerned, they are mine." He took her hand and led her to the pile of cushions and pillows he'd arranged on the rug in front of the hearth. As he knelt down into them, tugging for her to follow, he motioned toward a pair of glasses and a bottle. "I thought we'd have a drink or two before we returned to bed, aye?"

Although his intent was most welcome, she glanced back at the boys' bedroom door. "What if we wake them?"

"We'll be quiet," he promised as he handed her a glass. He flipped the wrap away from her shoulders and tossed it aside. "And we'll keep yer wrap close just in case." He filled her glass, then his own.

She breathed in, still holding the liquid on her tongue. The robust flavor, not sweet but pleasingly full and aromatic, surprised her.

"Do ye like it?" He looked proud of himself. "It just arrived today."

"Aye, *mo chridhe*." And she meant it. This caring man was *her heart*.

A loud scratching sound from the direction of the main door to the suite startled them both.

"What could that be?" She made to rise, but he stopped her.

"Nay. Wait here." He took up the iron rod used to stir the hearth fire. With it held like a sword, he strode to the door and yanked it open.

His actions struck fear through her. They were in the keep. Their own quarters. Surely, they were safe here. She gathered up her wrap and threw it back around her shoulders, then hurried over to him. She'd never allow her husband to fight alone. Especially not in their home.

"Whoever was there is gone," he said as he closed the door. "But they left this." He turned the small parchment bundle over, scowling at it. The thick, folded square was crisscrossed with a black ribbon. Ian untied it and carefully opened the layers, revealing three neat bundles of different kinds of dried herbs.

Gretna knew those from afar. The sight of them made her heart pound wildly. "Dinna touch them." Taking care not to, she scooped the package out of his hands, ran across the room, and threw it into the fire. Uncontrollable shaking took hold as she hugged herself and struggled not to sob.

Strong arms wrapped around her and pulled her back against the familiar safety of a hard chest. Ian held her tight, his chin propped on her shoulder. "Tell me," he urged quietly. "Tell me what that was so I can ease yer fears."

"Rue, pondweed, and elder." She drew a shuddering breath. "All meant to drive away evil and repel witches." In the past, when the rumors were at their worst, she'd often returned home to find such bundles nailed to her door and piled on her windowsills.

He didn't comment, just held her tighter. Ominous silence took over as they stood staring into the fire.

"I will speak to Alexander," he finally said, gently turning her to face him. "We will find out who left that at our door, and it will be handled, ye ken?"

"I dinna fear for me." She glanced toward her sons' chamber. "I fear for the lads." Easing back, she pulled the wrap tighter about her. "If they're not safe inside the keep…"

Without a word, Ian disappeared into their bedchamber, then reappeared a few moments later with her shift and shawl in one hand. He'd dressed and sheathed his weapons to his belt. He held out her clothing. "We'll spend tonight here on the couch by their door, aye? I'll have my sword and pistols close and at the ready."

"Ye always know what to do to ease my worries." A tear slipped down her cheek before she could stop it.

"I swear to always try," he said softly as he caught her tear on his thumb and pressed it to his mouth. "Get dressed, love, so we can settle for the night."

With shaking hands, she donned her chemise, then wrapped herself in the soft folds of the knitted shawl. Ian waited on the couch, pulling her into the protective curve of his arm as she nestled against him. Even with her head resting against his chest, she knew sleep would never come. Not tonight. Her mind was too active.

Hours later, daylight struggled through the window. Steady rain still spattered against the panes. The dimness of the room eased its hold as morning came.

"If ye'll stir the fires, I'll fetch Magnus and Sutherland to engage the lads in some such activity and guard them while we meet with Alexander and Catriona. They need to know of this." Ian yanked on his boots. "Bolt the door while I'm gone. Open it for no one but those ye'd trust with yer life, understand?"

"Aye." Her fears had given over to a despondent weariness some time during the night. She had fought this battle before and prayed she'd never fight it again. It seemed worse this time. Danger inside the keep. Nowhere was safe. "I'd hoped we were at least safe here, but now..."

An urgent kiss confirmed Ian felt the same. Without another word, he hurried out the door. She let the heavy beam fall across the portal into the iron brackets. "Dinna lose hope," he said through the door. "I will make this right."

She didn't answer, just pressed her forehead against the wood as the sound of his steps faded. "Dinna lose hope," she repeated. Eyes closed, she struggled against a suffocating bitterness. She hadn't lost hope; it had simply been ripped away from her one bit at a time.

"They willna win," she muttered as she jerked away from the door. "I willna let them."

She tended the fires in each of the rooms. Still fast asleep in their beds, she left the boys to their dreams, propping their bedchamber door open to better hear the soothing sound of their steady breathing. She'd dress, then tend to some mending 'til they awakened, and Ian returned. There would be no need to break her fast today. Her appetite had left her.

A peck on the door interrupted the braiding of her hair.

She stared across the room and felt locked in place with indecision and fury at those who had dared make her feel unsafe in her own home.

The urgent rapping sounded again. This time a bit louder.

Securing her braid with a ribbon, she went to the door but didn't open it. "Aye?"

"A message for ye. Arrived just this morning, m'lady," said an unfamiliar voice. A young lass. Perhaps Catriona had kept on a new maid because the girl had done such good work during the feasting.

It didn't matter. Gretna didn't know the girl. Therefore, the door would not be opened. "Slide it under the door, aye? I'm not yet ready to greet the day."

"It willna fit, m'lady. 'Tis too thick a packet."

"Then leave it on the floor. I shall fetch it once I'm ready." She wasn't a fool. If it was too thick to slide beneath the door, it had to be another ill wish determined to shake her.

"As ye wish, m'lady. Good morning to ye."

The scurrying footsteps faded down into the stairwell.

Although she'd promised Ian to keep the door barred, Gretna ached to open it, fetch the thing, and toss it into the fire. Hands fisted, she stared at the base of the door. Finally, she shook her head and stepped back. *Nay.* She would not break her promise to Ian.

She finished putting up her hair and took up her mending just as the lads wandered from their room, rubbing their eyes. "About time ye decided to rise," she said, greeting them with a forced smile. "How are my wee sleepy heads this morning?"

"Where's Da?" Finn asked.

"Gone to fetch Magnus and Sutherland. I believe they've planned a day for ye," she lied.

A loud knock thumped the door. "'Tis me, lass," Ian called out from the other side.

"Why did ye lower the bar?" Evander asked, suspicion in his tone. The lad might only be eleven, but he never missed a thing, and, unfortunately, the child had seen much during his lifetime. "Ye never bar the door," he added.

"Never ye mind," she countered, waving him toward the door. "Let yer da in, aye? So, I dinna have to interrupt my mending."

Her eldest didn't believe her. She saw it in his eyes. Thankfully, he chose to remain silent in front of his brothers. Evander opened the door, glaring at the three men as they entered, all of them wearing tense smiles.

Setting aside her mending, Gretna rose. A glance at Ian's empty hands puzzled her. "Was there not a missive on the step or maybe beside the door?"

Ian frowned and looked back toward the entryway. "I saw no

missive." He pinned her with a fierce look. "Did ye hear the same scratching as before?"

Magnus strode to the door, Sutherland close behind. He yanked it open. Both men stepped out for a brief moment, then returned. "Nothing on the steps," Magnus reported.

"Was it the same as before?" Ian repeated, moving closer.

"Nay." She rushed across the room and stared out the door, unreasonably hoping the men had somehow overlooked it. "A maid knocked and bid me let her in to give me a message."

"Which maid?" Ian took hold of her arm and gently led her back to the sitting area.

Magnus snapped his fingers to get the attention of the three wide-eyed lads everyone had forgotten. "Come, lads. Let us go down to the hall and break our fast, then we'll think up some mischief to brighten this dreary day, aye?" He winked. "If the rain lets up, I'll show ye how I taught Merlin to dive at the guards when they're walking on the wall."

"I think I need to stay here with Mama," Evander said as he hurried over and took hold of her hand. "What is it that's troubling ye, Mama? What happened?"

Her brave son. In another year, the scrappy lad would be as tall as she. Maybe even taller. Gretna patted his hand. "Nothing for ye to worry after, aye?"

"I'm not a wee bairn anymore," the boy argued. God bless Evander. When he hardened that jaw and lifted his chin, he looked just like his father.

"I know ye're not a babe anymore. Ye're a fine young man." She pulled him into a hug. While she held him tight, she whispered, "Please go with the men now. For yer brothers' sake. I promise I will tell ye more later. Please?"

As he stepped away, he gave a reluctant nod, then turned to his brothers. "Come on."

"What about Mama?" Rory asked while Finn edged a step closer to Gretna.

"Master Ian will keep her safe," Evander said with a threatening glare toward him. He waved his brothers forward. "Come on now, the both of ye. Wait any longer, and the best bannocks will all be gone because I'll eat every one of them."

Without further argument, all three boys and both men hurried out the door.

"Now, which maid asked to come in?" Ian repeated.

"I didna know her voice, so I bid her place the packet on the floor. I told her I'd get it after I dressed." Gretna wrung her hands together. "She seemed agreeable enough and left."

"But she didna leave the message." Ian glared at the door as though willing it to tell all its secrets.

"It appears not." She shook away her worries, refusing to give them power. "Catriona will know who she is, and then we can speak to the girl, aye?"

"Come. They await us in their solar."

After locking the door to their suite, they hurried to Alexander and Catriona's private wing.

Young William met them at the door, his twin sister, Willa, close behind. "Ye didna bring the lads?" he asked, pushing around them to look into the hall.

"That is nay the proper way to greet visitors!" Willa scolded. She rolled her eyes and pulled him behind her. Taking the lead, she stood tall and politely ushered them inside. "Please forgive my rude brother. Good morning to ye and do come in. Mama and Da are at their private breakfast."

"Thank ye, Willa." Gretna did her best to refrain from smiling and hurting poor William's pride further.

"The boys have gone downstairs to break their fast, if ye wish to find them," Ian whispered to the scowling boy. He snagged hold of

William's arm just as the child started to dart out the door. "Best ask yer da first."

William gave a quick nod, then charged around his sister. "Da, can I go downstairs to break my fast?" He turned and glared at his sister. "*Without* Willa?"

"William!" Catriona called. "Ye *will* take yer sister along with ye, or ye willna go." She turned to Willa. "If ye dinna treat the lads with kindness, young lady, ye will find yerself with no one to play with other than the wee ones. Is that what ye wish? Now, stop bein' such a cross hen."

"I'll do better," Willa promised in an unconvincing tone. She turned to her twin. "Sorry, brother."

Jaw set, William held out his hand and waited without accepting or refusing his sister's less-than-sincere apology. Smugly victorious, Willa took her brother's hand, and the two scurried off to find their friends.

"God help me if this be another set of twins," Catriona said with a glance down at her rounded middle. Her glare lifted to Alexander. "I might be forced to kill ye."

"Now, love." Unfazed at the death threat, Alexander smiled, kissed her hand, then motioned toward a pair of chairs at the table. "Please, join us. Cook always sends up plenty."

"Forgive us for interrupting ye," Gretna said as Ian helped her into a chair, then seated himself. A wave of guilt washed across her. She hated to cast a pall over their pleasant morning. "It's about the new servant."

"What new servant?" Catriona asked as she drizzled butter mixed with honey over a steaming bannock.

"The new maid ye kept on after the festival," Ian supplied, pushing back the tankard of ale Alexander had poured for him.

Catriona frowned, studying them both for a long, tense moment. "Neither I nor Mrs. Fitzgerald have added anyone to the staff."

"What is this about, Ian?" Alexander sat back in his chair, breakfast forgotten.

"Last night, someone scratched on our door and left an ill wish behind. A packet of herbs made specially to repel witches," Ian said, his tone rumbling with barely controlled rage. "This morning, while I fetched Magnus and Sutherland to watch after the boys, a young woman claimed to have another packet to deliver. Gretna refused to let her in. Told her to leave it beside the door."

"What was it?" Catriona asked, setting her knife down and clasping her hands atop the table.

"I dinna ken," Gretna said. She hugged herself, fighting to keep her voice steady. "Nothing was left outside the door even though the girl told me she'd do it." She understood now why Finn rocked when he was upset. She was tempted to do so herself. Massaging her temples, she wished the aching from lack of sleep would go away so she might think straight. "I'd hoped ye had kept one of the new girls who had worked so well during the feast. But now, I fear evil is afoot."

"And it appears that evil is within our own keep," Ian added. He took hold of Gretna's hand and gave it a reassuring squeeze. "I canna prove it, but I dinna believe Colin Neal left *Ruadh* so easily."

"As much gold as ye gave him, why would he not?" Alexander asked.

"Because he's always been a greedy bastard," Catriona supplied as she reached over and took Gretna's other hand. "I wouldna put it past him to see if he might squeeze more profit from the situation." Her look hardened even more. "And dinna forget, he's a Neal. A more headstrong lot, ye'll never meet."

Graham stormed into the solar without knocking. He came up short at the sight of Gretna and Ian at the breakfast table. "Forgive me for interrupting, but reivers struck again last night. East end of the glen. Set three of the herders' crofts afire and made off with at least a dozen mares."

"Within *our* glen?" Alexander rose so fast his chair toppled over.

"Aye." Graham rested his hands atop the hafts of his dirk and claymore sheathed at his waist. "It appears the more of them we kill, the more brazen they become."

Gretna suddenly felt very guilty for raising such a fuss over someone's cruel idea of mischief. Her problem seemed very small compared to such a strike against the clan. "The herders. Are they all right? Do any need healing?"

"We brought in three wounded, but none so severe as to need yer care. The lads are fine—just enraged." Graham turned back to Alexander. "I say we go on a devil hunt, aye?"

"Aye," Alexander answered without hesitation. "Clan MacCoinnich doesna take such an affront lightly."

As the three men drew closer with their planning, Gretna helped Catriona rise from the table and move to the other side of the solar.

"And what shall we do about yer messenger?" Catriona asked as they settled on the couch beside the fire.

Gretna smiled. She'd been known to plan a battle or two herself. "I say we act as though nothing has happened. Make them think their ploys have either failed or gone ignored."

CHAPTER ELEVEN

ONE SIDE OF the main hall had been turned into a ward for the wounded. Ian had never seen such carnage from what should have been a simple reining in of a band of horse thieves. This looked more like a clan war. As a matter of fact, that's what it had become, a full-blown feud. Word had reached them that a group of the Neals, who had never truly pledged fealty to the MacCoinnichs when Alexander and Catriona married, had joined with the bloody Campbells in an effort to lay claim to *Tor Ruadh*.

Ian had a fair idea which Neal had stirred all this trouble. None of this unrest had been apparent before Colin returned from the dead.

A blast of cold, wet air swept into the room as a young man, soaked to the skin and covered with mud, pushed into the keep. He clutched a leather satchel to his middle, a long strap securing it across his body.

Ian had never seen this messenger before, but he supposed old Fergail Parsons had gotten too far on in years to handle such a daunting task. He strode forward to help the lad, waving down a maid in the process. "Whisky for the messenger. Poor man's chilled to the bone."

The girl scurried off to fetch it.

"Thank ye kindly, sir." The bedraggled man plopped the dripping satchel on the hearth and backed up to the fire. He nodded toward the bulging leather bag. "Quite a bit this time. Glad the heavy snows havena hit yet. Mostly just sleet and a few snowy patches here and there right now." He accepted the whisky from the maid and downed it.

"Bring the lad the bottle, aye?" Ian moved a wooden bench closer to the fire so the man could sit while warming himself. "Anything for Ian Cameron?"

"I believe so." The messenger unbuckled the bag's flap and pawed through the contents, which looked amazingly dry. "Ah…here 'tis." He handed over a thick envelope bearing a familiar seal. "Straight from Edinburgh looks like."

"Keep the witch away from me!" The loud demand silenced all conversation in the bustling room.

Ian shoved the packet inside his waistcoat and charged to defend Gretna. She and Elena Bickerstaff, the elderly healer nearly too old and ill-tempered to tend to the wounded, stood beside a man whose leg had required amputation the day before.

"Now, now. None o' that," Elena shoved around Gretna and leaned over the man. "Ye're safe now, lad. Drink this so ye might rest and heal." Without a word, she snatched away the cup Gretna had been offering him. "I'll tend this one," she said in a gruff tone. "Go see to the ones who'll take yer help, ye ken?"

Without a word, Gretna nodded and backed away. The look on her face broke Ian's heart. How dare they treat his dear one that way. She labored for hours at their sides, ignoring her own weariness until it toppled her over. He took hold of her elbow and led her to the other side of the room. "A packet came from Edinburgh," he announced as he pulled the missive from his waistcoat. He hoped the news would get her mind off the ignorance taking over the clan like a plague. Alexander had tamped it down as much as possible, but a constant undercurrent of the vicious rumors still simmered strong.

Gretna didn't even attempt a smile, just stood with shoulders sagging as though bearing the weight of the world. She looked up from wiping her hands on her apron. "Aye?"

Ian prayed the good news would bolster her spirits. He had recognized Alasdair's seal. Surely, his brother had sent word that the divorce was final, and a wedding could now be planned. They all needed something to celebrate.

"Everyone!" Alexander called out, hammering on the head table with an empty tankard. "There is news of King James." A hush fell. Alexander looked around the room, then nodded at the messenger, now standing at his side. "Tell them what ye just told me."

"James VII, deposed King of Scotland, in exile in France, has died. Back in September. His son, James Francis Edward Stuart has declared himself James VIII." The man cast a nervous look at all the faces turned his way. Such an open announcement could be dangerous, even seen as Jacobite sympathies.

Murmurs filled the room like the rumbling of thunder.

"I need to get back to changing bandages," Gretna gently reminded with a nod toward the message.

Ian broke the seal, unfolded the parchment, and smiled as soon as he read the first few words. "Ye're mine for true now, lass. We best be telling Father William we're ready to say our vows."

Her smile he'd been seeking finally appeared for a moment. Gretna hugged him and even rested her head on his chest. "Fetch him now, so we might do it today," she said, squeezing him tight.

"Ye dinna wish a fine wedding in the chapel?" he cradled her close, reluctant to release her. This was the first time in weeks he'd felt the slightest easing of the tension plaguing her.

Gretna shifted against him. "Nay, I dinna need a chapel wedding, and Catriona's abed until the wee one comes." She lifted her head and treated him to another grin. "She'd miss seeing us say our vows." Her smile flickered away, and the shadows returned to her eyes. "And it seems selfish to celebrate with so much unrest right now." She squeezed his hands. "All we need are the boys, some witnesses, and the priest."

"What are we witnessing?" Alexander asked as he joined them. "Something good, I hope. This place is in dire need of good news for a change."

Ian handed over the document, feeling the same as Alexander and grateful to be able to provide some much-needed relief. "Good news, indeed. Place those in the clan records, my chieftain. Gretna Neal is no longer Colin Neal's wife, and we seek to change her name to Cameron this verra day."

Alexander brightened and clapped him on the back. "Fine news, for certain!" He scooped up Gretna's hand and kissed it. "Allow me to be the first to congratulate ye and also ask a favor?"

Gretna gave him a leery look. "A favor?"

"Would ye consider speaking yer vows in front of Catriona. Trapped in the bed, she's fretting so much, I fear for her and the unborn babe. It would truly brighten her day to have the honor of being one of yer witnesses." Alexander glanced at Ian. "Would the two of ye consider such?"

"All these happy faces," Graham said as he interrupted the conversation. "Would ye share the good news? I tire of dealing with feuding clans, vicious rumors, and wintry storms." Magnus and Sutherland followed close behind.

"Shall I make this easier and announce it to one and all?" Ian asked.

His heart lifted at the spark of happiness returning to Gretna. Even during Hogmanay, her liveliness had dulled, and endless weariness had visibly subdued her. The troubling times had worn ill on all in the keep, muting the normally joyous celebration of welcoming in the new year. Vows affirming their hope for the future might help strike down the worrisome evil hanging so heavy over the keep. "I'll stand on the table and tell everyone, aye?"

"Aye," Gretna said. "Share our wondrous news with all." She glanced around. "The boys should be here, though. I dinna wish them to hear it from anyone but ourselves."

"Last I saw them, they were in the kitchens begging scraps from Cook," Sutherland said.

"If they're hungry, they shouldna have to beg for scraps. Does this need to be addressed?" Alexander demanded. "I'll not have the lads mistreated by anyone fool enough to listen to those damned rumors of witchery."

Ian agreed and was just as frustrated as Alexander over the seemingly impossible to squelch gossip. If they could but find the source of the accusations, then they could end them.

"Well?" Alexander prodded when no one answered.

"The scraps are for their rats," Magnus explained, looking as though he was struggling not to laugh and quite possibly seeking the quickest escape from the room. He cleared his throat and shrugged. "Those three have lined their pockets quite nicely with the coins they've earned by racing the vermin they trap and accepting bets."

"I shall talk with them," Ian hurried to say before anyone else commented. He'd meant to speak to the lads before now about their emptying the pockets of those who had a bit too much ale in the evenings, but he'd been a mite busy with everything else.

"I thought ye already had," Gretna scolded under her breath.

Sutherland laughed and nudged Ian. "Ye already sound married to me, but I suppose Father William needs to make it official in the eyes of God, aye?"

"Fetch them," Magnus instructed his falcon. Merlin took off, soaring through the kitchen archway. "They'll be here in no time. Merlin gets a share of the rats, so he's quite fond of the lads."

All of the older children of the keep came running, led by the regal bird. The six had become fast friends, and one was rarely seen without the others close behind.

"Father William!" Gretna called out. The small, wiry priest rose from beside the patient he'd been reading to from his prayer book.

"Aye?" he responded as he reached them.

Gretna leaned over and whispered something in his ear.

The priest gave a solemn nod after patting the pocket of his simple brown robe, then took hold of the wooden cross hanging around his neck and kissed it. "Leave it to me, lass."

"And ye said what to him?" Ian asked. He and Father William had never quite gotten along ever since he informed the man that a truly loving God would never allow so much pain in the world.

"Ye shall see," Gretna promised as she looped her arm through his and turned toward the chieftain's table. "Make yer announcement, husband, and then we shall go upstairs to Catriona to make it official."

Heart full and happy that at least this battle had been won, Ian silenced the room with a hard thump on the chief's table. He kept an arm around Gretna as he held up the parchment for all to see. "Gretna Neal is officially divorced from Colin Neal, and within the hour, Father William will hear our vows to permanently seal the troth we plighted during our handfasting."

He paused and gave her a look he hoped she'd understand, a look that held all he felt for her. "I know it's not been a year and a day, but I dinna feel the need to wait. I love this woman. I wish her to be Gretna Cameron, my cherished wife." Most in the room cheered, but Ian couldn't help but notice that several remained quiet, fixing first Gretna and then the priest with wary looks.

Father William held up a hand. "It has been brought to my attention that some believe this fine woman to be a witch."

"What is he doing?" Ian whispered, drawing Gretna closer.

"What I asked him to do," she replied.

The holy man removed a small vial from his pocket, uncorked it, then started flinging the contents on both Gretna and Ian. "*Gloria Patris, et Filii, et Spiritus Sancti: Et nunc, et semper, et in saecula saeculo-*

rum. Ámen." The priest repeated the Gloria Patri as he walked around them. On his third and final circling, he repeated the words in English, "Glory to the Father, and to the Son, and to the Holy Spirit. Both now and always, and until the ages of ages. Amen."

Ian realized the man had showered them with holy water during the rite and immediately understood.

Upon completing the ritual, Father William faced the crowd. "If this good Christian woman was a witch, possessed by demons, or in league with Satan, do ye not think she wouldha burst into flames by now?" He flourished a wave of the holy water vial, scattering droplets from her feet to the top of her head. "This woman heals ye, helps ye, and serves our Lord with her sacrifices and services. Dinna insult her nor damn yer own souls to hell by feeding such vicious rumors about her. Ye best look to yer own actions and tend to how ye yerself live. Judge not lest ye be judged, ye fools!"

"Amen!" Sutherland shouted.

Ian bit his tongue to keep from laughing and receiving an eternal sentence of hellfire and damnation for himself. "Shall we go upstairs now to share our news with Catriona and speak our vows?"

"Aye." Gretna looped her arm through his.

With priest, children, and friends following close behind, Ian slowly shook his head as they led the way to the chieftain's chambers.

"What?" Gretna asked. "Has all the talk and trouble changed yer mind?" she whispered. She glanced behind them. "We should tell them now if that's so."

If not for the tremor in her voice and the fact she'd paled a bit, he'd think she wished for a way out herself. But no...he knew those shadows in her eyes. Gretna worried about him. He kissed her cheek as they reached the landing. "Nay, love. I was merely shaking my head because a scant six months ago, I wouldha never seen myself doing this—nor believe I could feel so at peace and happy with the doing of it."

"I'm glad."

"Aye. I am, too," Ian said as he opened the door to the solar and winked. "See if Catriona would mind a wee visit."

Gretna disappeared into the bedchamber. An excited squeal and clapping from within the room soon followed.

Father William smiled. "Maybe this excitement will convince that wee bairn it's time to be born." He gave Alexander a smug look. "Or the wee *bairns*, as the case may be."

Alexander groaned.

Ian laughed. "Aye, a third set of twins would be quite the blessing."

The priest arched a brow at Ian. "Mark my words. Ye'll be next." He motioned to the boys standing close by. "These three need a wee sister to protect. Do ye not, my lads?"

Evander, Rory, and Finn all looked at the holy man as though he'd just sprouted a second head.

"She's ready," Gretna announced, opening the bedchamber door wide and waving all forward.

As many as could crowded into the room. The rest remained in the solar. Catriona sat in the center of the bed, propped among piles of pillows, her face aglow. Ian took hold of Gretna's hand and squeezed as they faced Father William, who had taken a position beside the head of the bed.

Hands folded, the priest smiled at all in the room. "We are here to witness the vows of Ian and Gretna to each other. Their promise in front of our Lord." He leaned forward and lifted Ian and Gretna's joined hands, cupping his own around them. "The Lord bless thee and keep thee. The Lord make his face shine upon thee and be gracious unto thee. The Lord lift up his countenance upon thee and give thee peace." He nodded. "Speak yer words now, one to another. Ian?"

A loving contentment filled Ian as he soared into the brilliant blue of Gretna's gaze. He'd not felt this settled in a long while. *Aye*. This was right and true. He squeezed her hands. "Heart of my heart, soul of my soul, cherished forevermore. To thee I join, thee I love, until time is no more."

Gretna eased closer. "I shall stay at yer side, heart of my heart and soul of my soul. To thee I join, thee I love, until time is no more."

Father William gave an approving nod, then lifted a hand and held it over them. "I now pronounce these two as one, both in the eyes of our Lord and this world. Man and wife until death do part them. Let no man put asunder what God Himself hath joined." He nodded to Ian. "Ye may kiss yer bride."

"Gladly." Ian pulled her into his arms and claimed her with a kiss meant to meld them together for all time. "I love ye," he whispered.

"And I love ye." She closed her eyes and rested her head on his shoulder.

All in the room clapped and cheered. The happy sound rippled out into the solar, down the stairwell, and into the hall. Catriona cheered the loudest. From her position in the bed, she ruled as though it were her throne. "Alexander! Send for drinks. We must have a toast to celebrate."

Alexander hurried to do her bidding.

Ian motioned for Evander, Rory, and Finn to join them. The three had wedged themselves into a corner, flanked by their friends, as though they feared attack.

"Come, lads," Ian urged. "We're officially a family now." Finn had been calling him *Da* as though born to it. Rory called him that when he wanted something. Evander never veered from Master Ian or sir. Ian cared for all three and hoped someday they would *all* fully trust him and, at the very least, consider him a friend.

"Oh, dear!" Catriona stiffened and yanked up the covers, frowning as she peered beneath them.

"Oh, dear?" Gretna repeated. "Is it time?"

Catriona nodded. "Aye. My waters just soaked the bed."

Her cane lightly tapping out her path, Mercy headed for the door. "I'll alert Mrs. Fitzgerald that it's time."

"Have one of the maids fetch my basket, aye?" Gretna said as she started tugging at the bedclothes.

Catriona shifted, then flinched. "Merciful heavens, there's another rush of water. Should be the last of it."

"She's peed the bed. Twice? And with us standing right here?" Finn asked loud enough for all to hear.

"Everyone out!" Ian ordered before the lads made more observations.

The mysteries of bringing bairns into the world was best left to the women. Everyone rushed from the room, and the crowd waiting in the solar retreated, charging down to the hall below. Evander, Rory, and Finn looked like lost lambs separated from the herd. They hovered close to the outer door but stayed in the solar as though unsure as to what they were supposed to do. Sutherland, Magnus, Graham, and the priest remained. Ian closed the bedchamber door and blew out a relieved breath just as Alexander returned to the room, followed by several servants bearing trays of pitchers and tankards.

He came to a halt, frowning at the closed bedchamber door, then at those remaining in the room.

"It's time," Ian explained with a nod back at the door.

"Ahh…well, then." Alexander scrubbed his hands together. "Perhaps we'll save the toast to a good marriage for afterward. Once the women finish what they're doing." He motioned to the servants. "Set the drinks over there. I'm sure ye're needed elsewhere to bring up supplies for the bairn." He took a seat at the table beside the window, staring out at the icy rain streaking down the glass.

For a woman who had already been through this twice before, he seemed strangely detached from the entire situation. His jovial mood from the unexpected wedding had disappeared. Ian wondered if Catriona had experienced troubles during the times prior to this.

Bringing life into the world was deadly, indeed. He grabbed two tankards from a passing servant and joined his cousin at the table. "Take heart, man. All will be well. I'll consider nothing less on my wedding day."

Alexander rewarded the slight encouragement with a brief smile that shifted to a scowl. "It appears we were mistaken about who aligned the traitorous southern Neals with Clan Campbell's strength." He pulled his gaze away from the window and looked at Ian. "It's not Colin Neal keeping unrest stirred and leading the men in the plundering of our people."

"Who then?" Ian found that hard to believe. Colin had been reported among the renegades during every attack. The bastard had been spotted as he helped set fire to the houses of his own clan—those loyal to the MacCoinnichs. Ian had spied him while protecting the western tip of the village during the last raid. "I saw the man just days ago, riding with the Campbells."

Alexander shook his head. "I misspoke. Or at least, I didna make myself clear. Colin Neal does not act *alone* in splitting the unity of the MacCoinnich clan and trying to claim our lands."

Four maids rushed into the room, arms loaded with fresh linens, and two of them bearing kettles of steaming water. Mercy followed close behind, depending on her cane to find her way. All of them filed into the bedchamber. After several moments, the door opened again, and the maids hurried out, heading back downstairs.

Ian blinked away the interruption, flinching at the muffled sound of a woman's labored groans coming from the next room. He wished they'd all gone back downstairs to the hall. "What are ye trying to tell me, Alexander?" he asked, struggling to keep the man focused.

"Catriona's brothers," Alexander said through clenched teeth.

The statement pushed Ian back in his chair as though he'd been shoved. "Which brothers?"

Catriona's twin, the vile Calum Neal, had been killed while rescuing Catriona and saving the clan from his evil rule. The next brother in succession, Angus, just as wicked as Calum, but barely fifteen years old at the time, had disappeared during the battle. Her youngest brothers, Murray and Dougal, had only been nine at the time. Those two had been sent to relatives farther north, but as far as anyone knew, they had always claimed fealty to Catriona and Alexander. But ten years had passed. Enough time for boys to become men and old wounds to fester.

"All three of them. Angus, Murray, and Dougal," Alexander said. "Angus claims *Tor Ruadh* is rightfully his, and the other two support him."

"Chieftain Neal and Calum's cruel insanity has not been forgotten by the clan." Ian pushed one of the tankards toward Alexander. "Many of the Neals have shown their loyalty and sworn fealty to ye. They're happy with how ye've grown the clan and cared for the people."

"Many, but not all," Alexander said, then drained the cup. "If all were content, Colin wouldha failed at helping the brothers unite the Neals to the south, so Angus might rule over them. 'Tis also said Colin was the one to deal the Campbells into the fray."

"That bastard. We shouldha killed him when we had the chance." Ian shook his head. "All we can do now is best them, and best them we will."

A growling shriek echoed from the adjoining room. All the men stared at the bedchamber door as though it held a monster within.

"Is it always like this?" Ian whispered as he motioned for the children to run along and find something better to do. He feared the sound of Catriona's distress might trigger one of Finn's spells.

"Aye." Alexander stared at the door with a pained look. "It'll get worse toward the end. She'll stop groaning and go to cursing, then sobbing." He shrugged and attempted to settle more comfortably in the chair. "But once she holds the babe, all is well."

"Will ye tell her of her brothers?" Ian glanced around at those remaining in the room, Graham, Sutherland, Magnus, and Father William. All had been present during the battle ten years ago to cleanse the Neal clan of its demons.

Before Alexander could answer, an object crashed against the door and shattered.

"She often throws things whilst bringing our bairns into this world," Alexander explained with an impressive calmness. "She possesses the Neal temper."

God Almighty. Gretna's a MacNeilage. Almost one and the same. Ian rose and edged toward the solar's outer door. "Perhaps we should wait downstairs in the hall, aye?"

Alexander gave him a sympathetic smile. "Ye can all go if ye wish, but I'll be staying here. 'Tis the least I can do."

Ian sagged back down into his seat. He couldn't very well leave now and look the selfish coward.

Rising, Alexander went to the long buffet bearing several decanters. He poured drinks for everyone, waving them over to fetch them. "I appreciate all of ye here. Even though God has blessed Catriona with safe deliveries before…"

"All will be well," Ian repeated as he lifted his glass.

Everyone joined in with a hearty, "Aye!"

A robust wailing joined in.

"The babe," Alexander whispered with a step toward the door.

"Healthy," Ian said. "Listen."

The new life raged strong and fierce, and the child sounded thoroughly displeased with the world.

After what seemed like forever, the bedchamber door opened. Gretna searched out Alexander and waved him over. "Come, my chieftain. Ye have a fine, healthy daughter to meet."

"Just one," Alexander said, sounding relieved. "One daughter, aye?"

"Aye, just the one. But with the temper that wee one has, she'll be enough." Gretna stepped out of the way, nudged him into the room, then closed the door after Mercy joined her in the sitting room. She turned from the door and nodded toward the glass in Ian's hand. "We should all toast wee Mistress Maisie Leanna." She smiled. "And Mercy and I could use a drink as well."

"Indeed," Mercy agreed.

Magnus, Sutherland, Graham, and Father William gathered around as Ian poured drinks for all. With an arm around Gretna's waist, he lifted his glass high. "To Maisie Leanna." He hugged Gretna closer. "And to my lovely wife."

She beamed at him, lifting her glass alongside his. "And to the future…and precious, new life."

Ian paused with his glass midway to his mouth and gave Gretna a sharp look. *New life.* His gaze swept down to her middle. *Nay.* Surely, she meant the wee bairn she had just helped into the world.

"Aye!" everyone echoed, then downed their drinks.

An explosion, loud as cannon fire, shook through the keep.

CHAPTER TWELVE

*M*Y *SONS.* G*RETNA* ran for the door. Ian caught her by the arm and yanked her back. She struggled against his hold, yelling out her fears, "Let me go! I have to get to the boys!"

"Stay here," he ordered in a loud but calm tone. "I will find them and bring them to ye." He held her in place, watching her. *Damn him.* He knew her too well, knew as soon as he let her go, she'd run.

Sutherland and Magnus charged out the door, Father William on their heels.

Alexander raced past them with his sword drawn. He paused at the door and motioned toward the bedchamber. "Stay with Catriona and the babe. Please, Gretna, I beg ye."

"Both of ye stay with her," Graham said. He cupped Mercy's face. "Dinna worry. I'll bring the bairns to ye. Please, just stay here, aye?"

Mercy gave a quick nod. "Be safe, my love."

If Mercy stayed here, she could keep Catriona and the babe company. Gretna could see to her sons. As she edged toward the door and opened her mouth to offer this reasoning, Ian took hold of her other arm, too. "Nay, my stubborn love. I know damn good and well what ye're thinking. I *need* ye to stay here. I swear I will find them. They're my sons now, too, understand?"

He leaned in, forcing her to look him in the eyes. "I will find them," he repeated. He glared at her with bared teeth and nostrils flaring, then gave her a gentle shake to drive his words home. "Heed me, wife! For all our sakes, heed me!"

It took all her strength to force a nod and actually mean it. "Hurry." She shoved him away, then grabbed hold of his waistcoat and yanked him back for a kiss as harsh and hard as a slap. "But dinna ye dare get hurt," she warned as she pushed him away again. "If ye do, I'll force the vilest tonics I know down yer throat."

"Aye, m'lady," he promised with a grim smile. Before he closed the door behind him, he gave a warning tilt of his head. "Barricade it, ye ken? Open it for no one unless ye know them *and* trust them."

Gretna nodded, pushing against the door and dropping the bar across it before it clicked fully shut.

Ian's steps faded away. Faint shouts and an acrid scent of burnt gunpowder and smoke filtered in from elsewhere in the keep. *What in God's name had happened?* Her ache to rush out the door and find her babies raged fierce and strong. She pounded her fist against the wood. Not knowing ate away at her.

"Gretna?" Catriona's call from the bedchamber broke through her torment.

After stuffing a rolled tapestry against the bottom of the door to block any smoke, Gretna hurried to her. "I'm here."

Mercy sitting at her side, Catriona had curled against the head of the bed, clutching her sleeping baby close. "Thank ye for staying. I know the need to see to the children, but Alexander swore he'd have them all brought to us here. The men will see to our bairns."

Gretna sat at the foot of the bed, hugging herself as she strained to hear what might be happening below. Strangely, all seemed quiet now. That brought her some small hope. If they were under attack, surely the sound of battle would fill the keep. But if it wasn't an attack, what had it been? She knew the smell of spent gunpowder. It had filled the air enough to rise to the second floor. "I hate this." She rose and paced back and forth beside the bed.

"I know. A woman's lot isna fair during such a time," Catriona observed, staring sadly down at her new daughter. "My dear, sweet child, what sort of world have I brought ye into?"

Gretna pressed a hand to her still flat middle that wouldn't remain so in the coming months. *Aye, what a world indeed.* She possessed an enviable trait among women. Her courses flowed with the regularity of the moon's phases. They always had. She should've bled by now, should've bled a fortnight ago. With the experience of bearing three bairns, she was fairly certain another was on the way. She had planned to tell Ian the news today, but now she wondered if she should. He needed no distractions—especially not worrying about his wife and unborn child.

A pounding on the door caused all of them to jump and startled the babe. Gretna went to the door and leaned close. "Ian? Alexander? Graham?"

"They sent me," called out an unfamiliar voice. *A man.*

"Who are ye?" She stepped back from the door, glancing around the room for a weapon should she need it.

"One of the new guards. They bid me come and protect ye. Let me in, m'lady."

Liar. She glanced back at Catriona and Mercy, who had joined her in the sitting room. Catriona shook her head as she lowered herself into a chair.

"Ye can guard the room with yer back to the door. I'll open it for no one other than my husband." Gretna eyed the bar across the door. Heavy and thick, it should easily hold off one man. With her stare locked on the entryway, she backed across the room to the hearth and snatched up the fire iron to use as a weapon just in case.

"Smoke," Catriona whispered, pointing at the door. A wispy gray tendril filtered up from between the tapestry and the base of the door.

"The bastard started a fire." Gretna rushed to the bedchamber, grabbed two pitchers of water, and ran back to the door.

Kicking aside the tapestry, she sloshed the contents of both pitchers under the crack of the door, then shoved the cloth back in place. She fetched a bucket of wash water from beside the bed and used it to thoroughly wet the bunched-up weaving and the base of the door. Heart pounding, she backed away, staring at the soaked mess and praying she'd managed to put out the fire or at least slowed it until one of their men returned.

"Gretna!" Ian roared, pounding on the door and stamping his feet. "Open the door!"

Relief nearly knocked her down. She hurried to lift the bar. Ian stormed in, Finn in one arm, Rory and Evander at his side. Sutherland followed close behind with Willa and William.

"Praise God, ye're all right." Ian grabbed her up against his chest and kissed the top of her head as he held her close.

"The nursery?" Catriona asked as she hugged Willa and William. "Please tell me all my bairns are safe."

Sutherland nodded. "They're fine. Alexander is fetching Nanny with Grant and Maxwell, and Fenna is bringing wee Effie. Graham found Ramsay and will be here soon as well. All the bairns will be safe in this room."

Clutching Finn, Gretna found herself overtaken with relieved sobbing. She lowered herself to the couch and pulled all her sons close. "I was so afraid I'd lost ye. So verra afraid."

"We're fine, Mama," Evander reassured as he pulled away and stood beside Ian. "And we're going to help Da catch that bastard. I swear!"

Gretna smiled as she squeezed her brave son's arm. She'd not comment on his calling Ian, *Da*. She'd just accept it for the blessing it was. "I know ye will, son. I feel so much safer with the three of ye here."

"If I wouldha had my pistol, the son of a bitch would be dead right now," Ian swore. He pointed back at the door. "He ran as we topped the stair."

"'Tis a good thing ye heard him trying to set the fire," Sutherland observed as he kicked the soggy tapestry and scorched remains farther away from the door.

"He bade us let him in," Gretna said. She nodded at poor Catriona, growing paler by the minute. "But we refused." Strengthened by the knowledge her loved ones were safe, Gretna pushed up from the couch and helped Catriona back to bed. "Into the bed with ye, lass. God bless ye. This is no way to recover after having a bairn." She cast an eye over at tiny Maisie, sleeping soundly in her cradle. "Mercy and I will be just outside with the children, aye? Call out if ye need us."

"Aye," Catriona said as she settled down into the pillows.

Commotion out in the sitting room warned Gretna that Nanny, the youngest twins, and Effie had arrived. Graham had arrived with Ramsay, and Alexander had also brought along Fenna and another maid for reinforcements against such an army of young ones. Gretna smiled. No wonder the man was chieftain.

Ian met her at the bedchamber door as she closed it behind her. "I need to go back down and help Graham and Alexander. Sutherland's gone to fetch Sawny and Tom to guard the door. No one will get past them."

Sawny Fitzgerald had been nothing more than a twelve-year-old kitchen boy ten years ago when he and his best friend, Tom, had helped Catriona escape her evil brother's clutches. Their quick-wit and wiles had saved their mistress. Sawny and Tom were now well respected, high-ranking MacCoinnich guards.

"What in God's name was that explosion?" Gretna held tight to Ian's arm. He'd not escape her again without telling her what had happened.

"That damned messenger brought a bomb into our midst."

"A bomb?" Gretna recoiled as though the words themselves might explode. "How? Why on earth…"

"Because the cowards dinna like to fight us face to face." Rage echoed in Ian's voice. He flexed his hands as though anxious to take hold of his weapons. "They prefer burning homes at the edge of our lands, murdering defenseless folk caught out alone, and now, bombing the heart of our keep where we tend our wounded." He jerked a nod toward the outer door. "That same bastard set the fire at that door. Once we catch him, he'll rue the day he was born."

Gretna wrung her hands, shaking her head. *A bomb. Among the wounded. Among women and children.* As Ian turned and headed for the door, she ran after him. "I'm going with ye. I'm sure I'm needed below." She glanced back at the boys. All the children sat clustered around Mercy, Nanny, and the two maids. "Evander can help here and guard the others on this side of the entry. Can't ye, son?"

Evander nodded but didn't look all that certain.

Ian halted, scowling down at her for a long moment without saying a word. The muscles in his cheek ticked as his jaw hardened. "Perhaps, ye should." He pulled in a deep breath, the furrow in his brow deepening. "Ye should know that old Elena is dead. She was one of those closest to the messenger's pouch when it exploded."

"I see." Gretna supposed she should feel something because she'd been under Elena's tutelage for years. But she felt nothing more than regret for the wealth of knowledge and experience lost. The ill-tempered old woman had refused to write anything down and had been a renowned healer for ages. But she and Gretna had never been friends or allies. Most of the time, Gretna felt the wise woman barely tolerated her. She lifted her chin. "Then I will be needed down there even more."

"I suppose ye will," Ian said with a resigned sigh. "Come then."

"Please, wait just a moment." She rushed over to the boys and gathered them into a fierce hug. "Mind yer manners. Listen to Nanny, Fenna, and Lady Mercy, aye?" She nodded at Evander, then arched a brow at Rory and Finn. "And dinna vex yer brother. Evander is in charge of the both of ye. Do ye understand me?"

They all nodded, each of them still subdued by the day's events.

Gretna forced a reassuring smile, then hurried back to Ian.

"Bar the door," he instructed Fenna as they departed.

The closer they got to the main hall, the stronger the burnt smell permeated the air. Gretna wrinkled her nose, somewhat relieved at the conditions she found as they exited the stairwell. Not knowing had fueled horrendous imaginings of what she would find.

Most of the damage was contained to the sitting area beside one of the hearths. Thankfully, the ancient stones of the floor, the hearth itself, and the nearest columns and wall had handled the blast well. The area had survived with nary a severe crack, just a few chipped places, and quite a bit of soot. The same couldn't be said for the tables, chairs, and benches that had been close by. Piles of smoldering bits were still being gathered up and either extinguished or tossed into the hearth to burn.

As Gretna checked injuries, she discovered splintered wood had caused most of the damage. Elena's fatal end had been particularly grisly. A large wooden shard had been driven deep into the woman's chest. It was Divine Providence that hers had been the only death. Those already being treated for wounds had fared decently enough. Most were only covered with debris and needed clean beds and bandages.

An increase in the general noise filling the hall drew Gretna's attention to the front of the room. A sense of victory filled her. They had captured the wicked messenger. The vile man stood between a pair of MacCoinnich guards, struggling against their hold. She wiped her hands on her apron and moved closer. She'd paid little attention to the man before the attack. A better look was needed for this fool who had invaded them and dared commit such a heinous deed.

Alexander, with Graham and Ian on either side of him, waited as the guards forced their prisoner to stand before him. As soon as the man drew close enough, he lunged forward and spit at Alexander. "Ye dinna belong here! Ye're no' a Neal!"

The guards yanked him back a step, and one of them bent the man double with a punch in the gut. "Mind yer manners, fool, else I mind them for ye!"

Gretna eased closer still, an ominous chill settling across her. The stranger had a crazed look in his eyes, a look that said he didn't fear dying for his cause. She'd never seen him before. He was neither a Neal nor a MacNeilage.

"I canna decide whether to hang ye from the wall for all to see or send ye back to Angus Neal in a barrel." Alexander glared at him. His eyes narrowed to slits as he tilted his head. "Since ye taught us a valuable lesson today, I'll give ye the choice. Which way do ye prefer to die?"

"What lesson?" the man growled, hatred emanating from him.

"To trust no one," Ian interjected. "And close our gates to only those we know to be loyal."

The prisoner snorted. "Trust no one?" he repeated. "Ye've a witch in yer midst. With her bespelling ye, ye'll never survive no matter who ye trust."

Ian lunged forward, but Alexander held him back. "Not yet."

"The lot of ye heel like dogs," the man taunted. "At least Angus Neal doesna treat his men like lowly pets."

"I vote for the barrel," Ian growled. "Line it with spikes. We'll seal him inside and roll it down the hillside. They can fetch him if they like, wherever it happens to land."

"I agree," Graham chimed in. "And if they dinna fetch it after a few days, come spring, we'll set it afire to rid ourselves of it."

Alexander nodded. "A fine idea, indeed. It shall be done." He took a step closer, baring his teeth as he leaned toward the man. "Ye'll be a lesson for all. A message will be sent to Angus to ensure they learn of it."

The prisoner roared with a bloodcurdling cry as he stomped the instep of the guard to his right, then slammed his head back into the man's face. One arm freed, he twisted and grabbed the distracted guard's dirk, then dove for Alexander.

"Nay!" Gretna shrieked as Ian, with his dagger drawn, shoved forward and caught the slash of the crazed man's blade down the side of his face and chest. Ignoring the injury, Ian caught hold of the fiend's wrist before he could strike again and buried his blade deep in the devil's gut, spilling the man's bowels before stepping back and allowing the fool to fall to the floor.

"I guess it willna be the barrel for him after all," Ian observed, wincing as he attempted to staunch the blood streaming into his left eye.

Gretna rushed to him, taking hold of his arm. "Over here with ye, ye damned fool! What did I tell ye about not getting hurt?" She was torn between holding him tight and sobbing or shaking him, 'til his teeth rattled. How dare he make her feel this way. "Down here on this cot so I can see how many stitches ye'll be needing."

"It's not so ba—"

"Hush it!" She pulled his hand away from the bloody side of his face. The slash started well above his left brow, crossed over his eye, then split his face from the top of his cheek to his jawline. Praise God he had twisted in time to keep the blade from hitting his eye, although it did look as though the eyelid was slightly cut. The cut at the base of his throat might take a stitch or two, but luckily, his clothing had slowed the blade, and he'd not suffered from too deep of a wound. She peeled away the bloody edges of his waistcoat and tunic, checking all the damage.

"How bad?" Alexander asked from the other side of the cot.

"It's not ba—" Ian started to say before Gretna cut him off.

"Since ye're not the one lookin' at this bloody mess, I'll thank ye to shut it, Ian Cameron." She pressed a folded linen against his face and put his hand atop it. "Dinna talk, and keep pressure on it so the bleeding will slow." She lifted her gaze to Alexander. "Stitches and bandages will take care of it. A balm to keep away infection. He should be fine." She swallowed hard, struggling to keep from breaking down into tears. "With all the bleeding, the wound's cleansed itself better than I ever couldha."

Alexander nodded, then rested a hand on Ian's shoulder. "I'm indebted to ye, cousin. I know this isna the first time ye've fought at my side, but I do believe ye kept me from being gutted this time." He shook his head. "Damned fool that I was, setting my blade on the table rather than sheathing it at my belt and keeping it ready. Ye saved me."

"You wouldha done the same for me," Ian said after a fearful one-eyed glance at Gretna.

"He doesna need to speak." Gretna dampened a cloth with whisky and touched it to the shallowest end of the cut on his chest.

"Damn ye, woman!" Ian roared, flinching at the burn.

Served the man right. Scaring the life out of her. Her heart had nearly stopped beating as that dagger had slashed down across him. "Hold ye still." Her voice broke. Damned if she didn't need to weep out her feelings something fierce. She'd be lost if he died. A hiccupping sob escaped her.

"Shh… Forgive me." Ian laid a hand on her arm. "I didna mean to curse at ye." He peered up at her, then stretched to wipe the tears from her cheek. "Why do ye cry, love? Ye said I'd be fine."

"Because I love ye, dammit! More than I should. And I dinna wish our child to know the pain of growing up without a father!" As soon as the words escaped her, she bit her lip, wishing she had never said them.

Ian's uncovered eye widened, and he squeezed her arm. "What say ye?"

She pulled away, waving away the question. "Hush now. I need to fetch my basket, so I can stitch ye up and apply a balm to keep away infection." Still ignoring him, she waved down a passing servant. "Fetch the fresh linens from the kitchen. Cook said another batch that she boiled and dried by the fire should be ready by now."

"Aye, mistress." The lad gave both Ian and Gretna a duck of his head, then bounded off in that direction.

"Gretna."

While Ian's voice was soft and low, it held a thunderous power. Reluctantly, she turned back to him. "Aye?"

"Ye carry my child? *Our* child?"

"Aye. 'Tis early yet, but I believe I do." She gave up. She might as well tell him. Her body would betray her eventually.

His mouth snapped shut, and so did his eye that wasn't covered. "I thought ye said the herbs ye drank each morning kept a bairn from seeding?" he whispered.

His question cut her heart swifter than any blade. She almost choked on the hurt welling up in her throat. He didn't want the child. Maybe, he didn't really want her either. Maybe, his words had all been a great lie to get him through the winter. Then he'd slip away once summer came. "Nothing but abstinence is for certain," she said as she turned away. She refused to allow him to see how he'd hurt her. After all, she did have some pride.

"I see."

"Just what do ye see, Ian?" She couldn't help it. Her temper had always won out over her pride, and it demanded to have the last word. "Tell me, husband of mine, what do ye see? Do ye see a woman foolish enough to believe yer sweet words? A woman overjoyed at the thought of bearing the child of the man she loves?" She stepped closer, struggling to keep her voice low. "I'll tell ye what ye see if ye look close enough. Ye'll see a woman kicking herself for ever trusting ye. Dinna worry, Ian. One divorce was easily obtained. I'm sure a second can be gotten before summer comes, so ye can be on yer way as ye planned."

Before he could answer, she spun away and stormed over to the area of the hall where supplies were kept for the wounded. She got the attention of one of the maids, the older, awkward one who had shown herself to be quite adept at tending to injuries. "Flora! Master Cameron needs stitching, and his wound coated with the honey balm to prevent infection. See to it, so I can finish checking on these other poor souls, aye?"

"Ye wish me to take care of yer husband?" Flora repeated, doubt heavy in her tone.

"Aye. I said so, did I not?" Gretna snapped her fingers. "Be quick about it now. We've nay time to chat. Many need our care."

"Aye, Mistress Gretna." The woman bobbed a quick curtsy, grabbed up the needed materials, and scurried away.

"Gretna!" Ian had risen from his sickbed. He strode toward her, his wounds bleeding anew. "Ye will listen to me, *wife*. I can either shout what I have to say across this keep for all to hear, or ye can return to my side so I might speak with ye privately."

"Ye damned fool, ye shouldna be up. Ye've started the bleeding again." Gretna snatched up a cloth in each hand and held them out to him. "Hold these to yer face and get back to that cot. Now."

"I willna do so unless my beloved wife tends me," Ian continued in a dangerous tone. "I willna allow anyone but ye to touch me. Understand?"

He wasn't lying—of that she had no doubt. Gretna latched hold of his arm and yanked. "Fine. Now come." *Stubborn arse.* Well, she could be just as stubborn. She'd tend his wounds, but she'd not listen to anything he had to say. This time, she would know his words for the lies that they were.

Flora had already laid out everything needed on the table. She hurried away before Gretna had a chance to release her. Apparently, Ian's threat had been heard by all.

He sat on the bed and glared at her. "I chose my earlier words poorly, *mo ghràdh*. Allow me to explain."

Mo ghràdh. My love. A precious endearment now tainted with the truth. The words felt more like an insult to her intelligence. Gretna shrugged. "Do as ye wish, but lie back so I can clean the wound while ye talk." She dampened a cloth. "But make it brief. When I go to stitching ye back together, I'll need ye still—which means *silent*." A sense of victory filled her as he blew out a frustrated snort. *Good*. It was time he learned she'd not be taken for a fool again.

He reclined on the table converted to a padded area for tending the wounded. "I didna mean to sound so coarse and heartless," he said as he stared up at the ceiling. "It was neither lack of love nor joy that made me ask that cold question." His scowl shifted to her. "It was fear."

"A fearful mercenary," she mused in a disinterested tone as she cleaned his chest and face, then pressed another cloth in place to staunch the fresh bleeding. "When ye leave come summer, ye best take care that no one gets wind of such a weakness within ye. I'd think such a thing would sully yer reputation so much no one would wish to hire ye."

Ian grabbed hold of her wrist as she turned back to her worktable. "I know I hurt ye, and I am sorry. Sorrier than ye'll ever know." He held tight, preventing her from moving. "Ye've made me love ye, *mo chridhe*. A fierce love that scares me to death. I love the boys, too, and now ye've filled me with a love for my own child growing inside ye." His uncovered eye narrowed with a pained flinch, and his voice broke as he continued, "If I should lose any of ye—" He paused, tightening his hold. "I canna bear the thought of losing any of ye, and my greatest fear is my curse will steal ye from me."

Damned if his words didn't sound true, but then, so had all his others. Gretna fought to harden herself against him, but her heart wasn't in the battle. His excuse was legitimate. She tried to twist out of his grasp. "Let me go, aye? I need to finish cleaning away the blood."

After a long moment, he eased away his hand and rested it atop his stomach. "I dinna ken what it will take to make ye believe me, but know this—we've the rest of our lives together for me to convince ye." He latched hold of her arm again. "There will be no divorce. Not ever, ye ken? Ye're mine." He gently squeezed. "I love ye, whether ye believe me or no'."

Gretna tore her gaze from his and stared upward, begging the tears not to flow. They didn't listen. Instead, they streaked fast and hard down her face. "See what ye've done?" she scolded with an angry swipe of her hand across her eyes. "How am I to sew ye up when I canna see for the tears."

"I dinna care if ye ever stitch me," he said quietly as he pulled her down to his chest and held her. "All I care is that ye love me." He hugged her tighter. "Love me and forgive me, aye?"

"God help me—I do love ye!" Gretna gently pulled away and straightened. Her back already ached, and the fool man needed stitches. She rested a hand atop his chest. "But know this, if ye're lying to me, ye will regret it, understand?"

"Aye, love," Ian said. He flattened his hand on her stomach. "I understand." He gave a wincing, lopsided grin. "And I pray our son or daughter is born as fierce and courageous as their mother."

CHAPTER THIRTEEN

AT LEAST THE melting snow and persistent rains had slowed the fighting through most of March and into early April. Much of the glen had become a boggy mess that would suck the boots right off a man's feet. Ian frowned as he spotted Gretna trudging up the path from the village, skirts muddied to her knees. Her arisaid was hooded over her head as a useless shield against the steady drizzle.

She looked miserable. He'd speak to her about this, and she'd best heed him this time. The woman had no business tramping about with no regard to the hour or the weather. She'd been down in the village since well before dawn, and here it was almost sunset. He'd not have her catching her death while seeing to someone else's ailments. Aye, it was a selfish thought, and he fully admitted it. But fate and ill luck had taken more than their fair share from him. He'd not willingly pay them anymore.

He exited the guard tower and met her at the gate, pointing at the entrance to the keep. "To our rooms with ye now. While ye change into dry clothes, I'll send for hot broth and pour ye a whisky, and then ye'll keep yer stubborn arse by the fire until time for yer supper, ye ken?" He relieved her of her basket and hefted it up and down. "Are ye carrying stones now? Ye've no business carting about such weight. Why did ye not take Flora to help ye?" Offering his arm, he fixed her with a stern look. "We'll be talking about yer careless ways once I get ye dry and warm. Ye're going to start treating yerself with more care, or I'm locking ye in the bedchamber. Do ye hear me, wife?"

"My, my, such a warm greeting." Gretna's tone implied she still possessed enough energy to unleash her temper. "It is good to see ye, too, dear husband. Might I advise that ye'd do well to save yer nagging for another time? I'm nay in the mood for it, nor will I abide it."

While he admired her dedication and fire, he refused to allow her to keep putting both herself and the wee one at risk. Since the scolding she deserved appeared to make her even more bull-headed, he'd have to get wilier to make her behave. He caught the attention of a passing maid. "A hearty broth and bread for the mistress. Up to our rooms as soon as possible, aye?"

"Aye, sir." The lass curtsied and hurried off toward the kitchens.

Holding tight to Gretna's hand on his arm, he forced himself to hold his tongue for the remainder of their walk up to their rooms.

Gretna leaned against him, worrying him even more. "Has Mercy heard the news yet?" she asked with a weariness that sounded bone-deep.

"Aye. Graham told her this morning after the messenger left." Ian set Gretna's medicine basket on the table beside the door and helped her remove her soaked arisaid. As he shook it out and hung it on the drying rack beside the fire, he shook his head. "She mourns the loss of her godfather, but if ye ask me, the man's happier now that he's dead. Most say he never got over Queen Mary's passing."

King William had died from a lung inflammation, a complication from injuries he received when he fell from his horse. With no heir to take his place, his late wife's sister, Anne, was now queen regent over England, Scotland, and Ireland. This could bode ill for Clan MacCo-innich. Mercy had been King William's only goddaughter, and that connection had shielded them somewhat from the king's harsh opinion of Highlanders.

Ian poured a glass of whisky and followed Gretna into the bed-chamber. He pushed it into her hand. "Drink this while I undo yer laces. Yer wee fingers look red as fire and feel cold as ice."

Thankfully, she complied without arguing.

"Did it go well with Jenny? Graham said Sawny was so beside himself that he was useless on the practice field today. Nearly caught a sword in his ribs." He yanked at the wet knots of her laces, ready to be done with the blasted things and just slice them with his dagger.

Gretna lifted her arm higher to aid him in undoing the side laces that allowed her bodice to adjust to her growing middle. "Aye. Sawny is now the proud uncle of a healthy niece, and Jenny's overjoyed to finally have a girl in her brood of wee lads."

Successful at removing the garment, Ian hung it by the fire, then added more wood to the flames. The log crackled and hissed, sending steam into the air. Nothing escaped the weather, everything was damp. Prepared to launch a more careful reprimand of her stubborn ways, he straightened from the fire but was struck mute at the wondrous sight before him.

Gretna stood in nothing but her shift, the soft linen molding to the fine abundance of her breasts made even fuller by her pregnancy. Her stomach had started rounding with a small promising mound. She shifted in place, taking another sip of her drink as she turned aside to avoid his stare. "Stop lookin' so hard at me. Ye look like a hungry wolf about to rip into a wee hare."

"Ye're such a beauty." Ian led her to the chair closest to the fire. "I canna help it, love. Yer beauty makes me…fills me with…" He shrugged and shook his head. "It makes me unable to speak."

She smiled and seemed to melt into the cushions, gently stroking a hand down the slight curve of her stomach. "Aye, we'll see how ye feel when I'm waddling around big as a horse."

"More of ye means more beauty to behold." He kissed her sound-ly, aching to scoop her up and take her to bed. *Nay.* To do such would be selfish. She was exhausted. The dark circles under her eyes concerned him.

A knock sounded from the main door.

"'Tis probably yer broth. I'll fetch it for ye." He scooped up the dry shift she'd laid across the foot of the bed and draped it across the chair beside her, then scooted it closer to the fire. "We'll warm it here. Wait a bit to put it on, aye?"

"Aye, love." She'd already leaned her head back against the pillowed chair and closed her eyes.

The knock came again.

"Hold now!" He pulled the bedchamber door closed but didn't latch it as he left the room. Upon opening the hall door, he found himself in the middle of Sutherland's wooing of the young maid bearing a tray of food. Ian rescued it. "Here. Give me that before it spills."

The girl blushed, ducked her head, then scurried off.

"Ye scared her away," Sutherland scolded.

Ian ignored him and nodded at the decanters. "Pour yerself a drink. I need to get this to Gretna before she falls asleep." He hurried back to the bedchamber.

Gretna had already changed into the dry shift and climbed into bed.

"Prop yerself up, lass." Ian thumped the bed with his knee. If he didn't hurry, she'd be fast asleep for sure.

"I just want to sleep," she said as she curled onto her side.

"Ye need to eat—for the babe," he ordered. "And I'm not leaving or letting ye be until ye do so."

"Ye're an arse. Ye know that?" She glared at him as she shoved herself to a seated position back against the headboard.

"Aye. I'm an arse who loves ye." He balanced the tray across her lap. "Ye need this to warm ye and for strength. Ye know that as well as I." He stepped back. "Sutherland awaits me in the other room. Eat this, and then I'll leave ye in peace for a while, agreed?"

She rolled her eyes and lifted the steaming bowl toward her mouth. "Agreed."

He kissed her forehead, pleased that although her hair and face were still a bit damp, she remained cool to the touch. He might not be a healer, but even he knew an expectant mother worn to exhaustion risked falling victim to a fever.

"I love ye," he whispered so softly she didn't hear. It mattered not as long as she felt it. A sense of peace settled across him as he left the room and softly clicked the door shut behind him.

Sutherland stood by the window, staring at the raindrops racing down the glass. He turned to Ian. "She's not ill, is she?"

"Not yet." Ian shook his head. "If she doesna listen and take care of herself, she soon will be."

"She trained up Flora pretty well. Could the maid not handle some of the load?" Sutherland meandered back to the row of decanters on the cabinet and poured himself another drink.

"I'm sure Flora could if my stubborn wife would let her." Ian gave a curt nod as his cousin held up a glass. "Aye, I'll have one."

"Ye'll need more than one after ye hear the news I bring."

"What now?" Ian accepted the drink, then moved to stand in front of the fire. He'd gotten a might damp himself.

"Angus Neal has requested a meeting." Sutherland backed up to the fire next to Ian. "At Kilchurn."

"Campbell's keep." Hatred rushed through Ian, heating him faster than the whisky or the fire. Ever since Glencoe, ever since Janet's death, he'd sooner gut a Campbell as to look at one. "What's the bastard playing at?"

Sutherland shrugged. "His message said he's willing to call off the warring if an agreement can be reached. My guess is, he's going to demand what he feels is rightfully his, since he was next in line to claim the chieftainship after we killed that vile brother of his." He sipped his whisky and shrugged again. "But the message merely said *an agreement.*"

"An agreement." Ian tossed back his drink and strode to the cabinet for another. "I trust that whoreson about as much as I trust the bloody Campbells. What does Alexander say?"

"After talking to Graham and the other advisors, he's willing to hear the man out." Sutherland joined him and held out his empty glass. "Me? I'm against it. It smacks of treachery." He shook his head. "But the others feel if a suitable accord might be reached, we should attempt it, for the sake of the people."

Ian stared down at his glass. They'd all be lying if they didn't acknowledge that Angus's attacks had brought a fair share of suffering to many in the clan. If it continued, dissension and unrest would seed and grow among those who had always been faithful to the MacCoinnichs. All options had to be considered—for the survival of Clan MacCoinnich. He blew out a heavy sigh. "When does Alexander leave?"

"Not just Alexander." Sutherland lifted his glass in a mock toast. "You were requested, by name, as well. Magnus, along with several guards, will accompany ye both, while Graham and I remain here to guard the keep."

"Why me?" Ian asked, suspicion growing.

"None of this unrest occurred until Colin Neal returned from the dead." Sutherland meandered back to his spot in front of the fire and looked at Ian with a knowing scowl. "It is my opinion all this trouble has something to do with that bastard. After all, we'd heard nary a peep out of any of Catriona's brothers or the supposedly disgruntled Neals until now. I believe he's at the core of all this strife—whether he's doing it out of spite or because he's hungry for power." He shrugged. "A man like Colin goes through gold quickly—even the amount ye gave him."

This most definitely had to be a trap. Why else would Angus Neal request the chieftain's cousin attend? Ian shook his head. "And Alexander still feels we should go? Even under such suspicious circumstances?"

"Alexander knows he mustn't ignore any opportunity to stave off further attacks. Too many have lost their homes and their lives."

Ian scrubbed a hand down his face. "When do we leave?"

"Dawn." Sutherland walked over and clapped a hand on Ian's shoulder. "Take every weapon ye've got, and trust no one, aye?"

"That goes without saying." Ian stared at the bedchamber door. The idea of leaving Gretna alone filled him with gut-churning unease.

Father William's rite of sprinkling her with holy water had tamped down the witchery rumors somewhat, but a malicious undercurrent still flowed through the clan. Nothing outright but it was there all the same. Most seemed to appreciate Gretna, but there were still some who openly shunned her—mainly Colin's blood kin. "Keep close watch on Gretna, aye? And the boys?"

"That goes without sayin'." Sutherland headed for the hall door, pausing when he reached it. "The lads and I get along well. They like Magnus better because of that damn bird, but we get on just the same."

"I dinna care if they like ye or not. Just keep my family safe, aye? Even if ye have to lock them up here in our chambers." Ian meant every word. If Sutherland was forced to isolate them to this wing, there'd be hell to pay when Ian returned, but at least Gretna and the lads would be safe.

"I understand." Sutherland made a somber bow. "I'll speak to Alexander and Graham about tightening the guard around the keep until the two of ye return." He winked as he pulled open the door. "We can attempt to keep Gretna and the wee scamps inside the skirting wall. Easier to keep up with them that way."

"Whatever it takes." Ian turned toward the bedchamber. "Now, pray I survive telling my wife of what is to come, including the fact that ye will be her official keeper, and she's restricted to the keep until I return."

"God help ye, man." Sutherland made the sign of the cross in midair, then left, as though he feared getting caught in what would surely be a stormy conversation.

Ian eased into the room, pausing to see if Gretna was still awake. The crackling fire and the rain pattering against the window were the only sounds in the dimly lit chamber. She'd shoved her tray to the foot of the bed and curled beneath the covers.

As quietly as possible, he removed the tray and carried it to the table beside the door. At least she'd finished her broth and eaten all the bread. He returned to the bedside, sitting in the chair on the other side of the nightstand. Watching her sleep always filled him with a sense of peace. He'd sit here a while, then see to the lads' supper and getting them asleep.

As if hearing his thoughts, Gretna stirred, floundering among the pillows to push herself upright. "I need to round up the boys and get them fed."

Ian sat on the edge of the bed. "Nay. Stay abed. I'll see to them." He repressed a smile when she immediately sank back into the pillows. Her weariness must be fierce. She never gave in so easily when it came to caring for the bairns.

"I love ye. Ye know that, aye?" She smiled up at him with sleepy eyes that made her even more beautiful.

"And I love ye more." He leaned closer and rested a hand on the small swell of her stomach. "And this wee one, too."

She laid her hand atop his and squeezed. "I felt the quickening today. Soon, ye'll be able to feel the child moving, too."

He had no words. Instead, he leaned forward and poured all he felt into the tenderest of kisses. Such a glorious, precious woman. Breaking the connection before it inflamed him beyond control, he pressed his forehead to hers. "Ye've made me whole," he whispered as he lifted his head to fix his gaze with hers. "Mended my brokenness and healed my soul."

Tears welled in her eyes, making them glisten in the candlelight. She cradled his cheek in one hand, her thumb tickling along his jawline. "Ye rescued me from my dark loneliness. Ye are my light."

"Mama?" A gentle peck at the door broke the lovely spell.

Ian dropped his chin to his chest and laughed. Such was a life with bairns, and he wouldn't have it any other way.

"Come in, Evander," Gretna called out, pulling the covers higher.

The door creaked open. Evander, followed by Rory, then Finn, made their way into the room. The lads looked as though they'd done something they shouldn't have and were about to confess it.

"Mam Hattie said to fetch ye for Master Fergus down at the miller. Said he's feeling poorly," Evander reported with a half-hearted shrug.

"She said Master Hugh said he'd pay double 'cause he's so worried about his brother," Rory added quietly.

Before Gretna could answer or rise from the bed, Ian held up a hand to still them all. "Find Flora and tell her. Yer mother has done enough today and willna be doing a single thing more other than staying abed. She needs her rest."

"But Mam Hattie said—" Rory started.

"I dinna care if Saint Peter himself needs a tonic, yer mother's not leaving this bed!" Ian stood and herded them back out the door. "Now, find Flora as I told ye, then ask Cook to give ye supper. Once ye've eaten, get back here with yer faces washed and yerselves readied for bed, ye ken?" He pointed at them. "Dinna make me come hunting ye."

"I told Mam Hattie that Mama was doing too much," Evander defended. "But she set to fussing and wouldna hush until we promised to tell her anyway."

"Ye leave Mam Hattie to me," Ian advised. He halted the three of them out in the hall. "Now, I want ye to heed what I'm about to tell ye, aye?" He waited for all three to nod. "Alexander, Magnus, and I must leave at dawn to attempt a treaty to stop the feud. I need the three of ye to watch over yer mother and do yer best to make sure she doesna do too much." It was a tall order, but Gretna needed more than just Sutherland attempting to tether her and make her rest. She'd listen to her sons quicker than she'd listen to anyone, and these three were just as sly as she was. "Shield her any way ye can." He squeezed Evander's shoulder. "*Any* way ye have to," he repeated. "Do ye understand what I'm saying?"

Evander lifted his chin. "Aye. We'll take care of her. I swear it."

"If ye need anything, go to Sutherland. He's promised to watch over ye." Ian waited for three more nods before he continued. "The keep will be on complete lockdown while we're gone."

All three boys groaned.

"No village and no caves?" Rory complained. "What are we supposed to do all day?"

Ian glanced around, then leaned in close. "Until I return, ye have my permission to start up yer rat races again, but dinna let yer mother find out, and mind well who ye let in on the betting. I'll tell Sutherland it's fine. I'm sure he'll be delighted to help ye."

All three boys lit up, even quiet Finn. "Can we start tonight?" Evander asked, scrubbing his hands together.

"Nay." Ian pointed them toward the stairs. "Tonight, do as I've told ye. Ye can revive yer wee business tomorrow, aye?"

The trio responded with a chorus of hearty *ayes*, then stormed down the steps.

Hands on his hips, Ian watched them disappear, listening to their controlled chaos as they clattered down the stairs. Now, he had to tell Gretna. He prayed she'd take the news as well as the lads, but doubted that would happen. He returned to her bedside, half-hoping she'd fallen back to sleep. Unfortunately, she hadn't.

"And what did ye promise them if they behaved?" she asked as she settled more comfortably into her pillows.

"Why would ye ask such?" How the hell did she always know? Ian assumed an innocent facade.

"I heard the glee in their shouts clear in here," she explained. "They sounded as though they had just made a fine deal with the devil." She shifted higher in the bed, leaning back against the headboard. "Now, tell me what's going on."

Ian sat on the bed beside her after sending up a quick prayer for wisdom. "I merely told them the same thing I was about to tell ye before they interrupted us."

"Which was?"

"Angus Neal has requested we meet him at Kilchurn to discuss an agreement to stop the clan war. Alexander and I leave at dawn. Magnus and a small detachment of our best guards shall accompany us." He braced himself, resigned to the fact that no matter how he worded the news, it wouldn't be received well. "Graham and Sutherland will be here, overlooking an increased guard and a tighter lockdown of the keep.

Gretna glared at him. Even in the dim lighting, he could tell the color rode high on her cheeks. "Explain to me why ye're going rather than Graham. He's clan war chief."

He scooped up her hand and held it. "My presence was requested."

"By who?"

Ian could tell by the way she said the words, she already knew the answer. "We are to meet with Angus Neal."

"And Colin, I suppose?" She pulled her hand out of his.

"I dinna ken if Colin will be there or not." And he didn't. Sutherland hadn't said. But he wasn't a fool, and neither was Gretna. "But I feel certain he might be—as well as Catriona's younger brothers, Murray and Dougal."

Her gaze lowered to her tightly clasped hands in her lap. "I dinna want ye to go," she said quietly without lifting her head.

"Ye know I must."

"Why?" Her troubled look jerked upward, her eyes locking with his. "Alexander and Magnus can manage without ye. Graham could go along if ye stayed here."

"If I dinna go, at the very least, Angus could cancel the talks, at the worst, he could attack Alexander." He rested a hand atop hers. "What has been asked of me is no different than the trials that are asked of ye when ye're called to rise from yer bed no matter the hour, or brave any kind of weather, to see to those in need of healing. The risk is the same."

"It is not the same! I dinna risk attack or some such trap lying in wait for me upon my enemy's threshold."

"Be that as it may, I must go." He bent and kissed her fingers. "If this is a chance to reach an accord and stop the feuding, we must take it—for the sake of the people."

Her face crumpled as she bowed her head again. "I know the sense of it, but ye're filling my heart with fear."

He pulled her into his arms and held her, swaying from side to side as though she were a weeping bairn. "I know, love," he whispered with a kiss to the top of her head. "That same fear, the fear for yer safety and that of the boys', fills my heart, too." He hugged her tighter. "I know how ye hate it, but I need ye to stay inside the skirting wall. Please. If anyone in the village needs healing, send Flora. Ye've been called on too much of late. I worry for ye." He closed his eyes as he pressed his cheek to her silky hair. "Will ye do that for me?" Gently, he took hold of her shoulders and eased her away so he could look into her eyes. "Ye said yerself, Flora's training up well. Should the need come, let her prove herself, aye?"

After a long pause, she nodded. "I promise to let Flora do more." She lifted her chin. "But I demand a word from ye as well."

Ian waited, already knowing what she was about to say.

"Promise ye'll nay be the fool who rushes headlong into danger. Be a wise warrior. Braw and canny. Dinna be afraid to retreat when it would be wise to do so, aye?"

"Aye, m'love. I promise." He sealed the oath with a kiss, tasting her fear as strongly as his own.

"I need ye," she said in an urgent whisper against his mouth. "I need the feel of ye to give me strength." Her fingers flew down the front of his waistcoat, undoing the buttons.

He stilled her hands, then kissed them. "Ye're so weary, love. Are ye certain it wouldna be ill for yerself or the babe?" No matter how fiercely he wanted her, he'd do nothing to endanger either one of them.

"It willna hurt either of us," she promised as she slipped her chemise over her head and tossed it on the bed. With a sad smile, she framed his face in her hands. "Nothing could make me too weary for loving ye. Absolutely nothing."

That's all he needed to hear. He settled into her embrace, determined to think of nothing but the precious woman in his arms. Tomorrow's worries and fears could just be damned.

CHAPTER FOURTEEN

G RETNA LOOKED OUT the window as she placed the wooden bowls of herbs on her worktable. At least the rain had let up, and the sun was peeping through the clouds. Maybe she'd find time for a walk later once she'd finished her tasks. Perhaps the sun on her face would tamp down her worries and ease the feeling that something ill was afoot.

She'd taken refuge in the chamber located off the main kitchen, the room where she often saw to those in need of her healing skills. Bundles of dried roots and plants hung from the rafters. Shelves filled one wall, loaded down with crocks, jars, baskets, and bundles. A small cot was ready if needed. A long table, sturdy enough to hold a full-grown man, sat in the middle of the room. Catriona had even had Alexander provide her with a small desk, parchments, books, ink, and quills. Gretna was determined to record everything she knew in her journals. When the time came to pass on her responsibilities to the next clan healer, there would be written references to help them.

"All will be well, mistress. Mark my words."

Dear Flora. What would she do without that girl? Gretna could never remember Flora Stewart without a smile or an encouraging word. Strong, big-boned, and a squared jaw as stern as any warrior's, Flora would've made a handsome man. But the Almighty had seen fit to make her a woman, and the lass was a burst of sunshine to all she met.

"I hope so, Flora." Gretna added more dried lavender to the mortar and leaned into the pestle, grinding the leaves with all the anxiousness flowing through her. She'd almost sobbed when Ian had ridden away. He'd sworn they wouldn't be gone long. Three days. Five at the most. She didn't care. Until she saw him safe again, she wouldn't rest easy.

The babe within her stirred, the movements still a delicate fluttering, but there just the same. She straightened and pressed a hand to her middle, treasuring the miracle of new life.

"Are ye unwell, mistress?" Flora paused in her folding of linens. "Sit and rest. I can grind the herbs whilst ye look on to make sure I do them proper."

"I'm fine." Gretna forced a smile. "Dinna fret about me. The good Lord made me for birthin' bairns. I always have an easy time of it."

"As ye wish." Flora placed the linens in a covered basket and turned back to the rack of boiled strips of cloth drying by the small brazier in the corner.

"And ye know as well as I that there'd be no need for me to watch ye work the herbs. Ye've come along quite well with yer training." Gretna didn't want the lass to think she had no faith in her. In the short time since Flora had started, she'd learned quickly and remembered everything after being told but once. The girl possessed a keen sense of figuring out ailments and more compassion than anyone Gretna had ever met. "I dinna ken what I'd do without ye, lass. Ye're a blessing."

Flora's perpetual smile beamed even brighter. "Thank ye, mistress. I value such kind words, truly I do."

A knock at the door echoed through the chamber.

"Hold fast, mistress. I'll see to it." Flora hurried to the door. "Aye?"

"I've a message for Mistress Gretna."

Recognizing the voice, Gretna turned, wiping her hands in her apron. "What is it, Sawny?" She prayed nothing had gone amiss with Jenny or the new babe. "Is it yer sister? The bairn?"

The braw warrior, tall and manly but still stricken with the freckles and unruly hair of his youth, strode into the room with a wide grin. "Nay, mistress. I saw both her and my new niece last night. Both are hale and hearty." His smile faded. "Another runner from the village is at the gate. He bids ye come quick. Says this time it's Mam Hattie calling for ye, and she's said she'll see no one but yerself. Said not to send Mistress Flora. The runner said she's quarrelsome as can be and stricken with a terrible ague. Worse than the others Mistress Flora's already seen." He stood taller and resettled his stance. "I told the man to wait so ye could send her a tonic or some such poultice to help whatever ails her. The chieftain and Master Ian were clear. Mistress Flora can see to the village, but ye're supposed to rest and stay inside the wall."

Flora had just returned from the village earlier. She had reported they hadn't seemed all that sick when she arrived, but all three had sworn they felt poorly. And now Mam Hattie stricken with some sort of ague? That cantankerous old woman hadn't been ill a day in her life. Gretna prayed this wasn't the beginnings of some sort of plague. She went to the shelf holding the treatments for aching in the head and fever. She glanced back at Sawny. "Did the messenger say exactly what was troubling her other than her mood? Tell ye any of her other symptoms?"

He shifted in place, looking as though he wished he was someplace else. With a shrug, he shook his head. "He didna say, and I didna ask him anything else. Sorry."

Gretna turned back to the shelves, took up a small leather pouch, and stuffed it with a handful of carefully scraped and trimmed tree bark. The messenger had said *ague*. That usually meant fever and feeling poorly all over. Willow bark would help an aching head, pain in the bones, and fever... That's what Flora had given the others as well. Cinching the pouch shut, she handed it to Sawny. "Steep in hot water 'til the water changes color, then one small cup taken only every few hours. Plenty of broth. Plenty of water. Blankets. A good hot fire. Tell the messenger to fetch Mistress Agnes to help Hattie. Those two take care of each other like pups from the same litter."

Sawny nodded as he backed out the door. "I'll tell him everything ye said. Thank ye for not making me lock ye in yer chambers to keep ye inside." His mouth snapped shut, and his eyes went wide. Sawny always had been one to say more than he should.

"Lock me in my chambers?" Gretna repeated, halting Sawny as he tried to escape. "Did Master Ian tell ye to do that?"

He shrugged. "Him and Master Sutherland both—but only if ye tried to go beyond the protection of the wall."

"Ye best run while ye can, lad," Flora called out from the drying rack. "Ye've allowed yer mouth to overload yer plate again, and it's about to spill into yer lap."

"Good day to ye both!" Sawny took Flora's advice and loped down the hallway before Gretna could say another word.

"Lock me in my chambers." Gretna shook her head. While the audacity of the order tempted her to defy it, she knew it came from a place of love. Although she couldn't say that if something dire happened in the village, she wouldn't go down there, anyway. No one would bother her. The rumors had calmed somewhat since Father William's blessing with the holy water. If someone truly needed her, she had to go. It was her Christian duty.

She returned to her worktable and resumed grinding the herbs. A worrisome fidgety-ness filled her. The workroom usually brought her a feeling of surety and peace, but today, especially with Ian's departure, the place felt more like a prison than a sanctuary. She pushed her tools aside. "Since the rain's stopped, I'm going outside for a while. I need to move around and breathe. Come with me if ye'd like."

Flora smiled and set aside the basket of rolled bandages. "I believe I will."

Gretna donned her heavy shawl and arm warmers, leaving her arisaid on the peg by the door. With the sun breaking through the clouds, such attire should be warm enough, especially for a brisk walk through the gardens.

As they cut through the kitchens to access the rear door leading outside, Gretna spotted Finn and Cook deep in conversation over some sort of bundle the lad held between his hands. The child looked up at the portly woman with rapt attention, nodding as Cook tapped on the parcel and chattered away. Gretna smiled. Sweet Finn had blossomed under Ian's care. All her sons had. She almost laughed aloud. Mercy and Catriona had been right. She and Ian had needed one another and hadn't even known it.

Scooping up one of the baskets by the door, Gretna settled it in the crook of her elbow. Might as well do a bit of foraging in the gardens. Some tender young greens, just now pushing up through the soil, would be a tasty respite from broth and stewed meat. Flora took a basket, too, and followed along, humming a happy tune under her breath.

Gretna lifted her face to the sunshine, closed her eyes, and pulled in a deep breath of the cool, crisp air. The world had a fertile earthiness to it after all the rains. It smelled of new life ready to spring forth. She smiled at Flora as they added leafy shoots of cress to their baskets.

"I wish we could hunt for fiddleheads where the wall joins the mountain." Her mouth watered at the thought of steaming the delicate green curls and drowning them in butter. "We've had enough warm days for them. The ferns should be putting out their new fronds by now. Dinna ye think so?"

"Aye, they should be sproutin' good by now." Flora frowned at the border gardens along the inside of the wall. "I wish they'd thought to transplant some to grow inside the wall. 'Tis shady enough beyond those trees. But they didna, so I guess we best be thankful for the parsley and cress we do have. Looks like quite a bit is in the plot over there. There's wild garlic along the hedge, too."

Now that she'd thought of the fiddleheads, Gretna wanted them badly—craved them in an uncontrollable way. Knowing better than to even attempt it, she watched the guard walking along the top of the wall, surveying the land beyond. "I dinna see why we couldna look for some greens on the mountainside. If we keep close to the wall, the guards can watch over us easy enough. As long as we keep within arrow range, aye? That way, if anyone thought to do us ill, the MacCoinnichs could easily shoot them."

Flora gave her a dubious look. "Shame on ye, Mistress Gretna. Ye'd tan yer sons' arses for such a stretching of the rules."

Gretna chose to ignore that remark. "Of course, I'd ask Graham and Sutherland's permission first." *Maybe*, she silently added. She could sway Sawny to her side much easier than those two. All she wanted was for a stroll outside the wall. Up the mountain a short way. Not far at all. Where was the harm in that? Besides, if she didn't get a dish of buttered fiddleheads, she'd surely die. "Come. I have to at least try."

"Are ye sure?" Flora glanced around as though they were plotting a crime.

"Aye. Quite sure." She could taste those fiddleheads already.

Gretna hurried to the east gate. Graham and Sutherland were most likely in the guard tower at the main entrance, but Sawny usually guarded the gate to the east and should've made it back to his post by now. It was just as well. The mountainside to the east of the keep usually offered the most to choose from when it came to fiddleheads because a hearty grove of rowan trees had been planted there when *Tor Ruadh* was built.

Scanning the wall, she shielded her eyes from the sun. There stood Sawny, apparently discussing a longbow held between himself and another guard. "Sawny!" She waved him down.

He left the bow with the guard and climbed down from the lookout post above the eastern gate. "Aye, mistress?"

Pulling Flora a step closer, Gretna gave Sawny her most beguiling smile. "I came to ask a wee favor."

"A favor?" Sawny shifted back a step and looked ready to bolt.

"Do ye like tender, spring fiddleheads, Sawny? Browned in a skillet of fat for just a moment or two, then smothered in butter?" Lord have mercy, if she kept talking like that, she'd have her mouth watering so much she'd drown.

"Aye. I suppose so." Sawny glanced over at Flora, who gave a quick shake of her head.

Gretna closed the distance between them and stole a look toward the gate. "There's ferns aplenty in the woods just beyond that wall. New greens, ramps, and wild garlic, too." Assuming as innocent a look as she could muster, Gretna motioned toward the gate with her basket. "Where would be the harm in letting us forage among yon trees for a wee bit? Ye could watch over us from atop the wall, ye ken? We promise to stay within arrow range."

Sawny snapped his head back and forth. "Nay. Master Ian would have my arse, and when he was done with it, if anything was left, the chieftain would finish me off." Shaking his head again, he backed up another step. "Graham and Sutherland would be after me, too. There wouldna be enough of me left to pray over by the time all of them got done with me."

"We'd stay within arrow range," she promised again. "Right close to the wall." Determination mounting, Gretna surged forward another pace. She had to have those greens. "The trees are nay even fully leafed yet. Ye'd be able to see us clearly." She smiled and patted her hair. "I'll be sure and keep my head uncovered. Ye canna miss this red hair against the greening of the mountain."

"Nay," he said, but his denial sounded weaker. "Dinna ask this of me, mistress. What if something ill happened? I'd never forgive myself."

"Something ill? On this side of the mountain? What could possibly happen?" She jutted her chin upward and glared at him with the same look she used to strike fear into her sons. Sawny might be a man grown, but it would work on him, too.

"Attack." Sawny stood taller. "What if someone attacked while ye were in the wood?"

"They'd not be close enough to do us harm before we made it back inside the gate. Ye know that as well as I. The east side is so steep, they canna attack from above, nor from farther east. The only way to storm the keep is from the south. I'm not a fool, Sawny. I've survived attacks here before." Gretna sidled closer to the gate. "And there's naught but one cave on this side of the keep. A small one up the mountain a little way. Word has it that it's too small to be good for anything, so I doubt any danger hides in its shadows."

Scrubbing his face with both hands, he let out a frustrated growl. "Why do ye need these greens so badly? There's food aplenty in the kitchens."

"Do ye not remember always having to fetch extra pickled eggs and cabbage for Jenny? Had to get her enough to feed the entirety of the Highlands because she couldna get her fill of them?" Gretna waited. Sawny's defenses were weakening. The fiddleheads were as good as hers.

His shoulders slumping, he stared at her for a long moment, then turned and glared at the gate. He shook his head and threw up his hands. "I yield." With a stern scowl, he pointed at the gate. "But ye stay close to the wall, and dinna stay out there long. The quicker the better. I'm a dead man if they find out, ye ken?"

"Nothing will happen," Gretna assured as she hurried forward, waving for Flora to follow.

Chains rattled as the heavy wood gates swung open, and the iron portcullis lifted. Sawny shooed them forward. "If aught happens, and I call ye to come, will ye at least do me the courtesy of listening and hie yerselves back inside?"

"I swear it." Gretna gathered up her skirts and ran out the gate like a lassie escaping her chores. She and Flora hurried into the trees before Sawny changed his mind.

Flora chuckled. "No wonder yer bairns are such feisty lads. They get it from their mother."

"Perhaps." Gretna took that as a compliment. "Look! I knew it! Loads of fiddleheads." A carpet of ferns grew around the base of several trees, all of them putting up new sprouts. Pulling her small knife from her belt, Gretna started harvesting them. One end of her basket was soon piled high with the green spirals.

"Might there be enough so I could fix some for Hugh?" Flora asked as she clipped off more of the greens and piled them atop the ramps, cress, and wild garlic in her basket.

"Hugh?" Gretna straightened and fixed her full attention on Flora. "Hugh MacElroy?" She'd heard rumors about Flora and the overly short owner of MacElroy's Sundries but figured it a cruel jest by folk who had nothing better to do than say hurtful things about others.

Flora's cheeks grew rosier, and she ducked her head. "Aye. I know we're an odd match. Me, big and clumsy as I am, and Hugh short as a wee bairn, but he's a dear man filled with loving-kindness."

Gretna smiled, warmed by the news. "I wouldna say ye're an odd match at all." She picked her way around the ferns and reached for Flora's hand to give it a squeeze. "Kindred souls seek out their other half. When they find their match, they know it. It doesna matter the body that happens to house that soul." With a stern look, she shook her finger. "But if he ever treats ye ill, he'll have me to deal with!"

"Mistress Gretna!" The shout came from the path rounding the keep beside the skirting wall. "Ye must come quick!"

Gretna whirled about, the urgent cry sending her heart to her throat. Were they under attack? She'd heard nothing. "What is it?" She and Flora rushed to meet the man trotting toward them.

"Thank the Almighty I spotted ye on my way up the lane!" Lonnie McNaughton, waving both hands and gasping for breath, had apparently run all the way from the village. "It's Rannoch Mac-Neilage's lad, Roddie. Fell to the ground while fetching water. White as a ghost. Foam coming out his mouth and fightin' away any who try to help him."

Without hesitation, Gretna handed her basket to Flora, grabbed up her skirts, and turned toward the village, pausing long enough to shout instructions over her shoulder, "Fetch my bag, aye?" Although Lonnie McNaughton had always been close to Colin, first cousin, in fact, he seemed sincere in his panic about Roddie.

Sawny roared from atop the skirting wall. "Nay, Mistress Gretna! Ye must stop!"

Ignoring him, Gretna only slowed enough to pick her way around a muddy patch stretching out from the wall. Poor Roddie MacNeilage had never been a healthy lad. He was the same age as Finn and had suffered from these spells before. She had to get him calmed down before the entire village decided he was possessed by demons and tried to drown him again. They'd nearly killed the wee boy last time. Mugwort seemed to help the lad. His situation was dire enough to make her break her oath to her husband.

She'd not let the boy suffer from the prejudices some of these superstitious villagers had.

The main gate's horns sounded, blasting out the alarm signaling an attack. Still hurrying along, Gretna scanned the area. Few were about. The closest folks were a pair of men in a cart, driving along at a leisurely pace on the path to the village. She and Lonnie would soon pass them. Surely, Graham and Sutherland hadn't sounded the alarm because of her leaving the keep?

She rushed onward, glancing over at Lonnie as she swerved around several mud holes. "How long since the boy took ill?"

The man bared his teeth and loomed closer. "Got ye now, witch!

Lured ye away from yer safe nest where ye bespelled all yer protectors."

"What?" Too late, the trap became all too clear.

As she dodged him, Lonnie caught hold of her skirts and threw her to the ground.

Before she could rise and escape, someone behind her yanked a cloth sack over her head. Rough hands grabbed at her legs and arms. Another pair of hands rudely groped and dragged her across the ground. A rope or some sort of cord jammed across her face, parting her teeth and gagging her with the sack.

She tried to scream, fighting as ties wound around her body. *God help me.* She screamed again, whipping her head back and forth in vain. Did they mean to drown her? Who were these vile people?

"Make sure ye've tied that gag good and tight. We dinna want her speakin' no spells over us, now do we?"

Gretna stopped struggling, terror striking clear to her heart. It was another Neal she knew. But these were her people, too. Her own clan. How could they? That bastard Colin had rallied his blood kin to carry out his revenge.

"Ye didna tell us she was with child," said a different voice, a man she didn't recognize. "No trials nor executions are allowed by our laws if they be carrying new life in their bellies."

"Even if it might be Satan's seed?" Lonnie asked in an ominous tone.

Grinding her teeth into the gag, Gretna wished she'd killed her former husband in his sleep when she'd had the chance.

"Nay. We wait until the babe is born and examine it close. If both the child and its caul appear normal, the bairn is allowed to live. Then the witch is tried and burned." The unknown man snorted out a laugh. "Inverness prefers burning to crushing with stones or drownings. Fire ensures the evil is ousted for good."

They tossed her, and she landed hard against what felt like boards.

Probably the cart she'd seen the men driving. A brief silence followed. Gretna strained to hear the conversation above the rattling of the wheels.

"We could try her now, but it's nay near as easy to get a confession without a bit a torture," the stranger wheezed, then barked out a series of groaning coughs. "And the witch pricker doesna like to leave Inverness. Says the pits be full of Satan's whores needing his tests."

God help me. She prayed Sawny or someone from the wall had seen what had taken place. They'd not been that far from the keep. Aye, she'd broken her word and gone past arrow range, but surely if they had seen what had happened, someone would overtake them soon. She could tell by the hard jolts bouncing her across the boards of the wagon that they'd left the road and picked up their pace.

The thundering of horses closing in all around gave her hope. She pulled in a deep breath, thankfulness surging through her. It sounded like entire herds, coming from more than one direction. *Thank the Almighty.* The more the better to overcome these fools.

Gunfire split the air. The wagon lurched to a halt, and something hard poked against the side of her head. "Cease yer shootin' or she dies without benefit of trial." It was Lonnie again, holding a gun to her temple.

The sharp tip of a knife pricked through the cloth sack covering her face, cutting into the soft flesh under her chin. "We can either slit her throat or shoot her if ye refuse us safe passage. The choice is yers," said the bored voice of the stranger who had talked about the witch pricker.

Gretna swallowed hard, her head tipped back by the knife. She became aware of loud murmurings all around. It sounded as though they were surrounded by a restless crowd. But how? They'd left the lane and taken to the field for a short way. They had to be somewhere deeper in the glen. MacCoinnich guards followed orders in silence. Who were these people sounding like an angry mob?

"Release her or die," Graham said.

Relief washed across her. If the damned rope wasn't between her teeth, she'd sob aloud. Gretna fisted her hands, digging her nails into her palms. *Take the chance. Shoot both the bastards.* But she knew better. None of them would risk it.

"Ye dare defy us? The royal commission?" said another voice she didn't recognize.

"We are the army of witch hunters ordained by God and country," said a third who was also a stranger.

Had Colin actually gone so far as to rally those who traveled across the land, eking out terror in the name of the Almighty and the crown?

The nasally voice she'd first heard now sounded much closer as the man spoke again, "Ye do realize yer doing such will bring undue scrutiny upon Clan MacCoinnich. The highest in our ranks attends court on a daily basis and reports our findings to Her Majesty. We have the royal ear."

Gretna shut her eyes tighter, wishing she could awaken from this nightmare. If Graham refused to let them take her, the entire welfare of the clan could be at risk—including her sweet sons.

"Who charges this woman?" Graham demanded. "Ye actually take the word of a bastard who faked his death for six years and abandoned his bairns and his wife? Is that the only complaint against Clan MacCoinnich's finest healer?"

"It's nay only Colin's word, though that be good enough, I reckon." Lonnie bumped the end of the gun barrel against her skull. "I speak for all the Neals fighting to regain our lands while we cleanse it from this evil. I possess signed statements from a dozen or more in the village. One of them even witnessed the witch casting her spells and calling up demons to reside in her own son. Colin plans to return and have the poor lad exorcised as soon as we finish with this one in Inverness."

A brief pause followed this announcement. A pause long enough for Gretna to count her pounding heartbeats. Her Finn. They intended to hurt her sweet Finn. She thrashed against the thought. A hard blow against her head filled her ears with a muffled buzzing.

Lonnie continued, "We'll be bringing a priest from Inverness to handle it. It's obvious this whore of Satan has bewitched Father William. That man's in league with the devil, too."

Burning bile churned at the back of her throat. Gretna swallowed hard, unable to believe all this was happening.

"Who are these witnesses? Bastards ye paid?" The contempt in Graham's voice was plain. "Gold can make anything seen or heard."

Graham was stalling for time, trying to figure out what to do. Gretna could almost hear the underlying note of panic in his voice.

"Me! I seen her!" charged a familiar voice. "I be one of the witnesses who signed!"

Gretna opened her eyes, squinting through the loose weave of the cloth covering her head. Was that Hattie Neal, Mam Hattie herself? The woman who had shared her roof and helped with her sons?

"I seen her dancing naked with old Scratch during the full of the moon! Even heard her tell the Earl of Hell to take her youngest son as a vessel for his demons. Ye should hear that poor bairn scream on the nights they torment his soul." Venom dripped from Hattie's words as she continued, "And so jealous she was of nay being the chosen clan healer, she had old Elena struck dead. Drove a stake right through that good woman's heart without even being in the room! She's powerful wicked, she is. Mark my words!"

How could Hattie say such? The explosion from the messenger's bomb had killed Elena Bickerstaff, and how many times had Hattie helped her soothe Finn during his fits? Why would the spiteful woman do this?

Then it came to her. Gretna closed her eyes, feeling a complete fool. Hattie Neal was a distant relation to Colin and Coire but related by blood all the same. Old Hattie hadn't been the same since Colin showed back up, especially after Gretna had rebuffed him. The spinster also hated Ian. What better way to play out her wicked revenge than help Colin with this cruel plan? Hunger for revenge ran strong in that Neal bloodline.

The gun at her head clicked and nudged her skull hard enough to move her head. "What's it to be, MacCoinnich? My thumb grows tired of holding back this hammer. 'Twould be a shame for it to go off by accident."

"If ye're so convinced of her innocence," said the first man she hadn't recognized as the knife pricked her throat harder. "Come to her trial in Inverness." A wheezing laugh followed. "If the Almighty and the courts find her not guilty of the charges, ye can bring her home, and we'll trouble ye no more."

"Or we can kill her now," Lonnie said. "The choice is yers. I must say, a shot to the head would probably be a lot less painful than what's sure to happen to this wicked whore in Inverness." The gun shifted again, thumping against her temple. "What say ye?"

Before Graham could answer, the wheezing man coughed and choked so hard the wagon shook. The knife's tip slipped away from her throat as the stranger fought to catch his breath. The man gasped and groaned. Gretna heard a hard thud, then all went silent.

"He's dead!" someone called out in an awestruck tone.

The gun remained jabbed against the side of her head. "Ye see? The witch killed him! Do ye still doubt?"

"Burn her! Burn the witch now!" Hattie started the chant, but it wasn't long until the crowd joined in. "Burn the witch! Cleanse the clan."

Gretna closed her eyes and held her breath, her heart breaking. How had this happened? She'd only served these people with love and kindness.

"Enough!" Graham roared, a note of futility echoing in his tone. "Gretna Cameron has never done a one of ye wrong, yet ye'd condemn her to such a horrible fate?"

"Burn her! Cleanse the clan!" The chant started again, growing stronger, louder. More voices, voices Gretna recognized as those she'd lived and worked with all her life. She bit harder into the rope between her teeth, hot tears squeezing free of her closed eyes.

Suddenly, all went quiet. Gretna couldn't tell why, nor did she care. She was doomed to die. Condemned by her own, by those she'd helped and healed. *Please protect my sons*, she prayed. *Please keep them safe from these heartless fools.* It was a slim prayer that would most certainly require God's own miracle. Once the witch hunters were done with her, they'd surely come for her boys next. *Please comfort Ian, too*, she added. Her poor Ian. God help him.

"This guard shall ride with ye to ensure Mistress Cameron arrives safe and alive for her trial in Inverness," Graham said. "More MacCoinnichs will follow in a day's time—as well as her husband."

The gun barrel slid away from her head, and the wagon bed shifted. One of the men must've returned to the driver's seat. "Good enough, then," Lonnie said. "Tell Master Cameron to make haste if he wishes to see his wife alive one last time before she burns."

CHAPTER FIFTEEN

"'Y E'RE SURE THEY'LL send him back? Even if nothing's amiss?" Ian stared northward, scanning the sky. "The bird likes Finn almost as much as he likes ye."

"Merlin will return," Magnus assured, squinting at the horizon. "He knows we're on enemy ground and could need him."

Ian doubted the falcon had that much insight into the situation, but he kept it to himself. Everyone's nerves were raw. No need to nettle Magnus about his beliefs in his bird.

They stood on the balcony between two of Kilchurn Castle's tallest towers overlooking Loch Awe, most definitely the heart of hostile territory—Campbell land. Upon their arrival and during yesterday's tense, evening meal, Angus Neal had been unnervingly cordial, as had John Campbell, the first Earl of Breadalbane.

It had taken every ounce of self-control Ian possessed to refrain from drawing his sword and running Breadalbane through. The man was rumored to have had a part in the massacre at Glencoe. The bastard deserved to die, preferably a slow death, but Ian would take whatever form of demise opportunity offered.

Squinting against the brisk wind blustering in off the loch, Ian studied the surrounding area. The fortress had been converted into a proper garrison. Quarters large enough to house some two hundred men lined one side of the courtyard, and the place teemed with armed warriors. Ian recognized several from *Tor Ruadh*'s village. He hadn't realized so many Neals no longer wished to be counted among the MacCoinnichs. "What has Angus promised them to make them rise against us?"

Alexander looked as weary and beaten as if he'd fought a battle. "I've no idea." He blew out a heavy sigh. "Or it could be something as simple as pride in their bloodline." He leaned against the wall and stared out across the loch. "Their terms for peace surprised me. Far fewer demands than I expected. Half their ancestral lands, half the horses, and any Neal who wishes to join them be allowed to do so and take whatever they own when they move south. I'd assumed they'd demand some or all of the wealth we've attained over the past ten years, but they consider it Catriona's. A clean split from Clan MacCoinnich and a revival of their own line. How many times did they utter that?" He tilted his head and slowly shook it. "Angus Neal has come of age and appears to be a great deal more cunning than either his older brother or his father. Were we in his place, I wonder, would we ask for anything less?"

Ian agreed the terms had been surprising. In fact, their wants were so simple, they could've been sent in a message rather than this strange meeting. The situation still puzzled him. Had they been invited here merely to see that the Neals were allied with the Campbells? Ian took hold of Alexander's shoulder and squeezed, hating the internal struggle the man was going through. "Ye're actually considering what they ask?"

"There," Magnus interrupted, pointing at a spot above the horizon.

Shielding his eyes, Ian scanned the skyline. A dark speck raced toward them. Merlin's familiar cry pierced the air as the bird drew closer.

Magnus held out his arm and waited. The falcon chattered out a greeting, then landed. The bird stretched a moment, resettled his footing, then folded his wings. A scarlet ribbon was tied to his right leg. A dark look creasing his brow, Magnus nodded toward the tie. "I told both Sutherland and Finn to use the red ribbon to call us back. Something dire has happened."

"Riders approaching!" shouted a guard posted at the gate.

"Coming from the north," Alexander said as the three of them spotted the horse and rider speeding toward the keep at full gallop. "And they wear MacCoinnich colors."

Ian beat them all to the steps leading down to the courtyard. An ominous dread hammered through him with every heartbeat. He itched to draw his sword but refrained. If the bloody Neal and Campbell alliance had a part in whatever had befallen *Tor Ruadh*, he'd need to keep a level head to ensure none of them rushed any deeper into the trap that had been set.

"Ye'll not pass until ye're searched," shouted a Campbell guard.

"We're not bloody cowards like yer lot! I dinna have a bomb shoved up me arse to explode once I'm inside!"

Ian recognized the enraged voice. "Open the gate. They're MacCoinnichs!"

The garrison's gate swung open, and Sawny and Tom rode inside. "Master Ian!"

Sawny, greeting Ian before he greeted his chieftain, was not a good thing. Something was very wrong, and Ian knew in his heart it had to do with Gretna. "What is it? Tell me what's happened?"

After handing off his horse to one of the MacCoinnich guards who had traveled with them, Sawny strode over to Ian but didn't make eye contact. Instead, the young man stared downward and clenched his hands at his sides. "It's Mistress Gretna. They took her. A group of the traitor Neals joined with the witch hunters. They're headed to Inverness to judge her."

Rage hit him so strong and hard, Ian saw nothing but a red haze.

"How did they get in the keep?" he forced through clenched teeth, already knowing the answer. Gretna had gone outside the wall, and this spineless bastard standing before him had gone against direct orders and not stopped her.

Sawny shook his head, keeping it bowed. "They didna. Mistress Gretna had a powerful craving for greens from the eastern wood. She begged me to let her forage for a wee bit since the rains had stopped. Her and Flora." He shifted uneasily. "I didna see the harm. She swore she wouldna be long, and the east wall is always quiet. We watched over them from the wall." He lifted his head, regret and shame written across his face. "Then Lonnie McNaughton showed up and convinced her to run to the village. Flora said it was some such lie about a child Mistress Gretna had treated before. The bastards overpowered her on the road. Had her hooded, tied, and in a wagon quicker than a heartbeat. Graham and I rode out with guards to fetch her, but they held a gun to her head and a knife to her throat. Threatened to kill her right there if we attacked." Sawny shook his head. "We stood down to keep them from harming her."

Ian's heart burned with the pain of it. Without a word, he punched the lad and knocked him to the ground. He lunged forward to thrash the life out of this unthinking fool who had cost him his wife and unborn child. "I'll kill ye!" he shouted as he clutched Sawny by the throat and drew back his fist.

"Ian! Hold fast!" Alexander ordered as he and Magnus grabbed hold and pulled him back. "I understand yer anger, but ye canna believe Sawny meant any harm. Beating him to death willna solve anything. It's just a waste of precious time. Ye know that as well as I." Alexander shook him. "Think, man. Calm yerself and regain yer senses. All is not lost. She is not dead yet."

Ian tried yanking himself free, but both men held him firm, so he threw back his head and let out an enraged roar.

Rubbing his jaw, Sawny rose from the dirt. He bowed and backed up a step. "I canna beg yer forgiveness enough, Master Ian. I hate myself for being such a fool. I swear, I do." He kept his head lowered as he continued, "Sutherland is manning the keep. Graham and a troop of our guards have accompanied Mistress Gretna and those devils to Inverness to make sure she gets there alive." Sawny finally looked up, but he turned to Alexander. "A dozen or so from the village had signed statements against her, lies for the witch hunters to use as evidence. In yer name, Sutherland banished all who signed. The statements were all made by Neals connected to Colin. The heartless curs he banished are headed here to join with Angus."

"I'm surprised Sutherland didna execute them rather than banish them," Alexander said. He turned to Ian. "Take as many of the guards we have here as ye wish. Take them all, if ye want. Magnus and I will head back to *Tor Ruadh* to secure the clan even more, then we'll send more warriors yer way."

"I have one thing I must do first." Ian strode forward, plowing across the courtyard before anyone could stop him. Angus Neal had requested his presence at this meeting. Asked for him by name—and now Ian knew why. It had all been a part of that sniveling whoreson's game to torture Clan MacCoinnich by stealing away their talented healer and having her tried for witchcraft, then destroyed. He felt sure Colin Neal had convinced Angus to do such. Colin's life would end in Inverness. But before Ian left to save Gretna, Angus Neal needed to die, too.

Ian slowed his pace as he entered the main meeting hall. He'd learned last night that when Angus and Breadalbane weren't in their private chambers, both men stayed in the largest of Kilchurn's rooms. Last night, at supper, they had said so themselves, revealing their shared penchant for pouring over maps and plotting their holdings. They'd intended it as a veiled threat. Ian had taken it as the mistake it was—a wise man never revealed his habits to the enemy.

True to their word, Ian saw both men leaning over a table at the far end of the hall, a map spread out in front of them, beside a stack of parchments. Angus's younger brothers, twins Murray and Dougal, meandered around the room, their boredom obvious.

Anticipation and bloodlust mounting, Ian felt a calm settle across him—the familiar, deadly calm he always felt right before battle. A glance to his right assured him that the pompous bastards still hadn't stored away nor locked down their elaborate racks of throwing axes, halberds, and lochabers displayed on the entry wall. Even though their enemy was in their midst, they flaunted their collection of weaponry like arrogant fools.

And I thank them, Ian said to himself. Ripping an axe and a spear from the display, he surged forward, never slowing as he chucked the axe with all his might, then passed the spear to his throwing hand and hurled it as well. The axe head buried deep in Angus's chest. The spear passed through Breadalbane's left thigh, then embedded above his right knee, effectively stitching his legs together.

Ian frowned and unsheathed his sword. He'd never been very good with a spear. No matter. He'd finish off the bastard with his blade. The intimacy of steel cutting through a man's body was so much more satisfying than the impersonal method of gunfire. Besides, murdering quietly was a boon as well. No need to announce his actions to the entire garrison.

"Kill him!" Breadalbane shouted as he dragged himself backward, scuttling like a crippled spider. "Kill him and sound the alarm to take care of the rest."

A halberd shot past Ian and took down Dougal. A short sword whizzed through the air and took out Murray. Neither young man uttered a sound louder than a choking gurgle as they sagged to the floor. Ian glanced back at Magnus and Alexander. Each of them gave him a nod.

"Ian!" Magnus pointed to something beyond the map table, the direction Breadalbane had been dragging himself.

A heavy scraping, stone grinding against stone, confirmed the earl's escape. A long smear of blood across the floor abruptly stopped, disappearing under a block wall between two columns. He had left behind the spear that had ripped through his legs. Ian drew a little comfort from the knowledge that it had probably hurt like hell to remove it.

"There's no telling where that tunnel leads," Magnus said, frowning down at the bloodstained floor. "Hopefully, it's just a hole for hiding rather than a path to another room."

"Sawny should have the men and horses ready by now. I'd warned them all that we needed to be prepared to leave at a moment's notice." Alexander motioned for both Magnus and Ian to follow. "Come. We must get beyond the gate before the alarm sounds."

"Wait." Ian halted them. "We should do one more thing to throw them off when Breadalbane attempts to get the crown involved."

"What?" Alexander asked.

"Sign the agreement to split the clan. See if they left both copies over there beside the map. With the agreement signed, it'll look as though we had no issue with their terms." Ian went to the table, unrolled the pair of parchments, and tapped the bottom of each of the papers. "The arrogant arses already signed both of them, and their scribe witnessed it. Come look."

"Watch the door," Alexander ordered Magnus as he joined Ian at the table. He snatched up a quill, inked the nib, and signed his name to the bottom of each document right beside Angus's signature. Waving the paper to dry the ink before he folded it, Alexander nodded. "We'll be taking this copy with us."

"All is ready. Our men are waiting." Magnus urged them forward. "We must make haste."

Alexander and Ian hurried out, both assuming a calm, indifferent attitude as Ian closed the door behind them. They went to their horses and mounted as though nothing was amiss. Alexander nodded and led the group out the gates at an orderly pace. As soon as the last MacCoinnich had exited, they urged their horses to a full gallop and rode hard for as long as the beasts' strength held. There was no way of knowing when the Neal bodies might be discovered or Breadalbane would emerge from his hiding place to raise the alarm.

They reached Loch Tulla and stopped to give the horses a rest. Ian glanced up at the sun's position. They'd ridden a solid couple of hours. The surrounding area was clear enough, few trees and a gently rolling landscape. If anyone approached, they'd spot them easily. It was also a good place for him to leave the group and ride on to Inverness. He'd decided he'd take no men with him.

As a warrior, he'd always worked better alone. He also had no doubt that Gretna would have to be liberated from the jail using stealth rather than legalities. Such a job would require the wiliness of a man alone. He strode over to where Alexander and Magnus stood talking to Sawny and Tom. Ian completely ignored the two younger men, especially Sawny. It was the only way he could keep from killing him. "I'll be riding on to Inverness from here," he announced.

"How many do ye wish to take with ye?" Alexander asked.

"None." Ian looked across the blue-green waters of the loch, squinting at the sunlight dancing across the ripples. "I'm sure they'll be watching for me. I can slip in easier and steal her away if I'm alone."

"I shall go with ye," Sawny said, stepping forward and lifting his chin as though waiting for Ian to knock him on his arse again. "I'm as good as any when it comes to stealth. I helped Lady Catriona escape her brother's prison when I was but a wee lad."

"And I helped him," said Tom. Tom McNamara had been Sawny's best friend since they were bairns at their mothers' knees. The two were rarely seen apart. "Ye'll need more than just yerself to get Mistress Gretna away, and a lock doesna exist that I canna pick."

"Ye need someone with ye," Magnus said in a gentle prodding tone. "These two are as good as any since Alexander and I need to get back to the keep in case Breadalbane launches a full-on attack."

"I need ye to comfort Evander, Rory, and Finn." Ian shifted in place, ignoring the prospect of allowing Sawny and Tom to accompany him. He couldn't guarantee he wouldn't wring Sawny's neck if the fool came along. He nodded at the falcon perched on Magnus's shoulder. "Especially Finn. He seems to connect with ye much easier than Sutherland."

"It goes without saying I'll watch over the boys," Magnus said, then smiled at his bird. "And Merlin here will help me."

"I want ye to take Sawny and Tom," Alexander said in a tone that sounded more like an order than a request. "As soon as we assess the situation at *Tor Ruadh*, I'll send Sutherland with more men."

Ian glared at the two young men. He'd known them both since they were twelve years old. Liked them well enough. Watched them grow into men. And now he'd just as soon kill them as to look at them. He'd never been a forgiving man—especially when it came to someone who had caused his loved one's grief. "It is best I go alone."

Sawny stepped closer, dangerously close. "Ye can thrash me to death once we've saved her. At least then, I'll be able to be at peace in my grave because I'll know I undid the grievous wrong I committed with my poor judgment." He took another step, standing so close all Ian had to do was reach up and wrap his fingers around the lad's throat.

Ian felt the boy's regret and shame, for that's all Sawny really was—an overgrown boy who hated himself for failing. But it was Gretna and his unborn child who had been harmed. Neither his heart nor his conscience could let that fact go.

"Come on, man," Magnus urged. "Ye're wasting time. Dinna let yer stubbornness place yer lass in even greater danger."

That comment didn't deserve a response, not when Magnus would do the same were he in Ian's place. Without a word, Ian returned to his horse. Thankfully, his mount preferred motion to standing still and had already taken to fidgeting. Once in the saddle, he turned and looked back at Magnus and Alexander. "Tell my sons I'll bring their mother back to them soon. They're not to worry, aye?" He ground his teeth and forced out the words he prayed would never come to pass. "And tell them no matter what happens, they will always be my sons and have my protection."

"Aye, we will tell them," Alexander said. "Godspeed, and kill as many of them as ye can when ye save her, ye ken?"

"That I will do," Ian turned his horse northeast and took off at a ground-eating pace. A glance back told him that both Sawny and Tom had saddled up and followed. He shook his head. It was a hard ride to Inverness, a little over a day at best, and two full days at the worst, and that was riding through the night. He'd not waste time by stopping to beat the life out of those two, and they'd best be thankful for it.

As they traveled through the Highlands, Ian stayed in the lead, keeping the two young men slightly behind him. Ian sent out a silent plea to any benevolent power willing to listen and lend him aid. He promised to give anything he ever hoped to own, even swore to sell his soul. Anything to be granted the blessing of saving Gretna from those bastards' clutches.

"We should rest the horses a bit," Sawny called out. "And Tom and I can stand guard while ye rest a few hours before we reach Inverness."

"Aye," Tom added. "Ye need sleep to hone yer wits, ye ken?"

"And ye expect me to trust the two of ye to stand watch?" Ian shifted in the saddle, every muscle tensed and aching. As much as he hated to admit it, the two made sense. Both he and his horse had traveled about as far as they could stand for one day. Even with stopping for a while, they'd still easily reach Inverness before midday tomorrow.

"I willna fail ye again, Master Ian," Sawny said quietly. "I swear it by all that's holy."

"Neither will I," Tom said.

Both men peered at him through the darkness, neither of them climbing down from their saddles until he gave them permission.

"No fire," Ian ordered with a glance around. "Too little cover here."

"I'll take first watch," Sawny announced, swinging down out of the saddle and pulling his longbow from behind it. The bow was too cumbersome to shoot from horseback, but it was apparently Sawny's preferred weapon when he was on foot.

"I'll see to the horses," Tom volunteered. "Sounds like a spring trickling just past those rocks. I'll fill the water bags while I'm at it."

Ian didn't acknowledge their chatter nor their attempts to be useful, just dismounted and stretched. He wouldn't sleep. Wouldn't even bother trying. Ignoring the damp chill of the night, he made his way to a higher point and sat atop the largest of several limestones pushing up through the crest of the slope. He stared up at the stars, wondering if there really was anyone or anything watching the misery of this world and actually giving a damn.

"I can help ye get her," Sawny said as he joined Ian. "I know the wardhouse at Inverness. If that's where they took her."

Ian knew Inverness, too, but he feared the prison wasn't where Gretna was headed. "When were ye last in Inverness?"

"A year ago." Sawny stood with his bow hooked over one shoulder, scowling at the land around them. "They had the witch pit then, too. Two of'm, in fact. Down beside the docks."

The boy had spoken Ian's fears aloud. They kept the witch pits close to the docks because it was handier for their testing by water if a witch pricker wasn't available. Should the witch hunters fail to drown the accused, a great paved area had been built nearby, perfect for burning them at the stake or in barrels.

"Where will ye take her once we've gotten her freedom?" Sawny meandered back and forth atop the small knoll, constantly scanning the land. "The witch hunters will surely hunt her down again. If anything, to save their reputations. They willna let her live in peace at *Tor Ruadh*." He shook his head as he ran the curved wood of his bow through his hands. "Dinna ye reckon she'd not wish to return there anyway? How could she forgive the clan for nay stepping in to save her?" After a heavy sigh, he stubbed the toe of his boot against the ground. "How could she forgive any of us?"

Ian remained silent. He had shoved those very worries aside, but they'd nagged at his gut every moment of the journey. There were also the boys to consider. Wherever they went, whatever happened, Evander, Rory, and Finn couldn't be left behind at *Tor Ruadh* to suffer because of their mother. He scrubbed his face with both hands, then held his head as he propped his elbows on his knees. "I'll have to get her out of Scotland. Her and the lads."

"France?" Sawny asked.

"Nay." Ian rubbed his eyes, gritty from weariness and travel. "France is as bad as Scotland and England when it comes to the cruel practice of witch hunts. I willna risk the accusations following us to torment her there."

"I thought King Louis issued an ordinance forbidding the prosecution of witchcraft? I couldha sworn Lady Mercy mentioned it one day while she and Mistress Gretna were in the gardens."

Ian glared at the lad. Was the boy that big of a fool? "And I suppose France differs from other countries because the French never disobey any laws put forth by their king?"

Sawny ducked his head and ambled farther down the hillside. "Aye, I guess there is that." He glanced back. "Whatever ye decide, I'll help ye any way I can."

Ian didn't comment, just looked away, as though Sawny wasn't there. He had to concentrate on one thing at a time. The first matter at hand was getting Gretna out of the witch hunters' clutches before they tortured her with any of their cruel games. He'd get her safe and settled. Somewhere.

He rolled the weariness from his shoulders. Aye, he'd get her and the young ones settled, and then he'd find Colin Neal and do a little torturing of his own.

CHAPTER SIXTEEN

"BACK! BACK, I say! Hie yerselves back to the darkness or burn by the holy fire!" The gruff, booming voice had called out that same warning so many times, Gretna had lost count. She wished she had a bow to shoot the fool between his eyes.

"Gretna! Hurry!" Someone tugged at her arm in the dank darkness. "Ye heard the call. Ye're too close to the center!"

Gretna forced aside her weariness and found the strength to move. She half-crawled, half-rolled into the narrow tunnel previous prisoners had clawed into the side of the earthen cellar to shield themselves from the regular dumping of hot coals into their midst. According to the other women held captive with her, no one had ever been left in the pit long enough to escape. But each unfortunate soul damned to endure the place did their part and dug away more of the earth. They dug as long as their strength held, to hopefully help a future victim escape the vile treatment of the witch hunters.

After Gretna's first witnessing of the shower of live embers, Beitris, one of the other residents of the witch's hole, had told her the commission practiced the act to make sure the accused never slept. To sleep risked dreaming, and the hunters feared the power of a witch's dreams. Beitris confessed she knew this information because her husband, the man who had accused her of witchery when his cock refused to harden, was the overseer of the witches' fires.

"Heartless bastards!" shouted Effemy, another captive huddled with them in the tunnel. "A curse on ye all! May yer cocks shrivel to the size of a midge's arse and stay limp as worms!"

"Effemy!" scolded Teasag, the oldest of the three women sharing the stinking pit with Gretna.

"They're going to kill us anyway," Effemy defended. "Whether we cry, confess, or condemn them all to hell, they're still going to kill us."

"Aye, maybe so," Teasag replied with her right hand clutched to her chest. Her thumb and fingers had been crushed by the wicked thumbscrews. "But there's no reason to make them torture us even more before they decide to do it. Ye willna much care for the pilliwinks, I promise ye that."

"Aye," Beitris agreed. "And the witch pricker's still here, too. Ye saw what he did to me."

Gretna winced at the memory of Beitris's naked body, mottled red and purple from repeated stabbings of the witch pricker's long brass needle. It had been the day Gretna arrived. The last day she had experienced full-on daylight while being stripped naked along with the other women and paraded around the docks three times in a circle because of her captors' superstitions. They believed the humiliating act somehow protected them from a witch's vengeful curse.

Gretna's thirst for revenge had increased with every violation. She had been pinched, prodded, and spat upon, but at least the witch pricker had refused to use his cruel bodkin on an accused expecting a child. None of the others had seen fit to torture her with anything else either—not when both the pits held plenty of victims less likely to bring down any ill-luck upon their heads. They all believed the Almighty didn't look kindly on the torturing of an unborn child, even when the mother was a witch.

Instead, they'd handed her a grimy, half-burned shift with which to *hide the lewdness of her belly*, as they'd phrased it, before forcing her to climb down into the hole. The rest of the prisoners remained naked. She couldn't believe they'd taken such care to escort each of them down into the pit until she realized why. They wanted them alive and *somewhat* whole for torturing.

At the sound of the covering sliding away from the hole's opening, all but Gretna pressed farther back into the tunnel and shielded their faces with their arms. Gretna squatted at the tunnel's entrance. She readied herself in case a bouncing spark made it to her. No light streamed in before the pot of coals dumped. That meant it was night again. The lid to the prison was made of tightly woven thatch. Thankfully, it kept out most of the rain, but, sadly, kept out sunlight as well. She'd lost count of how long she'd been in this hell.

Fiery embers fell from above, sizzling and sending up sparks as they hit the damp ground, then spread. Gretna hurried to scrape up piles of dirt to push the coals back into the center. Earlier, they had all huddled together with the cold. At least now, they'd be warm for a little while. Her stomach clenched and emitted a loud, hungry growl as the four of them clustered around the heat.

"Yer babe thinks the fire means food," Beitris observed, her face dimly lit by the reddish glow of the coals. "I wish I'd had a babe," she added, staring sadly into the fire.

"Why?" Effemy growled. "So, yer bairn could watch ye burn?"

"Dinna be cruel," Gretna said, half tempted to scoop up a handful of dirt and throw it at Effemy. "We've enough evil to deal with from above. We dinna need it amongst ourselves, ye ken?"

"Gretna is right," Teasag said. "Now, draw closer to the warmth and sleep whilst we can. There could come a time when they dinna call out the warning and merely fill the hole with enough coals to be rid of us. They've outdone themselves with their gathering of souls to torture this spring. They put us in this old cistern because the other pit's so full no' another body could stand inside it."

"Aye," Beitris agreed. "My husband said they rarely use this one anymore because they've nay had time to fill in the tunnel. Reckon that means it's nearly made it beyond the wall?"

"I dinna ken. All I know is we need to keep digging after we've rested a bit." If Gretna had the energy, she'd dig right now while she raged at the vile injustice of these heartless bastards. But with little food and little sleep, she was so very tired.

Tears streamed down her face, and she didn't attempt to stop them. She missed Ian. Her sweet sons. Hated how her life would end all because she'd acted the stubborn fool and hadn't listened. She bowed her head and prayed that Colin Neal would burn in the hottest part of hell after suffering a painful death. The good book might preach forgiveness, but she didn't have a shred of it and never would. At least, if she was damned for not forgiving him, she'd witness Colin's suffering firsthand.

"I dinna understand why they're waiting so long to end us all," Beitris mused aloud as she scooted closer to the coals. "I been down here near on a sennight now, I think. Leastwise, that's what it feels like." She stretched her hands over the coals. "Wish they'd have the trial and go ahead and end us." With a shuddering sigh, she pressed her hands across her stomach. "No sense in me living on. The witch pricker shoved his needle extra deep into my belly. Now, I got a fever comin' on in my womb. I can feel it. I'll not be long for this world once it takes full hold." Her voice lowered as if she spoke more to herself than anyone else. "Tha's how my mam died when she had an old woman help her slip a bairn."

Beitris shrugged and poked at the embers with a stone. "After birthing a dozen and burying three, she said she couldna bear having another bairn. Bled like everything, she did, then took fever and died."

"Shut yer maw and go to sleep," Effemy said, but her tone was kinder than before. "We'll die when we die. No' a moment before. No sense worryin' 'bout it."

They lay in a circle around the dwindling embers, curled on their sides so each of them could offer their flank as a pillow to the next woman. With her head resting on Beitris's leg, Gretna stared into the coals, wondering if Ian had found out about what had happened to her yet. He was her only hope in this bleak darkness, and at least, if he couldn't rescue her, she knew in her heart, he'd protect her sons and raise them as his own.

She forced her eyes closed, determined to steal what rest she could for whatever lay ahead. For now, she couldn't depend on anyone but herself.

A scraping sound overhead jolted her back to alertness. She shook Beitris and nudged her leg out from under Teasag's head. "They're opening the grate again."

"To the tunnel. Hurry!" Teasag rasped as she crawled into the shadows. Beitris followed, then Effemy, but Gretna stayed put.

"Gretna!" Effemy barked in a harsh whisper. "Get yer arse over here."

"Nay." She'd had enough. Instead of skittering off to the tunnel and hiding like a frightened rat, she'd face her accusers and do her damnedest to fill them with fear. After all, as Effemy had said, they intended to kill her anyway. She crawled over to the wall and steadied herself as she rose to her feet. Head spinning, she waited for the dizziness to pass, trying not to think about how long it had been since they'd thrown down a few crusts of moldy bread.

The grating overhead eased back a few more inches. Scraps of low rumbling conversation floated down to her, but she couldn't tell what they said. No matter. She'd not wait for whatever wickedness they planned. Armed with a hand-sized stone, she stumbled over to the rubble piled against the wall. Those crumbling blocks had held her interest for a while now. Haphazardly stacked to the rim of the cistern, they were a better means of escape than the incomplete tunnel.

It was night. If she climbed to the top, she might be able to slip outside and take her chances. She had tried it once before and gotten a boot in her face for her efforts. The other women had pulled her back, begging her to stop her foolish attempts at escape. They'd said she'd bring the witch hunters' wrath down on all of them by acting in such a way. So, she'd stopped. But, she'd had enough now, and this time would be different. If the bastard kicked her in the face, she'd grab hold, pull him into the pit, then help the rest of the women out.

Just as she'd climbed to the rim, the covering slid all the way back. Gretna hugged the side of the pit, pressing back tight against the wall. Thankfully, light from the closest torch stand created a shadow in which she could hide.

"Where are they?" asked a familiar voice in a hushed tone. "Graham said he saw them put her and three other women in this one."

Gretna held her breath and didn't spring out of her shadow just yet. Was she dreaming? That had almost sounded like Sawny.

"I'm going down there to find her," said a voice that made her heart leap.

If she was asleep and having a dream, at least it was a happy one. "Ian," she called out softly as she risked rising up out of the shadows.

"*Mo chridhe!*" Ian dropped to one knee, grabbed hold of her shoulders, and yanked her out of the hole. "My dearest love," he murmured as he clutched her tight. "God Almighty, I feared they'd already done away wi' ye." Before she could speak, he stood, cradling her in his arms. "Sawny. Tom. Return the lid and come. There'll be a changing of the guards soon, and they'll find the bodies of this watch's witch hunters."

"Wait!" Gretna struggled to speak through the relief coursing through her. "Please. We must save the others, too—if we can. At least these three that were with me?"

Ian gave her such a grim look, for a moment, she feared he'd refuse. The thought of leaving Beitris, Teasag, and Effemy behind cast a pall across the joy of her own escape.

"Tom, Sawny." He nodded down into the prison. "Fetch them if ye can, but hurry."

The two disappeared into the darkness of the pit, returning moments later with Beitris and Teasag wrapped in Sawny's kilt, and Effemy wrapped in Tom's. Both young men had stripped down to their boots and lèines. All of them clambered out of the hole, then hurried out of the light of the torch stands blazing around each of the entrances to the prisons.

Gretna tucked tighter against Ian's chest. She hugged an arm around his neck and clutched his jacket in her hand. His embrace felt so good. Tears of happiness slipped from her closed eyes. She'd secretly feared never to feel his touch again.

When Ian bent to place her in the wagon, she refused to let go. "Nay! Can I please ride with ye?"

He kissed her forehead but gently pried her hands free as he settled her down into the hay lining the wagon bed. "Nay, m'love. The place we've secured is on the other side of the quay. Verra close. We must hide ye so ye willna be discovered. We can ill afford raising the alarm."

As much as she hated losing his touch, he was right. Gretna nodded and settled down beside the other three. Now was not the time to argue. After all, her bull-headed ways had gotten her into this mess.

The men retrieved their kilts, then covered the women with several blankets. After motioning for them to cover their heads with the cloth, they piled something soft atop them. Gretna wrinkled her nose, ran her hand out from under the blanket, and fingered the bundles. Wool. No one would suspect a wagonload of wool headed out.

"I canna believe we're safe," whispered Beitris.

"Shh," hissed Effemy and Teasag in unison.

Gretna agreed. Conversation at this time was too risky, no matter how relieved they all felt. They weren't out of harm's way just yet.

"Halt!" shouted a tired, disinterested voice. "Which ship be yer cargo headed?"

Gretna held her breath. Beitris grabbed hold of her hand and squeezed.

"No ship yet," Ian said. "This here load's headed for Mackenzie's warehouse."

"Mackenzie?" The voice sounded more interested now. "Since when does the Mackenzie trade in wool?"

Catching her bottom lip between her teeth, Gretna prayed the dock master's man wouldn't insist on searching the wagon. The Mackenzies were known smugglers of whisky, rum, and whatever else brought in the most coin. Ian's brother, Alasdair, was the Mackenzie's solicitor and made sure their profitable business dealings at least *appeared* legal.

"The Mackenzie deals in whatever he wishes," Ian replied in a cold, deadly tone. "Shall I tell him ye question his practices?"

Beitris trembled beside her, shaking so hard, the straw around them shushed like a hissing snake. Gretna squeezed the frightened lass's hand tighter. They had to stay calm. Panic would only give them away.

"Nay," the dock guard hurried to answer. "The Mackenzie can do whate'er he wishes. On wi' ye now."

Gretna eased out the breath she'd been holding. Thank goodness the reputation of the powerful Mackenzie clan had saved them from being searched. The wagon lurched into motion, continuing the slow, bumpy ride.

After a short time, the wagon halted again. The soft bundles atop them shifted, then lifted away, as did the blanket covering their faces. "Come to me, m'love," Ian said, reaching out to her. "Come and let me hold ye."

Gretna scrambled into his arms. An overjoyed sob escaped her. "Thank God for ye, *mo ghràdh*. I feared I'd never see ye again."

He lifted her out of the wagon, but rather than set her to her feet, held her tight. "I wouldha moved heaven and earth to save ye." He rained kisses across her upturned face. "I love ye fierce, *mo chridhe*." A sternness settled across him, drawing his brows together. "And I'll be hearing ye swear that ye'll listen to me from now on, aye?" He gave her a gentle shake. "I know ye're a wise woman who fears nothing, but I beg ye, for the sake of my heart, never go against what I ask of ye. Not ever again, understand?"

"I swear," she said without hesitation. "And I'm so verra sorry. Can ye ever forgive me?"

Ian answered with a kiss that made her wish they were back in their bed rather than standing in the middle of what looked to be a warehouse full of barrels, crates, and bundles.

A throat cleared somewhere behind them.

Ian slowly ended the kiss, and Gretna tucked her head to the crook of his neck. She reveled in his muscled hardness holding her. The scent of him. His warmth. She wept with joy for this man she loved so.

"Shall we fetch more supplies, Master Ian?" Sawny asked. "We werena expecting more than just Mistress Gretna."

"Aye," Tom said in a lowered voice. "We've no' got enough clothes, that's for certain."

The women stood huddled together, wrapped in the blankets.

"Let's get them settled first." Ian strode down a long, narrow aisle between wooden crates stacked almost to the rafters. He gave Gretna a smile that made her feel more than a little loved, then nodded toward the back portion of the massive building. "We've food and clothes. Enough for a wee start, anyway. We've much to discuss and decide."

"We'll not head back to *Tor Ruadh* right away?" Gretna wasn't sure how she felt about staying in Inverness. Was that truly the best plan? The need to see her sons safe was strong. She also worried that the despicable townsfolk of *Ruadh* might have gotten hold of her babies as well.

"The boys are fine," Ian assured as though reading her mind. "Alexander, Magnus, and Sutherland promised to guard them. Graham and the men will fetch them for us quick as they can. Tom's headed to Graham now to give them the word that ye're safe and to go get the lads."

"*Get* them?" Gretna hugged closer as Ian turned sideways with her to enter the narrow door of the warehouse office. "Why would Graham bring them back here?"

"Let's settle ye first, and then I'll explain." Ever so gently, he deposited her onto a cot against the back wall. He waved the trio of ladies, waiting just outside the doorway forward. "Come, ladies. Sit whilst I light the brazier and pour ye some ale."

Gretna's three former prison mates sat beside her, tucking their blankets close to hide their bare state as best they could. Teasag gave Gretna a shy nod. "Thank ye so much for no' leaving without us," she whispered. "Thank ye for caring."

"Ian," Gretna said with a smile. "Come close, m'love. Allow me to introduce ye to my friends."

Ian set aside the tinder box, added another brick of peat to the growing flames, then turned and gave all three a gallant bow as if he was meeting royalty. "Ladies. Ian Cameron, at yer service."

Gretna motioned to each of the women in turn. "Beitris Connor, Effemy Gordon, and Teasag Chisholm." She rested a hand on Beitris's trembling shoulder and nodded toward Teasag's mangled hand. "When ye send the lads for supplies, any sort of healing herbs or salves they could find would be most welcome as well."

Jaw hardening, Ian's eyes narrowed to angry slits, but he nodded. "I shall see it done." He rattled around the office, found enough drinking vessels, then filled them with ale. He followed that by pushing a small table over in front of them and uncovered a basket filled with bannocks, a wedge of cheese, and a small crock of honeyed butter. "Eat yer fill. There shall be plenty more. As much as ye wish. I'll see to that, too." He stepped outside the office for a moment, then stepped back in. "Sawny's gone to gather everything we might need."

Buttery bannocks washed down with ale had never tasted so good, but nothing satisfied Gretna as much as being back with Ian. She brushed the crumbs from her hands as she rose and eased her way around the table. Taking his hand, she pressed it to her heart. "I've had plenty for now. Let's leave them to eat in peace and dress themselves, aye?" Without waiting for his answer, she nodded at Teasag. "Eat yer fill, then parse out those clothes. I'll be just fine in this shift until Sawny brings us more."

Tears streaked down Teasag's face as she nodded, then gave Ian a tremulous smile. "Thank ye, Master Cameron. Ye couldha just as easily left us behind, but I'm more than grateful that ye didna. I'll serve ye the rest of my life. There's no way I can ever repay yer kindness."

"Aye," Effemy added. "Me, as well. Consider me yer servant for life."

"I'm beholden to ye, too, Master Cameron," Beitris said quietly. "I'm ever so proud Gretna's married to such a man as yerself."

"Ye are quite welcome, ladies. I'm glad we were able to save ye." He tucked Gretna's hand into the crook of his arm and escorted her to the door. "Come, dear one. I know of a perfect place for us while the ladies tend to their needs." With a grim look, he led her out and closed the door behind them. "I can tell ye're champing at the bit to talk about what comes next."

"Ye know me well, husband." Gretna leaned against him, the gnawing weariness so much easier to bear now that he was here.

"Come. Here's a pallet of wool and hides perfect for sitting, aye?" He helped her sit, then settled beside her and pulled her close.

She rested her head against his chest. "This is perfect," she said with a contented sigh. The steady sound of his beating heart beneath her cheek was the sweetest music. "Ye know I was ready to either yank ye in the pit or stone ye, ye ken? When ye pushed back the covering to save us?"

Ian rumbled with an impressed chuckle. "And I have no doubt ye could accomplish either attack ye had chosen, m'love."

"Ye were so quiet, and the guards had just dumped the coals among us. How did ye overcome all of them without a sound?" She struggled to keep her eyes open. The warmth and safety of his embrace was more relaxing than any drug.

"A man with a slit throat makes verra little noise." Ian hugged her tighter. "I just wish Colin Neal had been among them." He shifted again, as though fidgeting to serve out more revenge. "I shall see to Neal's fate before this is ended."

"I dinna wish to even think of that bastard now." Her eyelids grew heavier. She gave a very improper, hitching yawn, struggling to stay awake. "Now, tell me, why is Graham fetching the boys and bringing them to this evil place?"

"I'm nay so certain *Tor Ruadh* is safe for any of ye," Ian said quietly. "And I didna think ye'd wish to return to live among so many who had turned their backs on ye." He leaned forward and peered down into her face. "Do ye wish to go back there and start life anew? Would ye be able to move past how many in the village failed to lift a finger to help ye?"

"I dinna think all of them knew," she whispered, suddenly very much awake. "Mam Hattie was the only one I heard speak."

"Aye," Ian agreed. "But did anyone step forward to save ye? Did anyone other than Graham or the guards attempt to stop the witch hunters?"

"I heard none," she sadly admitted. "Mercy and Catriona would've fought for me had they been there. So would Flora." A few more names came to mind, but so very few, she kept them to herself. She sounded pathetic, like a wee child trying to convince herself that she had friends to play with. "But, if we dinna live there, where shall we go?" She'd never lived anywhere other than in the Highlands on the slopes of Ben Nevis.

"I've sent a message to Duncan MacCoinnich asking him if we

might come and live with him and his wife on their island." Ian tensed beneath her cheek.

Gretna sensed he feared her adamant refusal. A sad smile tickled its way across her lips. What Ian didn't realize was she'd learned her lesson and learned it well. She'd hear him out and give his words the thoughtfulness they deserved.

"Their island?" she repeated, more to herself than him.

"Aye."

"Isn't it past the East Indies somewhere? I believe that's where Catriona said."

"Aye." Ian paused. "The Archipelago of El Perdido, the Island of the Lost."

She'd never been on a ship. Never been outside of Scotland. And if they went, would it be forever? Would she never see her beloved Highlands again? "Catriona said Duncan's made himself a pirate now. Calls himself Devil Fraser Sullivan. Are ye saying ye wish to throw in with him and become a pirate, too? Ye'd stay asea most of the time? I'd rarely see ye?" Heart pounding, exhaustion victimized her with panic and fear.

"Shh, now, calm yerself, dearest. I'd never desert ye on an island." He caught her up and rocked her in his arms as though she were a fretting babe. "I didna say I'd become a pirate. All I know for sure is I'll be protecting my family by keeping them out of the clutches of those who would do them harm." He rocked slower. "After what I witnessed today and what Graham told me he discovered had been done to others in the name of hunting witches, I'd put nothing past those crazed men who seem to have no conscience. France wouldna be safe for the same reason. Neither would Ireland. Duncan is kin, my cousin, and I'm sure he'll help. He'll understand the situation completely."

"How will he understand? Was his wife been accused of witchery, too?" She sounded more shrill than she intended, but what Ian suggested was so…frightening.

"Nay." Ian cleared his throat. "Duncan is wanted for the murder of an English soldier. He was sentenced to hang and escaped. And that was under the benevolence of King William's reign. I'm nay so sure Queen Anne wouldna be worse."

The more Ian talked, the more confused Gretna became. She was the one who was wanted by the witch hunters commissioned by the crown. She hadn't killed anyone. Then it dawned on her. "Did ye kill an Englishman since last I saw ye?"

"Nay," Ian answered quietly. "At least, I dinna think so. The men I killed were all Scots. But, one I wounded was an earl known to have the ear of the crown."

Gretna went quiet, struggling to muddle through all Ian had proposed.

"Mo ghràdh?" He shifted her and pressed a tender kiss to her forehead. "Are ye all right?

"I dinna ken," she whispered, snuggling closer. "Just hold me, aye?"

"Aye, m'love. Gladly." He pressed his cheek against her and returned to slowly rocking. "I'll never let ye go again."

CHAPTER SEVENTEEN

A S THE DARK pillar of smoke widened and shifted directions, Ian snorted in a vain attempt to clear his nostrils. The smell of burnt flesh still tainted the air, but that hadn't been the worst of it. The tortured screams had taken far too long to die away. He glanced back at the warehouse, hoping it was far enough removed from the carnage to shield Gretna from what had happened. At least there were no windows on this side of the building.

After the witch hunters had discovered their guards murdered and their prisoners escaped, they'd wasted no time in executing their remaining captives. More than two dozen in all, Sawny had said. All of them burned without the benefit of strangling or having their throats slit first. Ian wished he could've saved them, but there had been no way.

Sawny and Tom hadn't handled Inverness's cruel cleansing of its witches well. Both had paled and vomited from what they had witnessed.

"Any rumors about the escape around the docks?" Ian asked. Maybe if he got the weak-stomached pair's minds on something other than the burning, they'd recover.

Sawny spit again and wiped his mouth on his sleeve. "Most say the witches flew away. Some say they changed into rats and got on one of the ships." He cleared his throat. "No word from *Tor Ruadh* yet. 'Course—Graham just left yesterday, so I reckon no sense in expecting word back this soon. How long will it take to hear from a place as far away as the Indies?"

"Could be a month or longer." Ian pulled his hat lower over his eyes and turned aside as a pair of men walked by. Gretna's safety depended on his not being recognized by anyone—especially not any rebel Neal bastards who might've arrived in Inverness.

He scratched his jaw as he strolled farther along the waterline, studying the area. His beard was still a mite sparse, but he'd done what he could to hide his identity by donning the clothes of a man working on the docks. Dark trews, worn jacket, threadbare tunic. Scuffed boots. Battered black tricorn. He'd left his kilt tucked around Gretna while she slept. Mistress Effemy had promised to tell her he'd be back shortly, if she awakened before he returned.

Turning to Sawny and Tom, he stole a glance back at the warehouse. "I dinna ken how long we'll be held up here waiting for word from Duncan or *Tor Ruadh*. That's why we must find other accommodations. Quickly. That building isna fit for a prolonged stay." The lads might be content enough with sleeping atop bales of wool in storage, but he needed the privacy of a room with his wife. Ian scowled at the bustling docks. They needed an entire house for four women and three men. And that didn't even take into account the three children that would be headed their way soon. He scrubbed his jaw again. *Damn, what a mess.*

"What will ye do with them when ye leave? The other women?" Sawny asked. "We hadna planned on saving anyone other than Mistress Gretna. Ye dinna think those three are real witches, do ye?"

"They seem pleasant enough," Tom said. "Will they be traveling to the East Indies with ye, too?" He sidled back and forth in a tight circle like a dog about to shite. "Or will we need to take them to their homes? Or maybe find them somewhere else to live? Do ye reckon their families will take them back? Or are they the ones that turned them over in the first place?"

"Shut it! Both of ye ask too damn many questions." Ian's head already ached from the past few days, and these two only made it pound worse. He should've left them to their puking so they couldn't speak. He pointed at the lane leading deeper into town. "Hie yerselves to the White Lion and ask for Mistress Morna Mackenzie. She's the Mackenzie's own sister and favorite aunt to Duncan's wife, Tilda. Tell her who we are and ask her if she knows of any lodging we might secure for a month or so. Make certain no one hears what ye're saying except her, ye ken? The lot of us canna stay at the White Lion. 'Tis too public. We've not only the witch hunters to avoid but the turncoat Neals, too. And Breadalbane might be a conceited bastard, but he's nay the fool. It willna take him and Colin long to realize the connection between clans MacCoinnich and Mackenzie." Ian cringed. Come to think of it, that was another reason to get out of the Mackenzie warehouse.

Looking relieved that they'd been given a task, the two hurried off.

"Christ Almighty," Ian grumbled under his breath as he headed back to the warehouse. Those two might be loyal clear to their bones, but they wore his nerves raw. He shook his head and pushed through the door. As soon as he entered, he could tell something was wrong. Panicked cries came from the end of the building where the office was located. Gretna shouted, something crashed, and the sound of breaking glass filled the air.

"Hell's fire." Ian drew both pistol and sword and charged forward. He kicked his way through the door, then came up short, not expecting what met him.

"Our Father...our Father, who art in...in," Beitris stammered and shouted snippets of the Lord's Prayer from atop a chair in the corner. She stomped in time with her words while covering her ears with both hands. Teasag and Gretna crouched over Effemy, trying in vain to hold the poor woman down as she thrashed uncontrollably. Blood-tinged spittle frothed from the corners of Effemy's mouth. Her eyes rolled back until only the whites could be seen as she repeatedly bashed her head against the floor.

"The demons are foaming out her mouth! They're coming after us all!" Beitris shouted, spinning about to face the corner and rock back and forth as she screamed the prayer even louder.

"It's not demons!" Gretna yelled. "She's bit her tongue and canna help it." She caught sight of Ian and jerked her head for him to help. "Teasag canna hold her because of her hand. We've got to keep the poor lass from hurting herself any worse until the attack passes."

Ian was more concerned about Effemy hurting Gretna. He strode forward and took hold, amazed at the strength of the woman's violent spasms. He held her down by the shoulders and pinned her flailing legs with his own.

Teasag backed away, clutching her crippled hand to her chest. She rushed to Beitris and backhanded her across the arse with her good hand. *"Haud yer wheesht!* Our poor Effemy's ailing. Dinna be such a damned fool!"

"It's not demons," Gretna repeated in a quieter tone as she held Effemy's head in one position. "If I could find her some mugwort, I've seen it calm others stricken like this. It might help her, too."

"Are ye all right? She hasna hurt ye or the babe?" Ian grunted and shifted positions as Effemy's jerking caught him in his man parts. Thankfully, the force of the strike wasn't hard. "Damnation! How long will this last?"

"It's gone on too long already. I fear for her," Gretna said. Still holding Effemy's head in place, she twisted and looked for Teasag. "We need a rag, aye? To force between her teeth." She jerked back around as the woman wheezed and gagged. "On her side! We must get her on her side, lest she swallow her tongue."

Ian rolled the twitching lass to her side, thankful that her fighting seemed to be growing less severe. Then he noticed her odd coloring and understood immediately why. The poor thing wasn't getting any air. "I fear it's too late, lass. She's not breathing."

"Dinna ye dare die on me, Effemy!" Gretna said as she struck the now still woman hard between her shoulder blades. "Pry open her mouth and pull her tongue forward!" she ordered as she hit her again. "Effemy! Breathe, woman! Dinna ye dare die after we went to the trouble of dragging yer stubborn arse out of that pit! I demand ye breathe right now! D'ye hear me?" She struck Effemy's back, over and over, to no avail.

As Gretna drew back to hit the lifeless lass again, Ian caught hold of her wrist. "Nay, love. She is gone. Let her leave us in peace, aye?"

Gretna sat back on her heels and allowed Effemy to gently roll to her back. "God bless ye, ye poor thing," she whispered as she closed Effemy's eyes, then rested her fingers on the woman's forehead for a brief moment. She crossed herself and clasped her hands to her chest. "Rest ye well, Effemy Gordon. I'm so sorry I couldna help ye. Please forgive me as ye go with God."

"She said her fits were why they thought her a witch," Teasag said quietly as she rose and tossed the rag back in a bowl of water. "The poor lamb was nay a witch, but she was surely cursed to bear such an affliction."

A noise from the corner made them all turn.

Beitris clambered down off the chair and hurried to Effemy's side. Kneeling down beside her, she scooped up Effemy's hand. "I'm so sorry I acted the fool, Effemy, but I hope my prayers helped the angels come to carry ye home."

Ian stood and gently pulled Gretna upward with him. He held her tight, selfishly thankful that at least both she and the babe were alive and well. A terrible fear struck him. "Her ailment..." How could he phrase this without sounding the callous bastard? "Can the rest of ye catch it? It's not some sort of...plague, is it?"

Gretna leaned back in his arms and looked up at him with a sad smile. "It's only a plague to those born with it. We canna catch it from her."

"How will we lay her to rest?" Beitris asked as she tucked Effemy's limp hand down at her side and smoothed the woman's clothes neatly in place.

Ian gently set Gretna aside, then bent and picked Effemy up. Opening the door wider with the toe of his boot, he paused and turned back. "Find a blanket to wrap her in. Tom and Sawny can lay her to rest in a kirkyard once night falls."

"But who'll pray over her and say the words?" Beitris argued, wringing her hands. "She willna be able to find her way to St. Peter if we dinna say the words to draw the light to her."

The more Ian was around Beitris, the more he wondered about the lass. She seemed more than a little odd, too childlike for a grown woman. He kept that in mind and chose his words with care. "Why dinna ye pray over her once we've settled her in the wagon? I think that'd be a kindly thing to send her on her way, aye?"

Beitris brightened and hurried to gather up a blanket.

Gretna gave him a grateful smile and followed him out to the wagon. It didn't take them long to settle Effemy Gordon for the last trip she would ever take.

Shouts from somewhere outside interrupted Beitris's singing of her prayers.

"All of ye into the office and bar the door, aye?" Ian ordered, realizing he'd left one of his pistols and his sword back there. It was just as well. The women could defend themselves if forced. He took hold of Gretna's hands. "One of ye take my pistol, the other the sword. I left them on the table." He eyed Beitris, then gave Gretna a pointed look. "Just yerself and Teasag, aye? Dinna give that lass a weapon."

Gretna held fast to his hands, refusing to let go. "Nay, come with us. Please dinna go out there."

He squeezed her hands, then led her a few steps in that direction. "I have to see what's astir outside. I'll be fine, but only if I know ye're safe. Now, please, go and bar the door, aye?" He could tell by the look on her face she was about to argue. "Did ye not promise ye'd do as I asked in times such as these?" He almost laughed aloud when she bared her clenched teeth.

"Aye," she fumed. "I did at that." She gave him a hard kiss across the mouth that was more like a smack than a sign of affection. As she headed toward the office, she looked back and shook her finger at him. "Dinna get hurt, ye ken?"

He pointed at the office door. "On wi' ye, woman. Now."

Once she'd finally disappeared into the room, he ran to the side of the warehouse where the shouts and cheers had grown louder. Unchaining a side door that opened into an alley, he slipped outside. Ruefully, he remembered that earlier he'd been glad there were no windows. Now, a peephole or two would've come in handy. He stole a glance around the corner of the building.

As it turned out, the crowd wasn't as close to them as the shouting had sounded. But the size of the amassed gathering was disturbing. The large group, both men and women, waved their fists overhead. They milled around a trio of men standing atop a stack of wooden crates on the walkway in front of a dock farther down the wharf. The three men were dressed all in black except for the lining of their cloaks, which were a dark crimson. The one on the left rang a small handbell as he sang out words Ian couldn't quite make out. Sounded like Latin. The man in the center held a thick book high overhead, and the one on the right held aloft a handful of unlit candles in one hand and a tinderbox in the other.

The man with the book waved and patted at the air for silence. Once the crowd had quieted somewhat, he spoke in a loud booming voice, "I swear on our Almighty Lord's word that we shall find these witches before they wreak any harm upon ye, good people of

Inverness!"

The mob cheered.

Once their cheers faded to a low rumble, the man continued, "We've already sent their sisters back to Satan. Once the four are captured, we'll banish them to the fires of Hell as well! The wicked ones shall trouble ye no more, good people! I do so swear it as the Witchfinder General!"

Ian peered closer at the group. He knew some of those folks. A few were Neals from *Ruadh. Aye.* And there was that bastard, Colin Neal, himself. The fool stood just behind the men stirring the crowd into a dangerous frenzy. Rage surged through Ian, tempting him to lift his remaining pistol and fire, but common sense stayed his hand. *Nay.* Colin was well out of range. Ian would leave nothing to chance when it came to killing that whoreson. Time would have to be bided on that score. The immediate problem was getting Gretna and the other two away from the docks since it sounded like the mob was about to search the area from top to bottom.

Sawny's familiar head of flaming red hair brought Ian relief this time rather than irritation. The young man stood head and shoulders above most of those clustered along the docks and was carefully weaving his way toward the warehouse. The sight of the lad keeping his chin tucked to his chest and his face hidden with one hand as though shielding his eyes from the sun gave Ian a new appreciation for the lad. The boy must've seen the Neals, too, and realized the danger of being recognized. Tom had to be close behind.

Ian hurried back inside, secured the alley door, and ran toward the small door they'd been using that overlooked the Mackenzie's two private docks. That end of the building was angled away from the crowd. Sawny and Tom entered just as he rounded a stack of barrels.

Sawny shook his head as he jabbed a thumb back toward the door. "I've never seen such a crazed bunch, and there's several Neals from *Ruadh* among them. They're talking of torching the warehouses to clear out the witches, as if those poor women are like the pox."

"Fear spreads faster than fleas, boy." Ian motioned him and Tom forward. "Pray, tell me that Mistress Mackenzie knew of a place we could go. Because go, we must. Now." He nodded at Sawny. "And we've got to get ye a hat or a bonnet to hide that hair. I'm surprised the Neals didna spot ye."

Sawny gave Ian an apologetic look. He pulled a knitted bonnet from where he had it tucked in the back of his belt and yanked it on, covering a good bit of his hair. "Mistress Mackenzie knew of a place right off. It's the building across the alley from the White Lion's stable. She said the Mackenzie just took it over to settle a debt, so verra few know he owns it. Said it's an old inn and completely empty. She's having it readied for us now."

Ian took the large key and hefted its weight in one hand. "If the two of ye continue to do this well, I might forgive ye yet." He walked faster. "Come. We'll get the lasses and be on our way." As they passed the wagon and its blanketed cargo, he remembered Effemy. "But there is one other thing."

"What's in the wagon?" Tom asked, his brows arching. "That looks like a body," he whispered.

"Effemy died earlier," Ian said. There was no easy way to tell it, and they didn't have time for gentleness. "She had an ailment Gretna couldna cure. Dinna talk of it, aye? I dinna want the women more upset than they already are."

"She was fine this morning," Sawny said, turning back to gawk at the long bundle laying in the hay. "How could she just die?"

"Ye'll find that happens more than ye know," Ian said, snatching hold of Sawny by the collar and nudging him onward. "Come. We've no time to delay.

Sawny glared at him as if he was the most cold-hearted man alive. It mattered not. All that mattered was getting Gretna to safety.

"Tonight, after we've safely settled at the inn, I want the two of ye to find a kirkyard and lay Effemy to rest. Can ye do that?" Ian asked, scowling back at the lad, then shifting the look to include Tom.

"A kirkyard at night?" Tom whispered, then crossed himself.

Sawny cut an impatient look at Tom, then turned back to Ian. "Only way we'll do it is if ye'll forgive us for allowing Mistress Gretna outside the keep. Forgive us and mention it no more, aye?" He lifted his chin. "I think we've proven our loyalty to ye and will continue to do so, but it's time ye treated us like men instead of the bumbling, snot-nosed lads we used to be."

Sawny made a fair point, and Ian admired the lad for speaking up. He agreed with a slow nod. "Ye have at that. Both of ye have, and I'm grateful." He nodded again. "Bury the lass on holy ground and consider yerselves forgiven, aye?"

"Only problem now is getting everyone out of here." Sawny nudged Tom. "Get the horses and hitch them up, aye?"

Tom headed for the corner of the warehouse they'd converted into temporary stalls for the livestock.

Ian strode to the back of the wagon, frowning at its current cargo of Effemy's remains and a great deal of loose straw. "We've got to make this look like a delivery for the White Lion."

Sawny glanced around, motioning toward the stacks of barrels, crates, and rolled bundles. "It's a tavern. What shall we load?"

"The problem is we need to hide so many." Ian nodded at the driver's seat of the wagon. "Two men on the driver seat. Any more than that would raise questions. One of us will have to ride in the back with the women."

"It should be yerself and Tom driving. Too many Neals recognize my height and hair. I'll pull my bonnet down low and crouch as small as I can." Sawny strolled over to a pile of barrels. "These barrels are awful big. If we try to make a pair of walls with them, there'll be no room left for four of us between them." He shook his head, scowling at the other goods stored in racks and rows. "A tavern would have no need for bundles of wool, and none of the rest would hide us verra well. Would it be too risky to just cover the wagon bed with a canvas?"

"Nay, I fear a canvas would tempt them to search underneath." Ian studied the massive barrels. Those just might do. "Four of those largest ones, the tuns, will fill the wagon and still leave room enough for ye to crouch between them as if ye're merely riding along to help unload the weighty cargo. The women can hide inside the casks. Tom and I will take the driver's seat."

"We can bash out one end of them." Sawny gave the barrels a dubious look. "How ill's the Mackenzie going to be over losing four tuns of wine. Tha's a dear price right there."

"I dinna ken, but I'll risk it," Ian said as he headed toward the office. "I'll fetch the women." He halted mid-step and turned back. "Hurry and load Effemy into the first barrel, aye? I'd just as soon the lasses didna witness that."

Sawny cast a squeamish glance back at the wagon. "Aye, we'll get to the task of Mistress Effemy first."

"Ye're a good man," Ian said and meant it. "I'll leave ye to it then. I'll bring the lasses out shortly."

The office door didn't budge when he tried to open it, and he was glad. She'd done as he'd asked. "It's me, Gretna. Open the door."

Furniture scraped, metal clicked, and then the door opened. Gretna rushed into his arms. "'Tis about time ye came for me. Shame on ye for making me wait so long. I should thrash yer arse for ye!"

The love in her scolding washed across him like a caress. He tipped her face up and drank in her sweetness with a long, slow kiss. Barely lifting his mouth from hers, he smiled down at her. "The lads found us a place to stay. A safe place," he said soft and low.

A quiet shuffling behind them reminded him that Beitris and Teasag were in the room. Regretfully, he eased back a step but kept Gretna in the curve of his arm. There was grim business to tend to. He needed to stay focused. "We need to leave here. Now. The witch hunters are stirring a crowd to search for ye." Thinking of the wine-soaked interiors of the barrels, he nodded toward the blankets folded atop the cot. "Each of ye snatch up a blanket, and we'll be on our way, aye?"

"Leaving in the middle of the day?" Teasag questioned. "Will they no' see us right off?"

"The lads and I have come up with a plan." Ian gave them a reassuring smile that he didn't quite feel. He hoped the young men had finished with the unsavory part of their task. He didn't want to stall much longer. "Come, let's get on with it. I fear the crowd will soon reach us."

The tension knotting him tighter than a bowstring lessened a notch as they neared the wagon. The air reeked with the sticky-sweet smell of wine. Three of the barrels were already loaded in the wagon. One barrel remained on the ground. Ian had a fair idea of what that fourth barrel held.

"Ye mean to stuff us in barrels?" Gretna asked, one hand held to her small yet rounding middle. Doubt shone in both her face and tone.

"Aye." Ian urged the three women forward. "'Tis the safest cover we could think of. Wrap yerself with a blanket to shield ye from the dampness, then crouch down, and we'll lower the barrel over each of ye."

"We knocked out the bunghole to give ye more air," Sawny said. "Be sure and face the back of the wagon when ye crouch down because we dinna wish anyone to see the open holes. Ye can keep yer faces pressed close to them so ye might breathe easier."

"What about Effemy?" Beitris asked. She walked over to the barrel still to be loaded and rested a hand atop it. "Ye put poor Effemy in here?" She bent and examined the barrel. "Ye didna knock out the hole for her!"

Teasag rushed forward, hugged an arm around Beitris, and walked her to the back of the wagon. "'Tis all right, lass. Effemy's watching us from heaven right now. Probably laughing with the angels." She paused and cast a glance over at Gretna. "Come. Let's get in the wagon so we can make a safe way to our new home, aye?"

Gretna hurried over and took hold of Beitris's other arm. "Aye, wee lassie. Up ye go now. Do ye no' wish to see our fine new home?"

"We're going home?" Beitris asked with a childlike smile. "A real home where no one will hurt us?"

Ian's heart ached for the poor lass. Her mind had taken all it could. "Aye, Beitris. No one will hurt any of ye ever again. The lads and I will guard ye well."

Beitris gave an excited nod, climbed up into the wagon, and allowed Tom to help her hide inside a barrel.

Teasag went next, crouching down with the blanket cloaked around her.

Ian gave Gretna a sound kiss, then lifted her up into the wagon. Tom gently settled the wooden cask down over her, then jumped down and helped Sawny load the fourth barrel.

With a grim nod, Sawny stuffed as much of his hair as he could up into his bonnet, then launched himself into the back of the wagon and crouched between the barrels.

Ian and Tom clambered up into the driver's seat. Ian took hold of the reins and steered the team through the wide bay doors on the end of the building opposite the dockside. After they'd exited, Ian halted the team long enough for Tom to close and lock the tall warehouse doors. As the lad returned to his seat, he nodded at a building farther down the way that was already ablaze. "Do the fools mean to burn all of Inverness?"

"I imagine the English as well as Mackenzie's men will arrive soon to halt this madness." Ian pulled his hat lower and urged the pair of horses down the nearest lane that would lead to the White Lion. The faster they put some distance between themselves and the docks, the better.

"Halt ye, I say!" One of the crimson-cloaked fools armed with a large group of men waving torches and an assortment of weapons, flooded into the lane in front of them. Those with the torches shoved them at the team of horses to halt them. "We would see yer cargo, sir. Four witches are afoot and must be captured."

"Witches?" Ian repeated in a gruff voice he used as part of his disguise. He wanted the bastards to think him a man of the sea working on the docks. "All we gots here be the Mackenzie's wine for the White Lion." He thought he'd spotted a Neal or two amongst the group, but didn't want to lift his head to study them closer.

"Them four casks be big enough to hide four witches!" someone shouted from behind the wagon.

Ian looked around. More of the crazed fools had streamed in behind them. "Get away from me cargo!" he shouted, drawing both pistols. "The Mackenzie'll have the lot of ye, but I'll pick off a few of yer arses first!" He'd not go down without a damned good fight.

Both sword and dagger drawn, Tom rose beside him. "First one touches our cargo loses a hand."

Sawny rose, hunched over as though permanently disfigured from hauling heavy loads. He wore his kilt up around his shoulders as though expecting foul weather. With an exaggerated limp, he gimped his way down the length of the wagon and thumped his fist atop the barrel holding Effemy's remains. He drew his dragger and pointed it at the group. "Crazy bastards. Finest wine, this be, and bound for the Mackenzie's own table."

"Prove it to us!" shouted the witch hunter as he pushed his way through the mob to stand at the end of the wagon. "Give me a taste of the Mackenzie's wine, and I shall allow ye to pass. Surely, a man as powerful as Chieftain Mackenzie would nay begrudge a holy man a sip of his wine."

Ian pulled back the hammers on both pistols. He knew the fight would be futile, but he'd be damned straight to hell if he'd give up easily.

Before Ian could take aim and fire, Sawny kicked open the back gate of the wagon and labored the cask around until the bunghole faced the crowd. He pointed his dagger at the witch hunter and sneered, "Gimme yer hat, ye doubtin' bastard."

Ian held his breath. What the hell was Sawny's plan? Had they actually submerged Effemy in the wine and resealed the top of the barrel? Impossible. It looked as tightly banded as all the rest. Only a cooper with all his tools and skills could manage such an act.

With a smug look, the hunter swept off his hat and handed it to Sawny. "Ye've nay got to fill it," he snidely advised. "A wee sip'll do."

Sawny stuck his knife into the wooden plug stoppering the bung-hole and worked it loose. Ruby liquid spewed forth into the hat. After he'd nearly filled it, Sawny stretched and slammed the hat back on the man's head, dousing him. "Good enough for ye?" he sneered as he jammed the bung back in the hole to stop the flow of wine.

The soaked man glared at him as he swiped wine out of his eyes. "Aye. Good enough, I reckon." He shook out the black book he held in one hand and waved it toward the docks. "Allow them to pass. Never let it be said that Thomas Nortonsby is nay a man of his word. Onward to the docks, my good people. Witches are still to be found!"

Sawny pulled up the gate, chained it in place, then nodded for Ian to go.

Ian spurred the team into motion at a rollicking gate.

"What did ye do with the lass's body?" Ian asked once they were out of earshot.

Tom grinned and pointed downward. "Pried loose the extra board and put her in the space under the seat. We didna have the heart to shove her into a barrel." He shrugged. "Seemed disrespectful and such, ye ken?"

"Yer cleverness saved our lives," Ian said. "I'm grateful to the both of ye."

Tom shrugged again as he held on tight to the swaying wagon. "'Twas Sawny's idea. He's a smarter than he looks."

"I heard that," Sawny shouted from the back of the wagon.

Ian laughed, genuinely thankful that fate had saddled him with the two.

CHAPTER EIGHTEEN

T HE MORE SHE thought about moving to some unknown place across the sea, the worse she felt. Gretna rolled to her side and concentrated on slow, deep breathing, in through her nose and out her mouth. She'd heaved so much her sides ached.

Ian pressed the cool cloth across her forehead and back under her hair against her nape. "Ye've been like this for days, m'love. Is there not some herb or root I can fetch to help ye feel any better and get past this? I'm sure Mistress Mackenzie can recommend a place I could go."

"The peppermint she sent over helps better than anything," Gretna whispered. "The queasiness eases as the day goes on. 'Tis just the wicked sickness that sometimes comes with having a bairn." She knew in her heart that's what it was. But she was also convinced that all the chaos had worn her down and made the queasy spells worse. The terrible need to retch had never plagued her this badly with the other three.

The other three. Her sweet sons. How much longer must she wait to see them? "Any word from *Tor Ruadh* yet? It's been well past a fortnight now. Closer to a month. Should we not have at least heard *something* from them? Did Graham not promise to fetch them quick as he could?" She hated the shrewish pitch to her tone, but she'd never waited for anything well. Patience was not among her virtues.

Ian gazed at her with the same infuriating smile he'd plagued her with ever since she'd started heaving through half the day. "All will be well, love. I promise."

"I am not a child, and that is not a proper answer!" She pushed up to a sitting position and immediately regretted it when her stomach churned anew.

Ian held the basin close and kept her hair out of the way as she gagged and spit. She appreciated his gentle attentiveness, but if anything, it made her feel worse. He shouldn't have to do such. But the stubborn man refused to let either Teasag or Beitris help, stating the bairn was his, and therefore, the sickness was his fault. Gretna fell back to the sweat-soaked pillow and propped an arm over her eyes. An old wives' tale played through her mind. "Ye know this means our bairn will be born with lots of hair?"

"Mam told me once that both Alasdair and I had full heads of hair when we were born. Said we looked like wee Highland coos." Ian took the basin to the other side of the room and fetched a clean one. "Seems like she said we both made her sicker than anything whilst still in her belly." He laughed. "Or maybe it was after when we grew big enough to vex her to no end."

"Speaking of vexing, ye didna answer me. Did ye send either Sawny or Tom to *Tor Ruadh* as ye'd promised?" She lifted her arm from across her eyes and glared at him. The six of them had lived at the former inn quite comfortably thanks to Mistress Mackenzie, but Gretna couldn't rest easy until her sons joined her. Surely, Ian understood that.

"Nay. Not yet." Ian slid an arm behind her head and lifted it, offering her a sip of water. "Inverness is just now settling down from the storm the witch hunters stirred. Tom found out today the crazed bastards finally left town yesterday. Apparently, they ran out of victims to torture in this area."

That news brought Gretna some comfort and also made her doubt their need to do something as drastic as seek sanctuary on an island in the East Indies. But if they didn't take shelter with Duncan MacCoinnich and his wife, where would they go? Would Ian be safe after wounding Breadalbane and killing the Neal brothers? According to him, he'd not acted alone. Alexander, Sutherland, and Magnus were just as guilty. If those three felt safe enough about remaining in Scotland, why couldn't she and Ian?

But she also had just as many doubts about returning to *Tor Ruadh* as she did about sailing halfway 'round the world. Her own kin had shown their true colors when they'd allowed her to be taken. She held her head, her conflicting emotions and confusion making it pound harder. "Ask Teasag to brew some willow bark tea, aye?" she whispered as Ian rested her back down to a fresh, dry pillow he'd stuffed behind her. She returned her arm across her eyes to block out the light, and with any luck, block out her thoughts as well.

Ian pecked a gentle kiss to her forearm. "I shall ask her now."

She must've dozed for a while because the next thing she knew, the shadows were longer in the room, and the evening candles had been lit. With a sheepish shrug, Ian handed her a cup. "I'm sure it's cold as a stone by now, but I didna have the heart to wake ye. Will it work just the same? Teasag left the bark steeping in it until just a short time ago."

Gretna pushed herself up and leaned back against the headboard. The ache in her head was long gone, and she didn't feel quite as cross. Apparently, she had just been feeling as quarrelsome as a tired bairn in need of a nap. Now, she felt nothing but guilty. "It'll be just fine, I'm sure." She accepted the cup with a smile and drank it even though she no longer needed it. It would do no harm. She patted the side of the bed, determined to make amends for her bad behavior. "Tell me what ye've done while I slept away the day."

Ian scooped up her hand and kissed it as he settled down beside her. "Sawny and I confirmed the rumor Tom heard in the pub. The witch hunters are for certain gone. But it appears they didna give up and leave Inverness of their own accord. The Mackenzies ousted them before they caused the city any more damage.

"Good." Gretna sipped at the cold herbal. "At least that worry is gone."

"And I have a surprise for ye." He leaned closer, impish devilry flashing in his eyes.

"What have ye done?" Gretna handed him the cup and shifted to sit on the side of the bed. Enough of this laziness. Even though the day was over half gone, she should still get up and be about a few chores. "Ye look like Rory when he's caught an overlarge rat for their races."

"Let's get ye into something other than yer shift so ye can find out." He held out his hand like a fine gentleman.

Interest stirred but still feeling a bit cranky, Gretna brushed his hand aside and hurried behind the fancy, triple-paneled screen hiding the chamber pot and washbasin from view. Apparently, the old inn had been quite the lavish place at one time to provide such unusual privacies. After taking care of necessities, she emerged from behind the screen with her stockings, skirt, and bodice already on, but it was too tight to pin the stomacher in place. She lifted an arm and turned to Ian. "Can ye loosen my side laces a bit? Yer bairn's growing."

"And that makes me more than a little glad," Ian said as he rested his hand on her stomach and stole a kiss before tending to her laces.

His loving enthusiasm filled her with pleasure and stirred the wee one to move. She held his hand tighter against her stomach and watched him. That bit of tumbling was strong enough for him to feel.

Wonderment filled Ian's face. He hurried to the sides of her rounded belly with both hands. "I feel him," he said in an awestruck whisper. "He's a braw, strong one he is!"

"Him?" Gretna laughed. "And how d'ye know it's not a fine las-sie?"

"Maybe it's one of each," he said as a simultaneous tap hit opposite sides of her stomach. "I felt two! Just then, I did, I swear it."

"Bite yer tongue! 'Twas but a wee fist and a foot," she scolded. "We dinna want twins. Ye've seen Catriona and Alexander's suffering."

He pulled her into a kiss, then held her close. "I will take whatever ye choose to give me, love, and I'm grateful for ye. I never dreamed to feel this much happiness ever again."

"I feel it as well," she whispered, but a faint sigh escaped her. "The only thing that would make my happiness complete is seeing my wee laddies again and knowing they're safe." She stepped back and turned away, a twinge of guilt shaming her. "Please dinna think I'm ungrateful or that I dinna love ye with all my heart. It's just that my sons will help me feel more settled. There's so much uncertainty here." She hugged herself against a sudden chill. "Uncertainties are so verra hard for me to bear—especially right now."

"I know, love." He pulled her back into his arms and brushed the gentlest of kisses to each of her eyes and then across her mouth—the holy trinity of loving, he'd always called it. "Hopefully, much of the uncertainty will settle itself soon." He took her hand. "Come. Time for yer surprise. Close yer eyes."

"Close my eyes?" She hated closing her eyes for surprises, and he knew it. Of course, whenever he'd had her close her eyes before, it had always turned out well. "Must I really?"

"Aye." He gave her a chiding look. "Ye must. Now close them." He took hold of both her hands. "I willna let ye bump into anything. I promise."

"Verra well." She closed her eyes, toying with the idea of cheating a wee bit and opening them just a sliver.

"Ach now! No cheating." Ian halted.

Damn him. She closed them firmly, so he'd get this ridiculous game over with.

He walked her forward over the threshold of the door. Gently steering her, he led her a short distance to the right, then squared her off by the shoulders and held her back. "We're going down the stairs to the sitting room. Can ye manage them with yer eyes closed? I dinna wish ye to tumble."

At least now she knew where she was headed. In fact, if she cheated now, she'd be able to see past the banister down into the room. Immediate guilt shot through her. *Nay.* She'd not cheat and steal his joy at surprising her. Eyes still tightly shut, she gave a nod. "I can manage them just fine."

After a few more steps that should've placed her well into the room, he stopped her again. "Hold out yer hands."

With an exasperated huff, she did as he asked.

A faint shuffling rustled in front of her, the sound of several petti coats on the move, then a pair of large calloused hands took hold of hers. "Ye can open yer eyes now, mistress," said a familiar voice.

"Flora!" Gretna threw her arms around the lass and rocked from side to side with her. "It is so verra good to see ye!" she cried, then a terrible thought came to her. She pulled back, holding Flora by the shoulders as she took a closer look at her. "Ye've not suffered for being my apprentice, have ye? Has anyone threatened ye? Ye've not been hurt?"

"Nay, mistress," Flora shook her head with a shy smile, then stole a glance behind her. "My sweet Hugh would never let anyone hurt me."

Hugh MacElroy stepped up to Flora's side. Even though the top of the man's head barely hit her at the waist, Hugh MacElroy portrayed nothing less than dignified composure. "Good day to ye, Mistress Cameron," he said with a polite nod. "We're verra glad to see ye've survived that horrendous ordeal so well. Ye've been in our prayers night and day since we discovered they took ye."

"Thank ye so much. If everyone in *Ruadh* possessed yer good hearts, such a terrible thing would never have happened," Gretna said.

She turned back to Ian and looped an arm through his. "Did ye ask them to come here?" she asked as she hugged him closer. While the sight of them delighted her, she couldn't help but wonder why they hadn't brought the boys, too? She didn't wish to seem ungrateful or rude, but why had they made the trip to Inverness if they hadn't brought her sons?

"The chieftain asked us to come," Flora answered before Ian could open his mouth. "And the Lady Catriona."

Ian gave Flora an encouraging nod as he patted Gretna's hand. "Flora can explain."

"They asked both of us to come, and we were happy to do so," Hugh said.

"Shall we all sit?" Ian asked as he led Gretna to a chair. "Teasag, Beitris, come join us, please."

"We'll fetch more refreshments, aye?" Teasag replied from the doorway. Beitris stood at her side, smiling as though she knew a secret.

Gretna noticed the tankards and plates dusted with crumbs on the tables next to the chairs. Apparently, Flora and Hugh had already had quite the visit with everyone except her. "Why did ye not wake me?" she asked, giving Ian's arm a pinch as he led her to the sofa closest to the hearth.

"Ye needed yer rest." He sat beside her, took hold of her hand, and held it tight. "No more pinching, ye wee vixen," he said with an affectionate scolding.

Teasag and Beitris reappeared, each of them with a pitcher of ale. They made their way around the room, refilling everyone's cup. Once they finished, they seated themselves and folded their hands in their laps. Both of them watched Gretna like dogs waiting for scraps to fall from the table.

"What is going on here?" She'd awakened from her overlong nap feeling better and suitably rested, but this quandary was about to put her back into an ill mood. "Each of ye look like ye've just stolen the royal jewels right out from under the queen's nose." She scooted to the edge of her seat, too anxious to relax into the pillows. "Now, tell me why Alexander and Catriona asked ye to come here?"

"Everyone wants ye to return to the glen, mistress," Flora said. "The keep's not the same without ye, and yer boys dinna wish to leave there either." She gave Gretna a pointed look. "They've made friends and havena been in any fights in quite the while. Ye know how rare that is. They dinna wish to live on an island where they'd never see their friends again."

"The keep isna my concern," Gretna said, regretting with all her heart that they might have to uproot the boys now that they'd finally settled. "It's the village." She shifted on the sofa, staring down at the tankard between her hands. "And I dare say, they havena fought in a while because they havena been allowed outside the keep. The people of *Ruadh*, my own kin, showed me exactly what they think of me. They wished me dead. I shall never trust them again."

"A fair bit of those particular townsfolk have left," Hugh said, then paused to take a sip of his drink. He frowned down at it as though pondering the flavor. "Sutherland banished them, and Alexander supported the decision. The rebel Neals have all gone to join with Angus, Dougal, and Murray."

Gretna turned to Ian. "Did ye not tell them those three are dead?"

"Let the man finish," Ian said with a smug look.

"The banished Neals willna be allowed back on MacCoinnich land," Hugh said. "And the Campbells have gone back on their alliance, leaving the traitors to defend themselves with what little they have. Another leader will have to pull together their *new* clan they wanted so badly." He shrugged. "The chieftain has a copy of the signed agreement granting them land and horses." He grinned and lifted his tankard in silent toast. "And he's already stationed guards along our new borders to ensure there'll be no more rieving or pillaging—not that the Neals have anyone capable of doing it. Trust me when I say most who betrayed ye are gone."

"*Most.*" Gretna shook her head, torn between returning to the only home she'd ever known or some unknown world across the sea.

Hugh gave her a kindly smile as he rose from his seat. "There will always be someone in this life who doesna like ye for whatever reason. Ye canna change people nor control their actions. But ye can control how ye react to whatever they do. I've endured narrow-minded, heartless fools all my life, and I'm certain I'll have to deal with more." He patted his chest. "But it is their loss when they ridicule me and judge me by my appearance." He tilted his head, hooked his thumb in his watch pocket, and meandered about the room. "I've been beaten, threatened, and nearly drowned once because they thought for sure I was some sort of demon because of my size." He stopped pacing and stared at her. "But I'll be damned straight to hell before I'll spend my life running from the bastards ever again." He winked. "I've learned how to deal with such folk in ways they'd never expect." He pointed at her. "Ye could do the same."

"And the chieftain has sworn to protect ye," Flora added. "Him, Lady Catriona, Master Graham, and Lady Mercy...all of them came up with and put a new clan law in place to handle witch accusations and rumors. A sound law, fair and good." After a curt dip of her chin, Flora continued, "Anyone in Clan MacCoinnich falsely accusing anyone of witchery or caught sending for the witch hunters shall spend at least a year in the dungeon—maybe longer depending on the circumstances." She gave another firm bob of her head. "The MacCoinnich had it all wrote up by the solicitor. Signed it in front of witnesses and had the crier read it to the clan and post it. Anyone disagreeing with the law was told to leave and never return."

"He gave those disagreeing with the edict the opportunity of joining the Neals to the south," Hugh added as he refilled his tankard, then returned to his seat.

Gretna massaged her temples. Her pounding headache had returned. She sagged back into the cushions, pulling in slow, deep breaths.

"Is the sickness coming back, love?" Ian scooted closer and rested a hand on her arm. "Usually, ye're better by this time of day. I fear something else is wrong. Shall I carry ye back to yer bed?"

"Nay," she whispered. "What I need ye to do is tell me what all this means. Are we returning to *Tor Ruadh* or sailing off for God knows where?"

"It is entirely up to yerself, m'love," Ian whispered. "Breadalbane hasna retaliated, and Alexander's at the ready if and when he does." He laughed as he gently brushed a stray curl from her face. "Our chieftain's missive was quite convincing and verra adamant that we return to *Tor Ruadh* rather than cross the sea." Contentment seemed to surround Ian. It reached out and touched her. His assured air eased her mind even more as he continued, "More of the clan remained and claimed fealty to the MacCoinnichs than left to become southern Neals. They know Alexander to be a fair chieftain. We've a safe home there if we wish it. Colin Neal wouldna dare step foot on MacCoinnich land ever again."

"Please stay," Flora pleaded.

"Aye, mistress. Dinna let the fools rob ye of yer joy." Hugh smiled. "The greatest revenge would be returning to *Ruadh*, adding a fine healthy bairn to yer family, and living out yer days in happiness." He took hold of Flora's hand and kissed it. "That is why we came here. To convince ye to return. Both Flora and I understand how folk can be when they think ye're different, but ye canna let them steal yer life by robbing ye of yer joy. Dinna give them that power over ye." He winked. "And besides—ye'd nay wish to miss our wedding, now would ye?"

"Of course not." She shifted on the pillows and touched Ian's cheek. "Ye're certain ye'd be safe if we stayed in Scotland? The English wouldna come to fetch ye for injuring Breadalbane or killing the Neals?"

Ian covered her hand with his, then kissed her palm. "The English dinna give a rat's arse when a Scot kills another Scot. Look what happened at Glencoe, and not a one was ever brought to justice."

"Then I dinna wish to leave Scotland," she whispered. "Can we go home?"

"Aye, love." He kissed her as though no one else was in the room. "We shall go to our home and never leave it again."

Chapter Nineteen

"WHEN NEXT MY brother meets here with the Mackenzie, give him this note, and he'll see to yer payment." Ian held out a folded parchment. His brother, Alasdair, was the Mackenzie's solicitor. Alasdair and Chieftain Mackenzie often met at the White Lion for business. "I've sent word to him of all ye've done for us. He's promised to reimburse ye well for yer generosity in our time of need. Stabling our horses. Food and housing for six of us for well over a fortnight—closer to a month, really. I canna thank ye enough, Mistress Mackenzie. I dinna ken what we would have done without yer kindness."

Morna Mackenzie, tall and foreboding in her black garb, gave a lofty sniff and pushed the note away. "Nay. 'Twas my Christian duty. After all, we are somewhat kin." She cocked a brow and primly clasped her hands in front of her. "Barely, but kin is kin since ye be cousin to my niece's husband."

The stubborn woman needed to take the promissory note. He always paid his way. Ian stepped closer and lifted the paper higher. "I insist, mistress. 'Tis a far sight too much to ask of anyone and a strain on the best of businesses."

"Ha!" Mistress Mackenzie peered at him with a look that made her resemble an insulted owl. "Ye insist nothing with a Mackenzie, Master

Cameron. Especially not myself. Ye'd do well to remember that." She shifted in the doorway and nodded toward the old inn that had proven quite the sanctuary at exactly the perfect time. "Besides, my maids tell me ye've left the place in a great deal better condition than ye found it. They tell me it's ready for business. All we need do is hang the signage over the door and open it." She waved toward the street. "Now, be gone wi' ye. I've business to attend to, ye ken?" Without another word, she stepped inside the White Lion and closed the door in his face.

"Well, I will be damned." Ian stared at the door. He did not take charity. Movement to the right caught his eye. The lad who worked at the stable was sweeping out the front entrance. "Boy! Come here."

With a swipe of his arm under his runny nose, the lad leaned his broom against the wall and came running. "Aye, sir?"

Ian fished a coin out of his pocket and handed it and the note to the young man. "Deliver this to Mistress Mackenzie *after* ye see me and my wagons have crossed over yon bridge, aye?"

"After," the boy repeated as he smiled at the money.

"Aye, after." Ian hurried down the steps and mounted his horse.

"It'll be done, sir!" the boy called out, stuffing the coin in his pocket.

Taking the lead, Ian waved for the others to follow. They made up quite the caravan. Two wagons. One driven by Hugh, carrying Gretna, Flora, Teasag, and Beitris. The other wagon was filled with enough supplies from Mistress Mackenzie to last them a month even though the trip to Ben Nevis was but a day and a half. The second wagon was driven by Tom, his horse tied to the back of it. Riding his mount, Sawny guarded the rear of the group. Even with the reports that the witch hunters were gone, Ian wouldn't let down his guard. Not until they reached MacCoinnich land. Thank goodness Inverness was northeast of Ben Nevis. They wouldn't be passing close to the traitorous Neals, whose new lands were farther south.

Ian lifted his face to the warm rays of the sun, thankful for the fair weather. Scotland could be fickle in making up its mind whether to rain, sleet, snow, or shine when it came to late spring and early summer. But the day was fine, Gretna hadn't heaved a single time, and they were finally on their way home.

Home. He'd never thought of *Tor Ruadh* as home before. In fact, he'd never thought of any place as home. His only stable place had always been his saddle. He glanced back. Gretna waved, smiling as the wind tugged at her hair. Then he realized it with a certainty that had always been there. It had just taken him a while to admit it. Gretna was his home. Wherever she was, that's where he belonged.

They traveled for hours. The road changed from cobblestones to packed earth riddled with ruts and holes, then it became a pair of narrow lanes through rolling glens, the sedge and bracken cut away by the wagons' wheels. As they came upon a gurgling burn, its crystal waters abundant, Ian held up his hand to stop. Surely, the women were ready for some relief from the rough ride.

"This looks to be a good place for a wee stretch of our legs. We'll rest a bit, then ride a few more hours before we set up camp for the night." He dismounted and helped Gretna down from the wagon.

She hurriedly brushed aside his arms and rushed to join the other women headed for the privacy of a cluster of bushes. With an apologetic glance back at him, she said, "Embraces in a bit, aye? I'm about to burst."

"Aye, m'love," he reassured, waving her onward. Happiness and contentment filled him. How had he ever doubted he needed this woman?

"Shall we water all the horses?" Tom asked. "Will we be here that long?"

The animals did look in need of rest after the hours of nonstop travel. Ian nodded. "Aye. We'll stay here a few hours and give the beasts their rest. We've made good time. In fact, I believe we're on

MacCoinnich land now, are we not? I dinna wish to camp here, but even if we tarry longer and camp later, we can still reach *Tor Ruadh* by midday tomorrow."

Sawny shaded his eyes with one hand and studied the landscape. "Aye. This is just inside our northern border. We've a watchtower hereabouts somewhere. Graham threatened to stick me in it if I failed to improve my aim."

Ian laughed. "So, I take it ye're a fine shot with both bow and pistol since ye're not a tower guard?"

Sawny winked. "Aye, I never miss." He took hold of both his and Ian's horse and headed toward the water.

Ian turned to help Hugh unhook his team, but was surprised to discover his help wasn't needed. The man already had his horses free of the wagon and halfway to the stream. Ian was amazed. How could a man challenged with such short stature, manage the task with such speed?

Catching Ian's shocked look, Hugh smiled. "A need or problem encourages a man to find his own solutions."

Ian studied the hardware on Hugh's wagon, then joined the man at the edge of the burn. "Where did ye get those things attached to the rigging? Those odd iron fasteners."

Hugh shrugged. "I drew up the design and worked with the smithy. After a few tests and changes, these clips ended up being the most useful and reliable for me when I need my wagon readied for travel."

"They look bloody brilliant to me," Ian said, deciding the invention could be adapted for numerous usages. "Ye must show them to Alexander."

"Ian!"

Gretna's shrill cry turned his blood colder than any Highland stream. Pistol in one hand, sword in the other, he charged in that direction. Over the slight hilltop and past the bushes, Ian halted, his blood no longer cold but boiling with rage.

Colin Neal held Gretna prisoner. With one hand knotted in her hair and the other holding a short sword to her throat, he walked her forward with a rude shove of her head. "Thought me gone, did ye?" With a crazed look, Colin panted out a strained laugh. "Thought them damn Mackenzies and lying Campbells had finished me off?" He coughed and stumbled a step, yanking Gretna sideways with him. "As ye can see, I'm harder to kill than a cat."

"I'm glad ye still live," Ian said, striding forward. "Gives me the chance to finish ye off myself." He dare not shoot the fool now for fear of hitting Gretna. But if he could get closer, he'd slice the bastard in two with his sword.

Colin stopped him by jabbing the blade hard enough into Gretna's side to make her cry out. "Come any closer, and I'll kill her and the bairn. I'll cut yer bastard right out of her." He sneered at Gretna and shook her. "I see it didna take ye long to seed the little whore." He jerked her by the head again, then smiled. "She always was a fertile little bitch. Worse than a rat." He nodded at Ian. "Ye should thank me for relieving ye of her. She'd birth ye a bairn every year. Ye'd never be able to feed them all."

Ian noticed the front of Colin's kilt was blood-soaked. It dripped with a regular rhythm on his boot. His wound had to be mortal. If he kept the bastard talking long enough, the blood loss would take him down. Ian could tell by Gretna's stoic calm that she knew it, too.

Colin blinked hard. His head bobbed, and he leaned against Gretna to steady himself. "Appears those Mackenzie devils might ha' wounded me worse than I first thought. Or maybe 'twas the Campbells." He shook his head. "It nay matters. I've still enough strength to get my revenge afore I die. That damned Angus was too big a fool to help me, and all Breadalbane cared about was the debt I owed him." He bared his teeth and drew back his weapon for the killing slash.

"No!" Ian roared, launching forward.

Colin's eyes bugged wide, and his mouth opened with a gasping groan as his blade fell from his hand. He released Gretna and sagged to his knees, staring down at the point of Sawny's sword emerging from his belly.

Ian finished the job by relieving Colin of his head.

Sawny yanked his sword out of the man's back and cleaned the blood from it with Colin's kilt. "'Tis a dead warrior indeed who doesna watch his rear and his flanks during an attack."

"Indeed," Ian observed, then dropped his weapons and ran to Gretna. He clutched her close, then held her at arm's length, framing her face with his hands. "Did the bastard hurt ye?"

Laughing, tears streamed down her face. "Nay. He didna hurt me. Just startled me a wee bit when he crept up behind us and took me by surprise."

"He wasna long for this world," Teasag said, pointing to a trail of dark splotches. "Look at all the blood. How did he know we'd travel this way? How did he know to wait for us here?"

"Maybe he's the witch 'stead of Gretna," Beitris said with a convincing nod. "That's why he helped the witch hunters catch her."

"He was probably trying to make his way to *Tor Ruadh* or maybe even farther south," Ian said, releasing Gretna to nudge Colin's body over to examine all his wounds. "Mistress Mackenzie must've mentioned the man's deed to the Mackenzie guards before they rousted the witch hunters from Inverness. I'd lay odds she sent them for him personally."

"Shall we bury him here or bring his body back to *Tor Ruadh?*" Tom asked. "I dinna ken if any of his closest kin are still there. Most probably left Clan MacCoinnich."

A cold hardness settled over Ian. "Leave him where he lies. I've never been a forgiving man, and I'm not about to start now." He returned to Gretna, wrapping an arm around her as he led her back to the wagons. "Are ye certain ye're all right?"

"I swear, I'm fine." She breathed in a deep breath and blew it out. "I'll have to seek out Father William for confession though." She shrugged and leaned forward, whispering, "I'm glad Colin's dead."

"As am I." Ian kissed her forehead, allowing himself to relax as he breathed in the scent of her. "Ye always smell of heather. Ye've the power to drive me mad, while at the same time, calm my soul."

Gretna wrapped her arms around his waist and hugged him, resting her cheek against his chest. "Good. I intend to drive ye mad until ye've grown old and gray." She gave a great sigh as she looked up at him. "I've but one regret."

Ian frowned. "A regret? Ye regret loving me? From the way she pressed her body against him, her actions belied her words.

"Nay, m'love." Gretna smiled with a suggestive wiggle. "I'll never be sorry for loving ye with all my heart and soul. My one regret is that Catriona and Mercy were right." She made a face. "Ye know what that means, aye?"

"What?" Ian asked, finding it increasingly difficult to pay attention to what Gretna was saying rather than how she was rubbing him in all the right places. Before they continued the trip homeward, a bit of privacy was most definitely in order. He filled both hands with her fine round arse and pressed her closer as he cleared his throat and struggled to concentrate. "Ye regret Catriona and Mercy being right, ye said. Why?"

"Because we'll be listening to them chant 'I told ye so' for the rest of our days."

"I dinna care," Ian said as he scooped her up into his arms and scanned their surroundings. *Aye.* That hill over yonder would do quite nicely. "Sawny!" he shouted as he started off in that direction.

"Aye?" Sawny called out from the other side of the burn.

"Man the camp, and keep all in this area until my wife and I return." Ian smiled down at Gretna, pleased to see wanting burning just as hot in her gaze.

"'Til ye return from where?" Sawny called out.

"None of yer affair, and if anyone disturbs us, I'll kill ye."

"Ian! Now, all will know what we're about to do," Gretna scolded, her cheeks flushing, but her eyes sparkling.

"Good. Then they'll also know their life is forfeit if they interrupt me loving my wife."

EPILOGUE

Glen Nevis, Scotland
August 1703

"COME ON, MALLIE! Come to me!" Finn held out his hands as he squatted a few feet away from his baby sister, doing his best to be the first brother she chose to walk to.

Gretna helped her almost-year-old daughter maintain her balance. Malina Kirsteen Cameron, wee Mallie for short, had just started walking and was very particular about who she trusted to catch her. She hadn't quite learned how to stop just yet. Instead, she dove forward with a delighted squeal. But so far, she only walked from her mother to her father. Little Malina preferred her Da above all others, whether walking or not, and Ian reveled in being her favorite.

"I bet the wee minx chooses Evander," Sutherland said. "She laughs easiest for him."

"I believe ye're right," Ian said from where they stood in the shadows of the covered walkway surrounding the garden. He had to stay out of sight, or Mallie would ignore all the others, and her brothers' contest would be over. "Dinna let Gretna know the lads have placed bets with each other, aye? She'll make them wash all the chamber pots as punishment. When she discovered how much they'd won with

255

their racing rats, she decided 'twas time to stop them from fleecing the clan."

"I dinna ken why," Sutherland said. "Those three are the shrewdest little buggers I've ever met when it comes to gaming, giving odds, and making a profit." He shook his head. "Hell's fire, I think we should back them in the opening of a pub with a game room. We'd all be up to our arses in coin in a year."

"Definitely dinna tell her that." Ian nodded toward the proceedings. "Finn's given up. Here comes Rory."

Sutherland studied the little girl as she cooed and waved her chubby little hands at her brother. "She might pick Rory. She's already learned he usually has something good to eat in his pockets."

"I doubt he's her pick." Ian tilted his head and pointed toward his daughter. "See the wee scab on her elbow? The little vixen was crawling too close to the hearth, and Rory pulled her back before she got burnt. She's quick as lighting, and the only way he could stop her in time was by catching hold of her ankles. Skinned her little arm in the process, and ye wouldha thought he was killing her. Never in my life have I heard such howling." Ian laughed. "I dinna think it really hurt her. I just think she was angry because he'd stopped her." Which reminded Ian of the latest rumor he'd heard about Sutherland. "By the way, what's this I hear that Lady Sorcha Greyloch has told her father, the chieftain, that if he allows ye on their land again, she'll shoot ye herself to protect the women of Clan Greyloch? What did ye do to anger her?"

Sutherland rolled his eyes and sidled a step closer. "I dinna ken what the hell's wrong with that woman. If her scornful looks dinna turn ye to cinders, the sting of her sharp tongue will. She's got the temperament of a swarm of bees protecting their hive." He shrugged. "Lady Sorcha Greyloch just hates me. I couldna begin to tell ye why."

That statement made Ian bark out a laugh. He thumped Sutherland's shoulder. "Is this not the same woman ye wagered ye'd bed under her father's verra own roof when ye delivered the horse he bought? In fact, is that not the reason ye offered to deliver the horse? Because ye'd heard of the lass's beauty and bragged ye'd have her bedded before Beltane?" Ian thumped him again. "Overplayed yer hand, did ye? She got wind of yer bragging, I'll wager? Never underestimate the speed of a rumor carried by maidservants."

Sutherland shot him a disgruntled look. "That damn wager cost me dear—an entire barrel of whisky."

"Ha!" Ian nudged him and pointed across the way. "Perhaps my sons could help ye when it comes to places bets. Maybe ye should seek their counsel."

With a delighted crowing, Mallie toddled the few steps across the grass straight into Evander's arms. He scooped her up, making her laugh even harder as he danced around with her.

"Well done, little sister!" Evander bragged as he jiggled the child until she clapped her hands with glee. "I always knew ye had the good sense to pick me."

"At least ye got that right," Ian told Sutherland. "Ye said she'd pick Evander."

An insistent babbling verging on an irritated yell warned Ian he'd been spotted. "I believe I'm being summoned," he said as he snagged hold of Sutherland's arm and pulled him along. "Come. 'Tis too fine a day to be spent grumbling about lost bets and women ye canna have."

Evander handed the squirming toddler over to Ian. "There's yer Da, ye spoiled minx."

"Ye're nay spoiled, are ye my fine wee one?" Ian tickled the babe under her chubby chin until she gurgled out a happy squeal.

"And did my ears deceive me? Did ye say a woman walks this earth that Sutherland canna have?" Gretna asked with a smirk.

"Never ye mind," Sutherland said, giving Gretna his back as he offered a finger for the babe to hold. "How is my wee Mallie today? Ye still love me, d'ye not?"

Grinning, the child pulled his finger into her mouth and bit it.

Sutherland grunted. "Yer bairn's got a fine new tooth coming in." He gently removed his finger and wiped it on his kilt.

Mallie cackled.

"She's as wicked as ye are," he said to Gretna, then gave them all a prim nod. "I shall take my leave now. Alexander said he wished to speak with me."

"Aye." Ian couldn't resist a smile. He knew exactly what that meeting was about. Sutherland would soon be fit to be tied. They'd probably be able to hear his roaring out here in the garden. "Godspeed to ye."

"Godspeed? What the hell do ye mean by that?" Sutherland asked as he headed toward the gate.

Ian just smiled and waved him onward.

"And why are ye grinning like a cat that's stolen the cream?" Gretna asked.

Hugging her to his side, Ian winked. "Alexander's sending Sutherland back to Clan Greyloch to negotiate an agreement for land sharing of the horses." After fluttering kisses into his daughter's hand until she tired of it, Ian switched to fluttering kisses into the crook of Gretna's neck.

She laughed, ducking her chin as she pushed him away. "Stop that now and tell me why Sutherland going to Clan Greyloch is so amusing."

"Because Lady Sorcha Greyloch is the woman Sutherland canna have. Says she hates him and will have him killed if he ever steps foot on Greyloch land again."

A devious look settled across Gretna as she snuggled up against him in a most inviting way. "I'll wager they're married before the year is out."

"Wager?" Ian hugged her closer, suddenly wishing his wee daughter would take a nap so he might have a bit of time with her mother. "I thought ye said there's to be no more wagering among the Camerons, or it'll be a month of cleaning the chamber pots?"

Gretna smiled at her daughter. "That rule is for yer avaricious sons." She cut her eyes over to him. "And I know about the bet regarding their sister walking to them." Her look softened. "But I'll allow that one since they love her so."

"What else might ye allow if this wee one agrees to take a nap?" Ian slid his hand down her back and cupped her rump.

"I'll allow anything ye please, dear husband." She slid her hand beneath his kilt. *"Anything* ye please."

About the Author

"No one has the power to shatter your dreams unless you give it to them." That's Maeve Greyson's mantra. She and her husband of almost forty years traveled around the world while in the U.S. Air Force. Now, they're settled in rural Kentucky where Maeve writes about her beloved Highlanders and the fearless women who tame them. When she's not plotting her next romantic Scottish tale, she can be found herding cats, grandchildren, and her husband—not necessarily in that order.

SOCIAL MEDIA LINKS:
Website: maevegreyson.com
Facebook Page: AuthorMaeveGreyson
Facebook Group: Maeve's Corner
facebook.com/groups/MaevesCorner
Twitter: @maevegreyson
Instagram: @maevegreyson
Amazon Author Page: amazon.com/Maeve-Greyson/e/B004PE9T9U
BookBub: bookbub.com/authors/maeve-greyson

Made in the USA
Las Vegas, NV
03 April 2021